NEECHIE HUSTLE

by Neal McLeod

Published by Kegedonce Press
11 Park Road
Friesens Printing
Neyaashiinigmiing, Ontario N0H 2T0
www.kegedonce.com
Administration Office/Book Orders
RR7 Owen Sound, ON N4K 6V5

Printed in Canada by
Cover Design: Eric Abram
Design: Eric Abram

Library and Archives Canada Cataloguing in Publication

McLeod, Neal, author
    Neechie hustle / Neal McLeod.

Includes some text in Cree.
ISBN 978–1–928120–09–4 (softcover)

    I. Title.

PS8625.L46N44 2017   C813'.6   C2017–903964–4

Sales and Distribution – http://www.lpg.ca/LitDistco:
For Customer Service/Orders
Tel 1–800–591–6250 Fax 1–800–591–6251
100 Armstrong Ave. Georgetown, ON L7G 5S4
Email orders@litdistco.ca

We acknowledge the support of the Canada Council for the Arts which last year
invested
$20.1 million in writing and publishing throughout Canada.

The Canada Council | Le Conseil des Arts
FOR THE ARTS | DU CANADA
SINCE 1957 | DEPUIS 1957

We would like to acknowledge funding support from the Ontario Arts Council, an
agency of the Government of Ontario.

ONTARIO ARTS COUNCIL
CONSEIL DES ARTS DE L'ONTARIO
50 YEARS OF ONTARIO GOVERNMENT SUPPORT OF THE ARTS
50 ANS DE SOUTIEN DU GOUVERNEMENT DE L'ONTARIO AUX ARTS

ACKNOWLEDGEMENTS

Mitoni kinanâskomitinâwâw mihcêtawak. There are many whom I wish to thank.

First, I owe special thanks to my friend Tim Fontaine who helped me imagine scenes with some of these characters in the early days of the now legendary Crow Hop Café. I would also like to thank various members of the Bionic Bannock Boys and Fair–Skinned Indians who brought these characters to life.

I would also like to thank Kegedonce Press for bringing this book to press. Special thanks to Kateri for being an amazing editor and to Renee for her support and work.

I would also like to thank Eric Abram for an amazing cover and for his design of the book. I would also like to thank nîciwâkan Randy Morin for helping to edit the Cree.

Finally, I would like to thank my nîcimos Natalie for supporting me in the final stages of the writing of this book.

— Neal McLeod, nihtâwikicikanisihk, 2017

DEDICATION

I dedicate this novel to two of my uncles,
Dale Durell and the late Burton Vandall,
who taught me the art of comedy.

NEECHIE HUSTLE

Table of Contents

INTRODUCTION

It was another day at the Third Hand Pawn Shop. The sky of the Broken Elbow reserve was always vibrant like a rich coloured tapestry. As Mervin approached the shop to interview the Senator, he saw the nêhiyawâhtik,[1] which had been the talk of so many fantastic stories and legends. Some say that it had been taken a couple of times over the years, but eventually the nêhiyawâhtik found its way back again. Many of the people around the reserve were too scared of its power to take it away.

Mervin was here to interview the Senator on the history of the Broken Elbow reserve. The Senator was getting older now, and he was having a harder time getting around. This was especially true since since he had his hip replacement surgery. The Senator had largely turned over the daily running of the Third Hand Pawn Shop to Jingles.

Things were okay for the Senator at the Old Folks home on the reserve. There were still people with whom he could speak Cree. There were shuffleboard games, good meals, and occasional fiddle dances, but the Senator missed the excitement of his earlier days. And, he missed his friends, even old Cash.

The Senator and Mervin's eyes caught each other for a moment, and they seemed to acknowledge each other. The Senator was the storyteller in the band, and he had a lot to say to people. Sometimes it was like words were just eating away at him and he needed to tell the people directly so that he could share his insights. It was like there was just too much for him to hold on to.

---

1   Wooden–indian

But then Mervin came with his questions:

"Senator, can you tell me about the time you guys tried to build a space rocket ship?"

"What about the time there were knights on the reserve?"

"How did the wooden Indian become the Chief?" With all of these questions the Senator felt alive again. The Senator smiled and said, "hâw mâka nôsim. ê–wî–âh–âcimoyân."[2]

---

2   "Yes, my grandson, I will tell you many stories."

THE EARLY DAYS

Mervin had the Senator thinking about the earlier days. He thought about all of the times in his earlier life when he had been truly happy. It was these times that gave him a foundation to understand the present. They would help him find a place to stand and also help him make sense of his world. Despite all of the things that had happened to him, the Senator was still fundamentally optimistic.

One of the things that had always been a source of great comfort to him were his memories of time spent with Nadine when they were children. He remembered that one time.

That one time Nadine's grandmother was up all night making bannock. Nadine's grandmother's name was Paskwâw–Iskwêw. She was making bannock for an exhibition and that was what brought in the crowds. People would get permits from the local sôniyâw okimâw, the dreaded Indian agent. Those that were fair complexioned would pretend that they were Metis so that they would not need a pass. Some of the Indian agents were hard working men, but to go against the system was very difficult. It was very difficult for them to stick their necks out. They had families and bills, and one thing that the Senator had learned early on, that once you had family and bills, you tended to take fewer chances.

That one day always brought a sweet smile to his face. He remembered not only the taste of the bannock but the way Nadine's long dark hair caught the light of the afternoon sun.

He had come by Nadine's ohkoma's[3] place. He could smell the bannock all of the way down from the top of the hill. The smell would waft down and fill the wind with the fragrance of grease and bannock. Wahwâ, he remembered that day.

He walked that winding path to the hills. He passed

3   Grandmother

through all of the little nooks and crannies, all of the places where Nadine's ohkoma had planted her feet over the past decades. The pathway was like a little map of all of those years and all of her great stories.

The Senator had gone to town the previous day, and he had put all of his money down to buy some grease for Nadine's grandmother. The best grease that the White women from town would use. They used it to make pastry that made the district famous for their baking. The ladies in the district had often won the baking contests during the exhibition.

He got to the door of Paskwâw–Iskwêw's house. He could smell bannock was lingering in the air. He could almost taste it. He could imagine the way Nadine must look now, little bits of flour on her face. He found that so cute.

He felt his heart racing to the point where he wanted to run, but he didn't seem able to run. His hand seemed to be guided by some unknown force– and while he tried to pull it back, he was not able. His hand hit the wood of the blue door which was the colour of a robin's egg, and he heard it echo through the house like a stray bullet.

He heard Nadine say, "nohkom. awiyak kâ–pê–matwêhikêt iskwahtêmihk."[4] After she said this, the Senator could imagine her hands making the bannock. "Hâw mâka nôsim,"[5] ohkoma[6] answered, and he could hear her shuffle to the door. He imagined her wiping the bannock dough off her fingers, readying herself to open the door. She always wore an apron, and he imagined her drying her hands on the apron. She was one of those kohkoms that kept her hair wrapped up, and had tied a scarf around her head. Usually the scarves were quite vibrant. A lot of the older ladies had their hair like that. It

---

4   "My grandmother, there is someone knocking at the front door."

5   "Okay my grandchild."

6   her grandmother

gave a certain look of dignity, and an aura of elegance.

Kohkom called out to the Senator, who was known then as Bobby Boy. "Cha! Bobby Boy kîkway ê–tôtâman?"[7]

Still, Bobby Boy continued to stare into the open space. He was dreaming someday of the things he would see in the world. He was dreaming of all of the travelling that he could do.

"Tânitê ê–ayâyân?"[8] said Bobby Boy.

"Nikihk, tawâw."[9]

Bobby Boy did not say anything. He just smacked his lips, looking at the bannock.

Nadine brought the jam to the area where Paskwâw–Iskwêw and Bobby Boy were standing, and she said, "Na."[10] She smiled and then offered Bobby Boy some of the bannock.

"Thank you very much for the bannock." Bobby Boy paused and looked a bit shy. He also paused to look at Nadine.

Paskwâw–Iskwêw replied, "You are welcome. aya, mêtoni, ê–miyo–kîskâk."[11]

"Mêtoni." He paused again. "I was wondering if you needed your pathway shovelled.

"Sure, that sounds good." She smiled because she knew why he was really here.

After he shovelled the path, and came back in, Bobby Boy was given more bannock. This went on all afternoon. Bobby Boy was playing it very smart because he knew the way to Nadine's heart was by doing things for her ohkoma.[12] He knew that if he could get her trust, he would be able to spend more time with Nadine. The key to any relationship on the reserve was not how fast one's horse

---

7   "Oh my goodness! What are you doing Bobby Boy?"

8   "Where am I?"

9   "At my house. Welcome."

10   "Here. Take it."

11   "It is truly a beautiful day."

12   her grandmother

was, but rather how good you treated their ohkoma. Even though Cash was better looking than Bobby Boy, Bobby Boy knew that the fact that he spent so much time with Nadine's ohkoma really helped him to spend time with Nadine. He would spend a lot of time there, drinking tea with them.

One time he even borrowed his uncle Pâcinîs's old car. He rode to town triumphantly. He had a permit from the Indian agent – which was something not everyone on the reserve could pull off. He started to sell more things when his grandmother died and he began to sell her beadwork. Over time, Bobby Boy had managed to save some money, and the one Indian agent used his connections to open up the European world to the beadwork that he possessed. Over the years, it allowed him to be economically independent, and also allowed him to bring Nadine's grandmother many beautiful things. Some of these things were genuine European imports.

Every time he felt his heart open to Nadine he remembered the first time he kissed her. They both had bannock grease on their lips. Nadine's okohma had gone out to feed the chickens. Over time their kisses had grown sweeter. It got to the point where he kept having to outdo himself with the gifts that he had been giving her old ohkoma.

NEECHIE KNIGHTS

Mervin came again to record the Senator.
"Senator," he said, "can you tell me about the time there were knights on the reserve?"

During the Second World War, there were a lot of teenagers who were too young to fight in the armies but too old to just sit around in the summer. They were active young men, but they didn't have a place to channel all of their energy.

One day a few of them were sitting around, and Uncle Pâcînîs said, "You know fellas. I feel pretty cooped up here."

Another said, "Yeah. I feel like a chicken in a chicken coop."

Pâcinîs continued again, "It is the damn Indian Act."

"It just gets so lonely here. Sometimes I just want to break free.," one of the older ones said.

Another replied, "Yeah, I want to see the world. A fella hears about all of them places and you just want to see them in real life. Sometimes I think it would be tâpwê miywâsin[13] to see the places in those magazines."

Old Moses, with his wide open eyes, added, "It is like those magazines are like time machines. They take you to places that you never thought were possible."

One of them older guys, Pâcinîs, said, "You know. For a long stretch I had a subscription to those military history magazines."

Old Moses laughed, "I remember one time when we ran out of the Sear's catalogue we had to use

---

13   truly good

that magazine of yours to wipe our cisks[14]... ahh, sweet Nanabush, it was so smooth. It was smooth tâpiskôc velvet. I felt like a big shot when I used that paper."

Pâcinîs said, "You were a takay[15] to do that. I had to use my Treaty money to get that magazine."

Old Moses said, "nimihtâtên ôma. I regret it. Look, I remember there was one of your magazines that I just couldn't bear to use in that way. I remember those pictures of old fashioned Englishmen. They looked real classy like. They had real fancied up horses, real shiny helmets and gosh when they pulled their visors down, you couldn't really tell who they were. They were kind of like the RCMP with sunglasses, eh?"

Moses said, "tâpwê anima. That is true what they say."

"They were like the Queen's little soldiers just like our boys overseas," the Senator replied.

"Tâpwê anima," Moses said.

Pâcinîs continued, "you know it was kind of inspiring when I saw those old English guys."

Old Moses didn't really understand "inspiring'" but he repeated it and added "tâpwê."[16] He seemed to think it was kind of like a magic bannock recipe. Whenever there was a tricky English word he thought that all he would have to do is add "tâpwê" to the tricky English word and others would believe him.

Pâcinîs kept weaving his tales, "When I saw old time kayâs ago Englishmen, I felt funny inside my heart because I thought to myself, "tânisi self," and my self said "tânisi" back, then I says "self, I bet that those old time English men in those shiny suits had a lot of honour like those old time long ago Englishmen at the Treaties. I kind

---

14   bums
15   dink
16   truly

of like to think of the way those old time Englishmen must have been."

"Tâpwê anima," Moses replied, "It is kind of like we are honouring them when we do it. It is like we are smudgin' up, when we do it."

"Ahâw," Pâcinîs said, they both felt like they were getting all sacred like.

Old Moses itwêw[17], "you know nîscâs, sometimes the way things are, it is kind of hard to see the goodness of the môniyâw[18] but I really try my best."

"Yeah," Pâcinîs agreed, "even though mitoni ayiman[19]. It's the way to go itikwê[20]. Otherwise you'll just get twisted up in anger like a wîhtikow."

Old Moses itwêw, "That is why we need something to do. Sometimes if you sit and just figure, it can drive you nuts."

Pâcinîs itwêw, "So here is what I was thinking. Maybe we could be like those English Knights and do these things they call jousting. They ride horses and hold these pointy sticks, and then they ride real fast, and crash into each other."

Old Moses itwêw, "cha. Kinda sounds like that game 'chicken' we used to play."

Pâcinîs itwêw, "Speaking of chicken, do you remember that time at the fair there was the sign that said, six foot tall man eating chicken?"

Old Moses itwêw, "Yeah, we were so scared but so excited at the same time, kind of like your first time."

Pâcinîs itwêw, "gee whiz. I just get so nervous." He paused. "But I talk in circles. We are all packed in there tighter than the contents of a Red River cart. Shucks, that

17   he says
18   White people
19   "It's very difficult."
20   I think

circus tent was just so full. The top of the canvas tent was fluttering in the wind – ever so Nadinely, ever so tenderly. Then people packed the rows so full that some of those big Metis bushmen with their tattoos even sat on each other's laps. Kind of strange if you ask me, but we were all so excited. We just couldn't wait. We were all so excited. People were trying to hold in their breath and sit still. The announcer came out crazy, like a drunk rodeo judge, and said, "now folks, I bring to you the six foot man eating chicken!" With that the crowd went wild. One old môniyâw farmer even got up and cheered. The curtains rustled a little bit, and we waited for more movement. Kind of like when the first bingo ball pops into the cage, and then you want more. Hush, hush went the crowd.

Then out came a man eating a piece of chicken. It was a drumstick in fact. One of the big Metis Bushmen yelled, "What the kind of show is this?" Another one yelled, "I thought it was going to be a crazy ass monster eating chicken – it is just a tall napêw."[21]

Pâcinîs replied, "'Cha, as if!' I heard an old man say."

Moses itwêw, "Yeah, a lot of those Big Metis lumberjacks got real riled up. It was kind of fun."

"That is the kind of fun I am talking about. A lot of boys are overseas, and they need something to centre themselves around," Pâcinîs said.

"I agree. What do you have in mind?"

"Well, I was thinking we could get fellas from nearby reserves – fellas from the district," Pâcinîs said with a rising pitch.

Old Moses laughed his hearty laugh, "You mean like pick–up shinny? But we dress up like those knight guys."

Pâcinîs raised his eyebrows. He was thinking

---

21   man

through this question on the spot, "Yeah, but if we play for money, people will bet on it."

"Tâpwê anima."[22]

"The day to do the jousting would be on Treaty Day. There are lots of folks out and about, and maybe the rodeo judges could judge the jousting contest," Pâcinîs itwêw.

"Yeah, tâpwê, on Treaty Day, everyone would be all cashed up." Old Moses gleamed when he said this.

"Well, let's get out there. Let's mingle with the people, and get it happening," Pâcinîs itwêw.

"We will need metal outfits."

"We can get Jimmy the welder to make them. And we can get scrap metal from some of those rez wrecks and from that old CN rail car."

Moses replied, "mêtoni miyohtâkwân. Sounds good!"

Pâcinîs smiled again and said, "Tâpwê. It will be a gooder."

---

22   "That indeed is true."

NEECHIE KNIGHTS: Part II

The day that everyone had waited for had arrived. People had gathered from far and wide to see the thing that everyone had been talking about. The thing that most of the people could not really pronounce. Many of the older ones who still spoke mostly Cree called it "chaw–stin" because there is no "j" in Cree. When one of the old timers first heard "chaw–sting" they thought it was some bad bite from some kind of bad monster that the money had dreamt up in some lab. Then when they heard what it was, one of the them said, "Cha" but most were really interested. And they all agreed that the reserve could use some fun.

On that day people gathered every possible chair that they could find. People formed a long line on the path where the jousting would happen. Some of the old timers even sat on logs. The sea of brown and brownish faces was interrupted by the occasional Scandinavian looking face. Those Swedes were 'spahk–môniyâw[23] people, the ones that tanned so heavily under the open prairie sun. The Chief had charged them a higher entry fee. Some of the things that the neechies were selling were: bannock in all shapes and forms, used radios, another counter which was selling fabrics and clothes – which was quite popular with the ladies.

There was a 25 cent entry fee which helped to cover some of the expenses of putting together the event. They had chosen this particular weekend because the Indian agent was known to be going away for to his summer vacation spot in Ontario. They didn't want the damn Indian agent wrecking their fun with some section of the Indian Act, or some subsection of this or that piece of legislation. Seems like those Indian agents were pretty booked up in the head, or least pretended to be booked up in the head, and they were kind of hard to outsmart sometimes. Some fellas like John Tootoosis seemed to be able to outsmart them, but

---

23   white people

sometimes the best strategy was simply to avoid them.

There was one young lady named Sophia who had gone to the big city of Toronto to study fashion. To bypass the Indian agents she pretended to be Metis, and thus avoided the need for a pass. That is one point where the Metis were lucky because they didn't have the same restrictions as people with Treaty cards. In many ways, one could say the whole system really didn't make sense. But at any rate Sophia had studied fashion and she was selling her stuff at the jousting match and was doing quite well. She kind of knew how to read the crowd. She had stitched together some medieval style clothing which was selling like crazy. Everyone wanted to dress like an old Englishman.

There was a boy who picked up a bit of trumpet playing from residential school. He was dressed up, all fancy-like, and began to trumpet away. The Chief was dressed up like a king and sat higher than everyone else in a bush tent which had its flaps opened up and was on a platform. He was dolled up like an old English big wig. He had powdered his face white, had magnificent lacy puffs around his neck area, and had very fancy leather shoes.

The crowd was seated in a somewhat scattered manner. One of the local rez carpenters put the people on double row seating in a few of the choice spots. It was a lot of the old ladies in wheelchairs who were sitting like this and some of them had moccasins with rubber boots. They wore their flowered dresses, and you could see by the looks on their faces that they felt quite grand. Some of the ladies had been through a lot and any day such as this was a grand day indeed.

When the boy started trumpeting, everyone in the crowd looked very solemn. It was somewhat strange how the Crees who were noted for their humour, could switch gears so abruptly and look so terribly serious. They usually looked serious like this whenever anything about the Queen was being invoked, or on Treaty day, or even when the results of the turkey shoots were announced on the reserve. The Chief undertook his duties very solemnly. It was that sense of solemn like when Crees sing Anglican hymns at a wake.

The Chief had a somewhat strange crown on, fashioned out of a pie plate with dried, glazed strawberries for jewels. The Swedish farmers who had paid money to see this were completely enthralled. They were seeing Indians be Englishmen– what more could they want? Some of the Swedish farmers came in their tractors, and one even came in his combine.

The crowd turned to the Chief. He looked like an old English mystic in the prairie field. The crowd waited for him to give the signal. The knights who were competing all waited, the metal of their armour glistening in the sun. Their armour itself was an interesting combination of metal from a variety of sources. The first knight had a garbage can lid for a shield. He used a long metal pole from a mining machine with an old army boot tied with moose sinew at the end. The "armour" on his body consisted of a bunch of metal shingles, which had been haphazardly stitched together. He had tied Sears catalogues to his shins, and he put parts of bath tubs on the armour of his body. He put fish netting around it to try and make it look like chain mail. A lame attempt, yes, but let us remember that these boys and girls were in the middle of nowhere, far from any city.

Old Moses was the first knight's opponent. Everyone gasped as he moved his horse into position. He wore a leather outfit and no helmet, but he had the fastest horse that the world had ever seen. Someone yelled at him, "Hey, why aren't you dressed like an English knight?"

Moses replied quickly, confidently but with a measured tone, which gave the impression that he was completely calm, "Because I am Cree, I have no desire to be an Englishman."

With that the crowd sighed. Even the Chief took a deep, deep breath.

The Chief put his hands in the air to get the

crowd's attention. "People," he said. The crowd cheered in response. "People," he said, and he kept his hands in the air and moved them back and forth. "We have ourselves a smart Indian." The crowd waited on his every word, their faces somewhere between a full smile and frenzy.

"Hey Chief. Kiss my ass!" said Moses.

The crowd was confused and not sure if this was part of the game.

The Chief tried very hard to be serious. It is uncertain where he got his sense of solemnity because it was before the internet, and before cheesy western movies were popular. He really had nowhere to find this image, yet he found it.

The knight stared down Moses. The sun illuminated the rusty metal and made it glisten under the sun. He looked like a champion and, by the sweet beard of Nanabush, he felt like one.

The Chief spoke again, and the crowd began to roar. The knight raised his lance and the King saluted him.

"My friends, my relatives, guests from nearby reserves in the district. Look around you. You are all red Englishmen. You are my little red White children."

An old lady laughed and elbowed another old lady who was sitting on the second level of the seating. She said, "Cha! The chief sure got around if we are all his children."

The other old woman said, "cha, as if. How can he even be my dad? Shit, I am older than that boy."

"Our champion, Sir Galahad, will smoke that red man on his horse."

"Ya! Ya!" the crowds yelled, "Get that red man!"

The one old lady elbowed the other one.

"Cha! Why would we want someone to beat a red man?"

The old lady laughed as she looked at her arms, "Cha! Don't worry. We are brown. They can get the red man. It would not affect us. We are brown." They both laughed.

"Our champion," the Chief said, "Sir Galahad will defeat this red savage."

The old ladies cheered and and one old kôhkom laughed so hard that her dentures went flying into someone else's tea. They tapped their canes on the floor. The Chief got up to the podium again. He cleared his voice and said, "Before we start can I ask everyone to stand while we sing 'God Save the Queen'." Everyone got up, dutifully and with neechie solemnity, began to sing that song.

Moses thought of all the things his mosôm[24] had told him about the old days of fighting the Blackfoot. He laughed at the hilarity of some of the stories, but he also remembered their bravery.

Sir Galahad's horse had been trained by an English fancy rider who lived near Prince Albert. The horse made fancy prancing motions. Once again, the sun hit the metal and created a lovely sheen, like the glistening blue of a summer lake.

Cân, the Chief's sidekick and first cousin shot his gun and the two jousters came barrelling towards each other.

Sir Galahad raced towards him with perfect form and Moses laughed. He took his horse and trotted slowly up with carefree laughter. This seemed to fire up the crowd and the Chief put his thumb down in disapproval. Galahad kept charging. A fair maiden yelled his name and said, "If you win, my father will give you his trap line." A furious roar emerged from the crowd. People spontaneously did "the wave" even though it was decades before it became popular in the land of the Wonderbread Eaters.

The two moved closer and closer. Sir Galahad raised his "jousting spear," in the way that the old English mosôms from a long time ago did. Moses didn't do that. He just kept riding towards him, exposed, without any armour. He did not raise his old hunting spear. No, not just yet. The crowd collectively gasped as the two warriors

24   grandfather

moved closer and closer. At this point in the event the vendors were not busy and they too were staring at the impending collision of horses and riders. The Swedish people were smiling, smiles as a broad as a Hutterite barn, and they were, in their excitement, speaking excitedly to one another in their language.

Sir Galahad lowered his spear to aim dead on Moses. He looked fine. His long hair, which he groomed regularly with bear grease, was fluttering in the wind. Some of the old ladies gasped, as a few of them had fathers who were in the old time Blackfoot wars. Some of those old timers spoke some of the Blackfoot languages. They really respected the Blackfoot, because they said they were such worthy opponents, and dammit they had good songs. But all that had changed. Now people just spoke Cree and, sadly, no Blackfoot. The sound on the reserves was now like a great forest that was missing many trees. Now, they had put aside some of the old songs, and instead sang "Onward Christian soldiers."

The crowd cheered, especially the old timers, when old Moses got up on his horse, stood straight up on the saddle and charged at full gallop towards Sir Galahad, who put his spear down just a little lower to zero in on Moses. Just as his spear was about to strike Moses, Moses jumped high, the spear passed through empty space and then Moses jumped back on the saddle. The crowd gasped. Even the Chief gasped. Sir Galahad was heard to cuss by those nearby him as he went thundering past and came to a crashing halt as he neared the end of the jousting runaway. Moses did a flip, and landed on the ground.

Moses' squire came up to him and said, "Moses, I thought that you had arthritis. How did you do such flips?"

Moses laughed and said, "Boy, the môniyâw may not have all of the answers, but one thing I will say is that WD40 will do wonders for the joints if applied generously and vigorously."

"Sir Galahad," said his squire, "did you see that

crazy jump? 'stakâc cî[25]?"

"Listen here, boy," said Sir Galahad as he lifted his metal visor, "I am not paying you to cheer for the other knight." The squire looked at him with a great deal of shame. "Now quit looking at me and earn your sôniyâw."[26]

"Okay," the boy said in a hushed voice, "that would have been a death blow."

Sir Galahad laughed. "Young man, that is more like it. Perhaps someday you will be one of the Knights of the Round Table."

The squire thought for a minute. He thought of all of the girls that would want to talk to him – all of the kôhkoms that would want him to meet their granddaughters. Maybe someday he would even give orders in battle. Maybe...

"We are about to start again."

The Swedes looked at each other and smiled. "Det är jävlig röligt den har indianer spel."[27]

"Det är jätte sant vad du säger."[28]

The old kôhkoms looked on. They were smiling – they were really getting into it – and they felt like big shots. People would bring their drinks in fancy cups and saucers that they bought in an antique shop in Montana. It was all a game of the old English people. They really liked playing at being White people.

The Chief had a huddle with his advisors. If young people today saw him, they would would say that he looked like a young Jabba the Hutt right before he got really fat. He had the chub of Jabba from episode 6, but the legs of the original Jabba as imagined by Lucas in the original scene cut in episode 4."Sir King, we need some contact. This ain't that damn Buffalo Bill show. People didn't come here to see some Indian do flips in the air."

---

25   "Isn't it truly amazing."

26   money

27   "This is darn entertaining, this Indian game."

28   "It is true what you said."

"That is true. What do you suggest?"

"I would recommend sir, that we tell Moses that if he does not play nice, that if he does not try to make impact, with his spear, that we will cut his rations." While this was intended as a game, it seemed that underhanded power politics were coming through.

"Okay," the King Chief tapped his royal walking stick twice on the ground, and nodded in agreement.

The King Chief sent someone down to give the message before they were to start their next run. When Moses got the message his instinct was to give the Chief the one finger salute, but he didn't want to, out of respect for the old people, and because so many Swedes were there. He didn't want to air out the community's dirty laundry in front of outsiders. He shook his head as he looked down and he realized what he had to do.

He grabbed his spear and remembered how he and his mosôm used to spear fish together in the spring. "Sir Galahad" had been too messed up by residential school to know much about hunting and that is probably why he got so into pretending to be an Englishman. Moses remembered the way his mosôm would concentrate so hard when he would spear fish. He would wait for the fish to get into the right spot. Waiting, waiting. Then when the fish was in just the right place, he would let the fish have it with one shot to its body. And in a second the fish's body would be lifeless. Moses thought that maybe if he tried to be like his mosôm in this challenge before him, then maybe, just maybe, he could win.

However, he did not want to hurt Sir Galahad. He just wanted to knock him off his horse. He wanted to hear the old timers in the back row yell and, by–the–sweet–beard–of–Nanabush, he wanted to not back down to the King Chief. He knew that the King Chief wanted to fix the game. He knew that if Sir Galahad won, then he would be in good with the folks there, and maybe, just maybe, the old timers would let him in on their secret fishing spot.

The knights, after refreshing and getting ready for

the next fight, faced each other. They had spoken to their squires, and the King Chief had even sent a runner to bring Sir Galahad a cup of rabbit root tea. The King Chief realized that the young knight was going to need that extra boost of strength, that extra boost of life, in order to face Moses.

For the last joust Moses asked his squire to come close to him. "My boy," Moses said, "Wâpahta nêtê!"[29] His squire looked towards the crowd and could see people standing up. He could see the old timers with their mosôm caps tugging at them lightly while a few of them rolled their own cigarettes. "Those old timers want something to believe in. They don't think so much of these progressives. People like the Chief who are trying to change things. They believe in the old ways, they believe in the way our warriors did things a long time ago." Moses paused for a moment and then looked into the eyes of the squire. "Mahti pê–wîcihin boy, itêw," he said. "Help me take this suit off." The squire looked at him quizzically at first and did not understand. "I want to face Sir Galahad like an old timer," Moses said. He paused. "I want to give those old timers something to believe in." With that, he took off his clothes, and he put on some old timer garb, and blackened his face like the old timers did.

At first Sir Galahad kind of laughed and did not know what to expect. Some of the crowd did not know what to do, nor did they fully understand. The Chief raised his hands in the air as though he did not understand what was going on, and the Swedes furiously started to bet again, and it was clear that some of them were betting heavy against Moses, except for Old Olaf, who was rumoured to still believe in Thor, and who was a fan of the old ways.

Sir Galahad put down his visor, and old Moses looked at him with great intensity. The kisêyiniwak[30] could not believe what they were seeing and they rose and <u>saluted old Moses</u>. One of them sent a runner to the Chief

29   "Look over here!"
30   Old men

and had him pause the proceedings. It was only because of his social weight in the community that he was able to do it. He rushed off to his house which was not far and came back with the lance of his grandfather that had actually been used in combat against the Blackfoot. He humbly presented it to old Moses, and then saluted him. Old Moses humbly grabbed it, and said, "kinanâskomitin."[31] He looked straight ahead, and then the Chief dropped his hand to tell the two knights to make the charge towards each other. The old people were cheering, and one of them pulled out his hand-drum, and started to sing. As the two riders approached each other, the sunlight glistened on Sir Galahad's helmet. The sunlight also caught the black face paint on old Moses. The two combatants moved towards each other, their horses pounding the ground beneath. As they approached each other Sir Galahad lowered his lance aiming it right for old Moses. With the old man singing in the stands, and at just the right time, Moses leapt into the air, did a flip, landed with his lance still in hand, and with a mighty swing knocked Sir Galahad ass-over-tea-kettle off his horse. Once he fell on the ground he saw stars. His armour was thrown around like pots in bush camp, catching the sun at different points and places.

At first, Sir Galahad was astonished that such a thing took place. The Chief was astonished. The Swedes were astonished, and there was a debate amongst them as to whether the move was legal. The old men in the stands smiled, and the old man put away his hand drum. As they left the arena, old Moses got off his horse, gave it to his squire and went to order some bannock from one of the stands. He had shown the Chief that maybe the old ways were still useful, that the old ways were just as a good as the môniyâw ways. That Indian warriors could defeat English gentleman.

---

31   Thank you

AFTER THE WAR:
NAPOLEON AND THE PASS SYSTEM

Mervin came to see the Senator again and wanted to know what happened after the war.

"My boy," the Senator itwêw, "mêtoni kî–ayimahk.[32] There was a time when things were different. That was in the kayâs ago days. In those days, the bannock tasted different. In those days, rez dogs barked louder. In those days, Chiefs didn't get paid to give speeches. In dem olden days, dem fellas would pass a hat around to raise money for their leaders. My gosh, dem old guys sure had to put up with a lot. They would leave the reserve sometimes in the middle of the night without a permit. Those boys would ride their horses so far to organize politically that the ones without saddles couldn't walk straight for a long time after."

The period after the Second World War saw a great deal of changes for a lot of people. When the Indian veterans came back, they could demand to be treated the same as anyone else. They could demand to be served in bars. They could demand to be able to sell their grain at an elevator without a permit. It wasn't because the Indian Act had been magically changed so that they were "permitted" to do these things. Rather, what had permitted them to do these things was their valour on the battlefield. It was their valour which was essentially their ticket to a new way of being – a new way of life. A way of life which was a lot more open than life had been before.

To fight was to try to make the new world. They wanted to make this place better, not only for themselves, but for their children. This was a fight where they had to dig deep.

The men had been gone for many years. After

---

32   Things were very difficult.

years of fighting the Krauts, a lot of the men were still wired for fighting. In some ways you could say that they couldn't really turn off that switch that helped them be good fighters. It was something that they would have to end by rewiring the whole structure. It was like rewiring a house. It was like having to gut a house, and then stringing decorations around the Christmas tree.

In those days, there was no running water, unless you counted the water that was running in the river. And of course, there was also no electricity. Many of the people still used old lanterns in order that they could see. Some of the men, like Napoleon, were filled with anger and just couldn't seem to find their place in the world after the war. They needed a switch to turn off the fire – a switch to turn off the anger. The switch that would just make everything quiet. It was all about turning off that switch which had made them such great fighters.

Despite not having electricity and not having running water, one of the things that seemed to keep people going was the smell of freshly made bannock. The smell of bannock would just sink into their skin. The smell was something that just seemed to soak into someone's being.

The best bannock on the reserve was, of course, made by Nadine's ohkoma – her grandmother. They say that her recipe was very old and its stretch of existence and transmission went back as far as anyone could remember – and for Cree people, that was a pretty long time of remembering.

She was a strong old woman, and she also had strong warm eyes. She pretty much stuck to her own business and no one really seemed to bother her. She had the warmest brown eyes that you ever saw, but you also knew that she would and could stand up to anyone who would get in her way – or anyone who might try to bully her. Preachers and Christian ministers came, the place of women became distorted, and seemed to be forgotten by many. The rightful place of our women was put aside like a forgotten love letter in an old box of letters that you might find in an estate sale.

Paskwâw–iskwêw had a strong, vibrant mind that moved through thoughts with great energy and force, like the movement of the prairie clouds across the prairie sky. It was the movement of her mouth and her eyes which were like clouds in the sky which broke up the blue space and carved forms through movement. She was quite a striking woman whose beauty came from her whole being. It was not just a physical beauty, it was a deep beauty, like that of the deep blue of the Saskatchewan River, where it seemed to be deepest where it curved.

Like the deep strength of deep water, Paskwâw–iskwêw moved through her life with conviction and power. In her life, she had stood up to Indian agents and the silly rules of the Indian Act. She had grown tired of the fences that the new rules had drawn onto the land. She was always firm like an old rock on a stretch of prairie earth. The words and laws of the Indian Act were like the wind, which blew against the rock. The wind would come and go on the surface of the rock, and the rock would remain.

The Senator, who was known as Bobby Boy when he was younger, would haul wood for her. The smell of freshly made bannock would fill the house, and make everything seem alright. It was a smell that meant safety. The first winter of residential school had been so hard on him. It was difficult to be away from the language of his reserve. During that time, he longed for the smell of bannock. The memory of his mom and gramma cooking bannock kept him warm when all of the heat seemed to be pulled from his body by the bitter cold of that lonely place.

The wiring of the minds of a lot of the soldiers could not handle the changes that occurred in the period after the war. It was both an opening up and a closing up at the same time. The war opened up their minds with possibilities, but it was also a closing because when the soldiers came back, they were not able to leave the reserve without a permit, they were not able to sell their grain without a permit, and these veterans who fought so bravely in other parts of the world found themselves trapped once they were home. They did not get the same benefits, in fact they received no benefits that the other soldiers received and that upset many of them including Napoleon. Of all of the people who felt this, it was Napoleon who was the most angered. He saw some of the toughest fighting of the war. He was one of the first men who landed on Juno Beach. The fighting was hard, and intense. Instead of being told to do things by the Indian agent, he was the one who was giving the orders, leading his troops through the small spaces between German bullets and shells. At first, a few of them did not want to follow an Indian. One of them even tried to fight him, but Napoleon hit clocked him, knocking him into the ground.

One of the things the Indian agent tried to do was to try to discredit him. He wanted to shut Napoleon down. Napoleon was involved in politics. They were trying to protect the Treaties, fighting for education, and struggling to get recognition for the old veterans. Despite the valour of many of the Indians, such as Napoleon, they were given a raw deal. Word got around that the Indian agent had not even been a soldier. They saw that the Indian agent had lied about his paperwork, and made up an excuse as to why he could not fight. Napoleon could not stomach that a coward such as him without honour would push him around. "It was bullshit," Napoleon would say. But the Indian agent found out that Napoleon knew the truth of his forged documents. He did not like the trouble that the organization was making, especially for Indian agents. The Indian agent wanted it to stop. He needed a plan.

His plan was simple and also very destructive. The Indian agent trumped up charges against Napoleon. He made up fake papers saying that Napoleon had sold a cow without his permission. He also said that Napoleon

had not gotten permission to leave the reserve. The truth of the matter was Napoleon asked for permission to leave the reserve to attend the funeral of one of his friends.
He never did receive the permission to go, but he went anyway. He didn't need a goddamn letter of permission from the Indian agent to attend the funeral of his friend, who also was a soldier. On the way back he tried to get into the Legion, but they wouldn't let him in. He was refused entry. To top it off, when he got back to the reserve there was a hand-written note saying that he was going to be charged under provisions of the Indian Act. After he read it, he crumpled up the paper, threw it on the ground, and said, "this is bullshit!" He marched over to the house of the Indian agent to give him a piece of his mind. But the Indian agent was no where to be found. That was the last straw for Napoleon.

He was going to town and he was going to make a goddamn splash on the scene. He drove his shiny yellow meteor car and went back to his house. He lit a cigarette outside of his house, and thought about what he needed to do. After he finished his cigarette, he went into his house. He put his suit on, and his hat. He looked at this hat in the mirror, and adjusted it. He smiled – he was a neechie dandy. He looked sharp in his pin stripe suit.

He drove the dusty roads into town. When he got to the Legion there were only a few other cars parked there. This time, maybe because there were not many people around, he was able to enter through the front door. He waved at a couple of his friends and they smiled and waved back. Lenny, a former soldier, was the bartender. He would often let Napoleon in and serve him drinks even though it was against the Indian Act. A police officer who had served in Napoleon's unit would never follow through on any charges, but there was a new officer, so Napoleon was not sure how this would play out. One time, there was a police officer who was visiting. The visiting officer wanted to charge him. But Lenny, who was washing the counter, had laughed and said, "Don't worry he's not Treaty. He is Metis." Napoleon did his best not to look at Lenny. He thought that if he looked at Lenny directly his smiling eyes might give away the truth. With that the visiting officer walked away and left a short time later after finishing his drink. He wouldn't be able to bully an Indian that day.

The police officer who was leaving had grown a bit chubby. He may have been an athlete at some point – perhaps an athlete of some skill, of some merit, but the days of his sporting glory had long since passed. Now, in the chubby present, he tried to find a bit of glory and power in other ways.

Now he sat in the bar thinking of his friend who had just passed. Napoleon sat there sipping from time to time, saying "hi" to his fellow soldiers. Most of them knew that Napoleon was really not supposed to be there according to the law. But, they didn't say anything because Napoleon had served the army, and he didn't bother anyone when he was drinking quietly, generally by himself, in the Legion.

Then something happened. The Indian agent from Broken Elbow came into the bar. Most of the vets didn't notice and the ones who did, didn't seem to care. The Indian agent was a noted coward. No one bothered him because he worked for the government. But they did not stop to take notice of the other person who came in with him. The other man was a big red headed man. He was in a police uniform, and Napoleon guessed that he was probably a veteran. He could tell this by the way he swaggered, and the way he seemed to have a single purpose in his eyes as he walked towards Napoleon. The Indian agent seemed small to Napoleon as he was pointing at him. He seemed small for a number of reasons – he was small against the large red headed man, and because Napoleon now knew that he must have been home when Napoleon had gone by his place.

"There he is," he said as he pointed to Napoleon.

Manny Davis, that was the name of the large police officer, had served overseas in the war, and had been wounded in France in the fighting after D–Day.

"Fresh off the reservation, eh?"

Lenny knew that there was going to be trouble, and he knew that he would not be able to convince this police officer like he had with the others. But he thought that he should try.

"Officer, that is Napoleon Sanderson. He is a veteran." Lenny said this half hoping that this might be able to make things okay for Napoleon.

Manny folded his arms, and looked right at Napoleon, "You some kind of Emperor, Napoleon?" He laughed and unfolded his arms, and looked at the Indian agent who also nervously laughed. The Indian agent always seemed to be so tentative in all of his laughing. He seemed to be so tentative in all of the things that he did. That is probably why the neechies of the Broken Elbow reserve were quick to launch into political activism. They saw this nature of his as a weakness. It was probably why someone in the Department of Indian Affairs was working hard to get some muscle into the situation. Someone like Manny Davies.

"No, I am no Emperor. I am just an Indian soldier from the Broken Elbow reserve." Napoleon knew that there would be no point of trying to conceal that he was a Treaty Indian. By these words, Manny Davis, made it clear that he knew and he was actually going to charge Napoleon. Also the Indian agent was there as well, and there could be no disputing his take on things. "I was actually a Lieutenant, and received a Victoria Cross for my combat experience." Napoleon paused without losing the focus of his stare. "You were a Sargent I hear."

Manny Davis was a bully, and he was not used to anyone standing up to him, "You want me to salute you?"

The Indian agent laughed nervously. Lenny gave the Indian agent an annoyed look and did not offer to serve him a drink.

Manny continued, "You think I am going to salute a Indian?" He asked with a rising intonation to show that he was in fact asking a question. At that point, Napoleon looked walked right up to him. Lenny raised his head from the counter. "Okay boys," he said, then paused, "we don't want any trouble in the Legion."

Manny pushed his body right into Napoleon's. "I want trouble," he said. "You are under arrest."

Napoleon laughed. "Arrest for what? Being too handsome?" The rest of the soldiers in the bar laughed. Manny tried to stare them down, but most of them did not look away. "Come with me," he said to Napoleon and he pushed his body into Napoleon's. He thought he would get Napoleon to punch him, but Napoleon didn't take the bait. He knew the routine. If he punched a police officer, the consequences would be grim – not unlike when he punched the priest at residential school. Manny Davis pushed into him again. No reaction. Stared at him. No reaction. Then Manny just seemed to lose his patience, and he tried to head butt Napoleon – but Napoleon dropped down, and then moved up again hitting Manny with a left fist to the ribs. Then a right jab to the face. A crack was heard, and blood poured down the officer's face.

Manny fell to his knees and yelled out, "He broke my nose." Then he paused briefly. "The Indian broke my nose." He looked around the bar, but the other vets were not going to have any part of it. In a quick, desperate panic, the Indian agent charged towards Napoleon, but Napoleon didn't even flinch. The Indian agent was going to punch, but then he hesitated. Napoleon didn't flinch. He just laughed. "When I faced the Germans on that one night in France they didn't hesitate, and I still took them out. They had years of combat experience in Russia. You look like you are fresh from your desk job at Indian Affairs. What do you think your chances are?"

Napoleon stood there for a long time without saying anything. He waited for either the Indian agent or

Manny Davis to say something. The silence grew, and the room was still, like water on a lake in the early morning sun. Manny whimpered in pain. The Indian agent backed down and moved towards Manny to see if he needed help, but Manny waved him away.

"Êkosi mâka,"[33] Napoleon said. He threw a bill on the counter and walked out. He kept a low profile for a while after. No charges were laid or pressed. It seemed like everyone just wanted to push it all aside and forget about it.

The story of the fight in that sleepy prairie town inspired a lot of neechies to stand their ground.

---

33   "Well that is it."

MOSES MOSTOS

Mervin came again, with his recorder, and made the Senator his tea. Mervin brought a tin of evaporated milk. It was a little difficult to find the evaporated milk sometimes, but he found it. This is the story that the Senator told him that day.

Everyone had known that Moses Mostos was very handy with electronics and technology, and he was able to fix many things. For instance, he was able to fix radios of all types. People would bring radios and other miscellaneous electronic items as well as small engines to him to fix. Even some of the Swedish farmers would bring their stuff to get fixed by Moses. He rigged it up so that Pacinîs could broadcast his stories to the reserve for two hours twice a week. The people really liked to hear those stories. A lot of the younger people enjoyed listening to them because they could brush up on their language skills. Sometimes Pacinîs would mix fiddle music into it. This would cause the old Swedes to listen because they liked fiddle music as well. Later on, Moses would learn how to fix TVs. When they got their first TV all that they could get was the French channel– but after Moses tinkered with it, they could get the channel in English too. But that is another story.

Moses Mostos had tried, as everyone knew, to build a metallic flying crane. The metallic crane had looked glorious, its shiny metal body, gleaming in the light of the sun. Moses had tried to launch the metallic crane from the top of the barn. Everyone had gathered to see the launch. It was a bright sunny day. People had beads of sweat on their foreheads as they waited to see the metallic bird fly. Moses had a couple of younger people tending to the fire so that Moses could try out the smoke signal remote controls. The science behind it was sound by all accounts, but the two young men were not experienced in fire keeping, and there was too much smoke. The excess smoke fired up the bird too high. The metallic crane shot straight into the sky. It was like the bird was heading directly for the sun and there was really nothing that could stop it. One of the older Swedes was looking right into the sky and said, "vad händer?"[34] Another of the old Swedes said, "Jag vet inte, men tror jag det flyggar för högt."[35] After a few more seconds, and a few more scattered words of speculation, the metallic crane went a bit further. The boys kept fanning the flames and the more that they did this, the higher the metallic bird flew. Finally, there was a great bang and the metallic bird came down harder than the balance sheets of the Broken Elbow reserve in the 1990s. But that is another story.

After everything cleared up, they assessed the situation. He realized that he was on to something. He realized that there indeed was something to his smoke signal remote control device. He realized that the wrong kind of wood had been used for the metallic bird's thrusters. Also, as everyone seemed to note, the boys who were tending the fire did not completely seem to know that they were doing.

A few days after, the TV Club got together to listen to the news on the radio. They called themselves the TV Club, even though they had no TV yet. They all knew the TV would replace their radio soon. There was another report about Sputnik. The TV Club speculated about the Senator's three-legged dog, Not-Even, going into space. "We gotta think like big time môniyâw show business people," Buddy Bradley said.

Pacinîs laughed and said, "tâpwê miywâsin ôma."[36]

Everyone was pretty sure Moses Mostos could build the ship, and all the parts and mechanisms that

---

34   "What is happening?"
35   "I don't know, but I think that it is flying too high."
36   "This is truly good."

were needed. There was something about the people of the Broken Elbow reserve. They did not feed the cultural anxiety that people on other reserves felt sometimes. The people on the Broken Elbow reserve never pushed their heads lower on the pavement to try to avoid white people. There was a stereotype, which had floated around in some môniyâw circles, that Indians never looked people in the eye. Instead they challenge white people. Some of the old timers like Pacînis were even know to say, "cha. I wonder why they think they are better than us? They are rejects from Europe," he would say. "They don't even have their own culture." Itêw, "They even try to be just English people," he would say.

"Aya, mosôm," said Moses. "Don't you remember back a few years ago when we pretended to be joust champions? We were all pretending to be English."

"Tâpwê," said the Senator. "Even the Chief was pretending to be King."

"Aya, kihci-okimâwihkâsow ana okimâhkân."[37] With that everyone laughed. Pacînis did not seem to have a retort. He just smiled and started to laugh with the others. Once he forgot that he was kind of embarrassed, then he really started to laugh.

_____

37   "Yes, that Chief was pretending to be a King."

MOSES MOSTOS: PART TWO

Everyone from the TV Club had decided that they were all going to commit to launching a rocket ship into space. Then they started to talk about where they would launch it from. The obvious place would be Blueberry Picking Hill which overlooked the whole area. It was the highest point in the whole district. This time, there would be no smoke signal remote control. Rather, Moses had figured out a way to make special wires that would help propel the metallic crane to space. One thing that they did well was that they were asked by Moses Mostos to save all of their farts in little jars. About a thousand pwêkito iskotêw[38] power would be needed to launch their ship into space. They needed to get into Prince Albert in order to get the special wiring that a Russian immigrant had conceived of, and who had custom made it. Buddy had met him on a comedy tour which the Indian agent had actually sanctioned by signing his pass.

Buddy borrowed Napoleon's car and drove into town. The car was flashy, and Buddy drove it in a flashy manner. One of the things about Buddy Bradley was that he did not really run into much trouble. No one ever told him that he did not belong. The reason why he did not run into any trouble was that he was fair, so he didn't stand out as an Indian. One time when he was he was at a redneck bar, someone yelled, "Get off the stage you damn Mexican!" Sometimes people would even think that perhaps he was French. A lot of people that were part Cree, and were fair, would try to pass as French or perhaps they would be taken as French, and their lives would be that much easier. He would never get stopped and asked questions about why he was off the reservation. He just passed the heart of whiteness without any problems and without anyone saying anything.

Buddy heard that the Prime Minister, who was famous for meeting neechies, would meet them on Central

---

38   fart

Avenue in kistapinânihk.[39] The Prime Minister would tell
and retell his story of shooting the other pilot down. The
older Crees really liked this story because they said it
reminded them of the old time stories. The old time stories
that old time grandfathers would tell them about. Those
old people called them the kihci–âcimowina,[40] the great
stories. They were the stories of when the Cree would fight
the Blackfoot. They were the stories about when the people
would get their honour, and from that honour they would
get respect from the people. They had proven their bravery,
had proven themselves to not be afraid of death. The Prime
Minister did not have any time for the mihkowâyawak[41]
that were like a blight upon Saskatchewan. He challenged
them in the open spaces of cafes and he would open up
the courts to the Indian people. The Prime Minister had
heard that the Cree people of the Broken Elbow reserve
had jousting tournaments in the 1940s, and they paid
for Pacinîs and a couple of the other old timers to go to
England where they were able to see some re–enactments
of jousting tournaments. Instead of being able to simply
watch the jousting tournament, Pâcinîs was asked to
tell "real red Indian stories," and to try to shape the
imaginations of the people about the real red Indians.
The Senator was also flown out so that he could translate
for the Pâcinîs. Pâcinîs went on a bit a talking tour, but
he refused to wear the headdress that they offered him.
Instead he wore his GWG work clothes, which were often
green. He then wore a Saskatchewan Wheat Pool hat. The
people loved him, but the British anthropologists were
disappointed because of the elements of modernity which
seemed to linger in him.

When Pâcinîs and other older Cree men visited with
the Prime Minister, they would meet at the one Chinese
restaurant. It was the kind of restaurant where a neechie
could feel comfortable – where a neechie could just sit

39   Prince Albert
40   the great storeis
41   rednecks

and relax. Where he or she wouldn't have to wait for the first redneck comment. They would talk about all kinds of things. They talked about the weather, about reserve life. The Prime Minister would tell them how he missed the prairies how he missed the lights of combines in the fields in the fall. Most of all he missed the chatter in the cafes. He even spoke of how he missed the Senator and the way he would clank and clank the side of his coffee cup. The Senator would fool around so much when he getting his coffee ready. The Prime Minister would laugh at all of Buddy's jokes.

Now, in the present, Buddy Bradley walked proudly down the street towards the hardware store with his permit in his hand. According to the permit, he had to be back to the reserve by the next day. He walked down the street whistling and feeling good. Sometimes because he was so fair skinned he felt like a spy – like he could slip into the world of the White people. His fair skin was like a camouflage that allowed him to get into the heart of whiteness.

He went to the hardware store to get the wires that Moses Mostos needed. He fished into his pockets to retrieve a crumpled piece of paper. Yellow wire for this, red wire for that, and blue wire for God knows what. Buddy Bradley had no idea how it would all fit together. Sometimes Buddy would just feel restless. He thought that Wîsahkêcahk had it a lot easier. All he had to do was to eat some beans or grab a crane by the leg. He didn't have to fool around with all of this wiring, all of these metal sheets, or all of the techno mumbo jumbo.

Sometimes Buddy Bradley would get restless, and he would get on a tractor and drive around until he ran out of road. However, there was only so much road on the reserve. That is why Buddy Bradley wanted so much to go into space. There was no limit to how far one could go. No one could run out of track. Buddy got all of the wires and a few of the parts that Moses Mostos needed and stayed at the hotel that people from Broken Elbow would stay at. Early the next day he went back to the reserve.

BUILDING THE BARN

After the Prime Minister himself had intervened, the Indian agent knew that he had to stay away from the TV Club boys, and perhaps most importantly and most pragmatically, he had to stay away from the barn by Pâcinîs place. The Indian agent, despite all of the restrictions, could not resist looking out his window. He could see the lights and hear the clank of metal. He caught himself saying to himself, "It sounds like those boys are having a little pow wow." He tried to think of sections of the Indian Act that he could possibly throw at them. Maybe he could get them for the fiddle music that Pâcinîs would play into the night. Maybe the Indian agent could get them on the grounds that it was taking away from the hard work that they should be doing. Maybe he could get Buddy Bradley on some kind of traffic violation for driving his tractor while eating bannock. Maybe he could get the TV Club, the Senator in particular, for the sale of food during the hockey games. But there was really nothing that he could do as long as the Prime Minister was backing them.

Meanwhile back at the barn of Pâcinîs, everyone was getting very tired, and was starting to doubt whether or not they could actually make it to outer space.

"How the hell do you think we will even make it?" one said.

"Well, the hill will give us a head start."

"Yeah, but don't you remember what happened when Moses tried to make the metal crane to fly to the moon."

"That is no excuse, Moses should have factored in for a margin of error." Moses didn't say anything – he just kept working on the wires. The Senator knew that he would have to get up and give a big speech:

"We have been trapped on this reserve for a long time. We were herded on here after the buffalo left the skin of the earth."

"Holeh Senator," said Buddy Bradley, "you sound like one of those fancy poets in one of those fancy books."

"Well," he paused, "aya. We have been trying to get off this reserve. There was a time when we were free, a time when our grandfathers and grandmothers did, in the old days of fighting the Blackfoot. We were free in those good olden days. When you could go out in the morning and get yourself a buffalo and then by night time a fella would be chewing away on buffalo stew. This was a good time. Mitoni kî–miywâsin ôma. Life was good." He paused for a bit. "Now I know some of you are doubting what we are doing." He looked around and some of the people actually looked down as his eyes met theirs. "Moses has an idea to get us off the reserve, ever since he saw the Sputnik rotating around the earth. We saw that metal stretching across the sky, stretching for its freedom. Moses has a dream – just like that flicker show we saw in town, with that guy with the stone plates, the other Moses, awa okwêmîsa. That one is the namesake of our Moses right here." Everyone seemed to pay even more attention to the Senator. Their eyes were fixed on him like he was some kind of movie star in one of those flicker shows.

"This Moses, this booked up neechie, will lead us to the promised land."

"Tântê êkwa?"[42] said one of the older men from the TV club.

"Nêtê,"[43] he said pointing to the sky, "ispimihk"[44]
"Kah,"[45] said Pâcinîs.

"This here acâhkosi–otâpânâsk,[46] this here star vehicle, that we are hammering away at, will reach to the stars." Everyone started to cheer. Everyone started to clap. The speech had worked. People were fired up. The Indian

42   "To where then?"
43   over there
44   up in the sky
45   "Wow"
46   space ship

38

agent heard all of the commotion, and opened his curtains again. The Senator continued. "He dreamed of building a rocket ship that could cross the stars. He wanted to make this here space teepee. We will build our encampment in the stars far away from here. Far away from the Indian agent, we can live free. Sure Buddy Bradley has gotten a bit of freedom on his comedy tours. When he leaves the reserve, he often does not have to get a pass because his fair skin allows him to go deep into the encampment of our pale face neighbours. And recently he went to Prince Albert with his pass in hand. He had a bit of freedom, and we know that with that freedom one will always have a bit of swagger in their walk."

The Senator continued. "But why limit ourselves to Prince Albert? Or Regina? Why should we even limit ourselves to Ottawa? Or maybe even to the land of the other tea drinkers – Peking China. Hell, let's go all of the way to Alpha Centauri. There must be some space buffalo that we could get, some space buffalo wiyâs.[47] And there wouldn't be a damn thing that the môniyâw government could do to stop us."

Everyone held a quiet little place in the spaces of his words and they stopped to look at the space teepee. Part of it was protruding out of a hole that was made in the barn. The teepee was made of scrap metal that had been been welded together. The various pieces of metal made it look like an old kôhkom quilt. There were metal poles which were like radio antennae which stood out. The whole structure was covered with a layer of bannock grease. The bannock grease would protect it as it moved through the atmosphere and would help hold in the warmth of the structure once they made it to outer space.

Ezekiel, one of the white hairs of the TV club, spoke. "Some of the old bush hunters used to see flying saucers in the bush. They would hover over those hunters sometimes, and they would even come off the water near

---

47   meat

the lake on the north side of the reserve. It was right where those hunters were fishing." He paused, and then Pacinîs spoke in Cree. "Aya, there must be something out there. Sometimes the Old Ones, I mean the Old Time Indians said the earth would be invaded by an army of crazy green men. They said, "they couldn't be worse than the môniyâw."

The Senator added one more thing. "Now kimosôminânaw[48] is good with numbers and such, and we have faith in him. He has all of those wires dangling, from his pocket, hanging out, different colours like a Christmas tree. Moses âstam pê–pîkiskwê!"[49]

Moses stepped forward adjusting his Indian Affairs glasses. They were black and heavy framed and were so damn thick that one time in the bush the TV Club had used them to start a bush fire. Moses seemed to squint a lot because he had been studying for the correspondence course out of Houston Texas. While he was not a smoker, he had found the address from a matchbox. It was one of those correspondence courses and sometimes it was tricky to come up with the extra postage to pay for the lessons, but he had persevered and had completed the course work. At one point, at one of the lowest points, when he just couldn't come up with the money, he had tricked the Indian agent into signing some forms to issue a cheque to cover the rest of the course.

Moses was not one to give great and big speeches so he cut to the chase. "I was thinking that the best place to launch the ship would be on the hill. We will just open up the ceiling a bit." Moses paused. "The key will be to distract the Indian agent while we launch the ship." The people talked for a bit and before too long, Nadine's mom came into the barn with some of her fresh bannock.

---

48   our grandfather
49   come and talk

BUILDING THE BARN: PART TWO

Napoleon had left to go to town and sit in the café. He went to the trouble of actually getting a pass from the Indian agent. The Indian agent didn't really say much. Napoleon just showed up and the Indian agent started to fill out the form. Napoleon was interested, like everyone, in the spaceship that Moses was building, but he didn't think that it would make it to the stars. He had seen too much in the war and in his life to put a lot of belief in things that might seem farfetched to others. He respected everyone in the TV Club and the others, but he just needed to get off the reserve, and blow off the steam. He wanted to relax, to try to forget things. Napoleon was fairly dark so when he went to town, there was no mistaking that he was an Indian. He didn't have much trouble because everyone knew that he had been a soldier. He came back from the war with a chest full of medals. He wanted to settle down and start a new life. He thought he might want to try to farm, but he never did get the same benefits as the other soldiers. That really pissed him off because he had fought as hard as anyone else.

Napoleon had risen to the rank of Lieutenant during the war. While there were limits to how far he could go up in the ranks, his raw talent could not be denied. No one could prevent him from becoming a Lieutenant. He had lied about his age. He had fought the Fritz at Vimy Ridge in WWI. He fought the Krauts when he landed on D–Day. He was in charge of a platoon. Those Germans were as tough as any Blackfoot in the old days. Some of the môniyâw didn't care too much for him being in command, but once he gave a few of them a bannock slap, they didn't have much more to say about that. It turned out that the Indian agent was worried that if Napoleon would give a môniyâw a bannock slap in the war, what would be the case in peace time? One time when Napoleon was in Prince Albert getting his yellow Meteor serviced, the sôniyâwikimâw people, said all kinds of things to get Napoleon in all kinds of trouble. The report was officially filed in Ottawa, but when their buddy, the Prime Minister took charge he had it officially removed from the record. This helped settle Napoleon a bit, but it also helped to level the standing that the Indian agent had with the people of the Broken Elbow reserve.

After Napoleon had his day in Prince Albert, he went back to the reserve. He went to the hill of Pacinîs and made his way to the barn. The barn was actually orange because that was the only colour of paint that they could get. There were a few people gathered outside the barn doors including Kihci Lars. They had asked him to say some old Viking prayers for the ships. Ezekiel was there and many of the others members of the TV Club. There was a hush when the barn doors opened and the Senator took off his purple velvet cape, which had been especially made by a Hutterite seamstress for his flight into space. Everyone in the TV Club figured that on account of his bush piloting experience, he would be the best one to try to fly the rocket ship. The velvet cape showed his place of importance. ê–pasikôniht awa.[50]

Everyone in the TV Club was there, Moses too, of course, and a Hutterite electrician who was helping with some of the tricky wiring. Everyone waited patiently while the Senator took off his cape, and fixed himself some tea from the campfire, which was in front of the barn. The Senator had always been very Nadinely when he did this, and there was the familiar clank, clank of his spoon against the cup. He would then pour a bit of Hutterite honey into the cup. He would lick his lips lightly then clank, clank, clank his spoon against the cup. The same

50   He was raised up in position.

with the whitener. Clank. Clank. Clank. It was really a long process. People sighed but tried not to sigh too deeply. They didn't want to make the Senator feel bad – nor did they want to take away from the magnificence of his purple velvet cape.

Then the Senator started to speak, "Boysak and iskwêwak. It is a good day that we are here. Drinking good tea, on this good day, in that good way. I say this all in that good way, my good relations."

Everyone kind of looked at each other, while everyone tried to pretend that they were not looking at each other, hoping that everyone was not looking each other, but they were ê–kimôhtêwâpimitocik. They were all looking at each other secretly.

"We are getting close to our launch date. Now, we all know that everyone has been working hard." He paused and felt the velvet of his purple cape.

His uncle Pacinîs started to speak and said, "cha, you mean after all of that clanking of your spoon against your coffee cup that is all that you have?"

The Senator laughed uncomfortably and said, "Tâpwê ôma. Êkwani piko. aya, ka–miywâsin kîspin Moses kêtahtawê ka–mâci–pîkiskwêt, pamwêyas, sôniyâwikimāaw ka–pê–itôhtêt ôta."[51]

Moses nodded and then said, "Thank you Senator. Now boysak and iskwêwak, this is a takahki–kîkway[52] thing that we are doing here. We all know that building a space rocket ship isn't something that we learned from old people, or that we learned in those damn residential schools. But dammit it is something that we can do – if we put our wits together and work together. As I said, before, the key is to keep the Indian agent distracted while we

---

51   "That's true. That's it. But it will be good if Moses can begin to speak before the Indian agent comes here."

52   Important thing

launch." He paused, hoping that someone would have an idea of what to do. People looked at each other and a couple of people just shrugged their shoulders.

Then Buddy Bradley came running to the barn. He wore his overalls too tight and wore them so he didn't have a moose toe, but rather had a buffalo hoof. Buddy came running in, heaving and breathing hard. While Buddy Bradley had a big heart, he had the grace of a wounded moose running in the forest. "I've got an idea," he said. "The Indian agent looks kind of down. It is his birthday."

Napoleon piped in, "Why the hell should we care if it is his birthday? He is a goddamn asshole."

Buddy, having been used to doing the rough comedy circuit said, "I hear you. I hear you and understand where you are coming from. But here is the situation. We need a distraction. Maybe if he had a talent show to honour him, then he would feel better and be distracted."

Kihci Lars said that this was a good idea and then everyone else seemed to agree with the idea. People talked about it after assuaging Napoleon's wounded pride. The main point of concern was that the Indian agent would be suspicious about why they were going to have a celebration for him.

Nadine's mom decided that the best course of action would be for them both to go to the Indian agent, and then they would tell him that the community was going to put on a talent show. When they did tell him, he was a little skeptical at first but after a few minutes the old kohkom won him over as kohkom generally do. By the end of it, he was actually kind of giggly.

People began to gather at the Band Hall. Buddy Bradley approached the hall where everyone was gathering. Old rez cars limped along the bumpy reserve roads and pulled up to the band hall, and flocks of young people with a lot of great energy piled out. Young napêwak[53] whose heads were heavy with Brill cream and bear grease ran to the large open doors, where the light of the hall poured out on the night scape. Buddy could make out the shadows of people, he could make out the silhouettes and outlines too. He heard the fragments of sound, both Cree and English merge into one. The young women were there too. They had come in swanky reserve garb. Their flowered dresses seemed to dance ever so gently in the summer air as they congregated and giggled when the young men walked by. Everyone brought some kind of present for the Indian agent and for the young people. The talent show had a bit more flash then the Tupperware socials which were then the rage, and were not really so much about selling Tupperware, at least in the minds of Reznecks (Broken Elbow slang for Rez people), but more for them to get together to engage in courting. It was tricky to find someone that you were not related to. Indians were weird, they would exaggerate how many relatives they had for politics, and then underplay those numbers for courting. Those neechies were always cooking the books.

Buddy moved towards the band hall. He could see the lights on top of the hill, and he smiled to himself knowing that the spaceship teepee was about to launch, that Crees were about to launch a new era, a time when they would pow wow amongst the stars.

From the top of the hill, the Senator looked down at the band hall and in a way he was happy that the Indian agent would feel a bit of happiness. The Senator had to smile and chuckle a little. The two Hutterite welders were sparking on the metal. Some of the group were wiring up the campfire at the base of the teepee. There was the cockpit, and that is where the Senator and Moses would sit. There was dried meat in middle compartments, and various

---

53   men

plants and medicines that would help them with space sickness were stored safely away. There were bows which Moses had made which would shoot out laser arrows. This required special wiring and a special soldering gun which they had to special order from the States. It was one of those mail order deals, and it took a long time for it to ship. They used Lars' post office box so as not to arouse the suspicion of the Indian agent. They had done that for a few of the unique parts that they had to send away for. They also had special suits. They were made of green material because that was the only colour that they could get of the special material that they needed to create their space suits. Napoleon and Ezekiel got into the suits as well as the Senator and Moses.

Moses Mostos had spent a great deal of time trying to concoct a synthetic form of bannock grease. He mixed it with a form of moose gravy, and dried berries, coupled with an old Swedish bush recipe. They figured that they would fire it up at the right time and there would be enough power in the thrusters to get them into space.

"Okay everyone," the Senator said, "Everything is in order. Now fire up the grease in the teepee fire chamber and we will be ready to go."

The Senator and Moses got ready, and worked their way up the windy stairs to the takay pit on the top of the teepee. The lights were on, and all the dials were lit up on the flight deck. The Senator looked out the window and could see everyone below. They gave each other the thumbs up. The middle chambers were where the supplies were put. The bottom level was where they would tell stories while they would fly into space. Above the space campfire was a stairwell that led to various sleeping chambers. For the journey into deep space, they had picked a special bush mushroom, which would put them into a hibernetic sleep for long stretches of time. Napoleon and Ezekiel were strapped into special seats that held them in place. Outside were three "lighting points" which three assistants moved toward the flames. Pacinîs motioned for them to move ahead and they placed the fire torches into the points. Everyone cheered, as the lighting points received the fire. The synthetic bannock grease, coupled with the other elements crackled, and the crackling spread towards the lowest fuel component. Pacinîs began the count down in old Indian sign language. Then the teepee blasted up through the open spaces of the barn. The Senator looked ahead, up through the upper windows, and the Senator said, "ahâw, kâ–miywâsin êkota." They looked at each other, and gave each other the biggest grin that any neechie ever gave someone. Then not even a few seconds later, a series of lights on the dash began to flash. The flight data was being recorded on the cutting edge technology of the day.

The Senator said, "kîkwây ispayin?"[54]

Moses replied, "môy 'skêyihtamân nitotêm!"[55]

They felt the teepee arch down towards the môniyâw town.

"By the sweet beard of Nanabush," said the Senator, "it looks like we are crashing straight into the Legion Hall."

"Holeh shit boy!" They both braced for impact and the crash of the teepee was intense. There was smoke all around.

"What the heck just happened?" someone said in a môniyâw voice.

"Must be some kinda commie attack," said another.

"Run for your lives. There are green men with some kinda weird injun–looking weapon," yelled a redneck. They could hear Napoleon laughing and shooting his space

54   "What is happening?"
55   "I don't know my friend."

bow into the ground.

"Let's get the heck out of here Senator!"

"Tâpwê my boy!"

"I have to get the flight recorder in the lunch kit box." Moses sounded so disappointed that the flight into the sky failed.

"Don't worry my boy. Kikohcihtân[56] boy, kikôhcitân!"

Moses grabbed the flight data in the lunch kit data box.

"They are goddamn aliens," they heard another môniyâw say. The Senator and Moses laughed knowing that Napoleon was having fun. Such was the day that they almost made it to the stars.

---

56   You try.

THE FIRST TV ON THE RESERVE

After the space ship incident, it took awhile
for things to settle down in the district. Pacinîs won a
competition that Indian Affairs had sponsored. Eager to get
back into the good books of the people on the reserve, the
Indian agent tried to rig things so that someone from the
reserve would win. Everyone on the reserve was so excited
to try to win. Everyone entered the competition. Many of
the people actually tried to put in multiple entries. Some
succeeded, some didn't. But everyone tried.

Some of the people on the reserve were sceptical
of the idea of the TV One old man thought that there were
going to be great changes brought about by television.
Some said that it wasn't right. They thought it was the
TV was capturing and putting people's souls into this
shadow maker, cikâstêpayihcikan. Some of the other old
people just said it was plain creepy. One old man said that
he found it creepy, "cha why the hell would I want some
random môniyâw voice travelling through the house. As
if!"

But a lot of the so-called progressive Indians on the
reserve wanted so badly to have the TV, including the TV
Club, that the Indian agent was making a competition for
one. They knew that they would have something that a lot
of white people have.

"Tânisi nôhcâwîs,"[57] itêw Senator.
"Kîkwây ê–nôhtê–kakwêcimiyin my nephew?"[58]
"Mêtoni ta–miywâsin kîspin ê–otahowiyahk ôma."[59]
"Kîkwây ôma??[60] Cikâstêpayihcikan cî ōma?? The

Shadow Maker."

---

57   "Hello my uncle."
58   "What do you want to ask me my nephew?"
59   "It would be good if we won."
60   "What is this thing?"

"Âha, êwako ôma."[61]

"Kah, tânêhki ê–nîhtawêyihtaman ôma?"[62]

"Ta–miywâsin ôma nôhcâwîs.[63] Pikwîtê ohci ta–pihtamahk âcimowina misiwêskamik."

"Tânêhki ê–nôhtê–pêhtaman ohci ôta iskonikanihk?"[64]

They debated the merits of whether or not they should get a TV or not. In the end, Pacinîs made his case, the Senator heard it, and he pretended to agree with it. Despite their long discussion the Senator could not resist submitting an application to the contest. He went to the band office that day and he secretly submitted his application. He hoped against hope that he would win the contest.

---

61   "Yes, that is the one"

62   "Wow, why do you want this?"

63   "This will be good my uncle, we will hear stories from all over the earth"

64   "Why do you want to hear stories from all over here on the reserve?"

THE FIRST TV ON THE RESERVE: PART TWO

In the following weeks, everyone on the reserve kept talking with great excitement about the contest. People shared their desires for a TV with one another and they also seemed to betray each other with their desires. Everyone pretended to be hoping that the other would win, but deep down everyone was trying to secretly slip in another ballot when no one else was looking. Some people were purported to have put upwards of 20 ballots in the box. In fact, some said that Cash and his family had put in over 40 ballots. However, the Senator liked to play by the rules. Pacinîs, his uncle, said that it was very bad karma to cheat in a contest. He said it was kind of like using hunting medicine. Even though the Senator knew that Cash was cheating in the contest and had even seen him, on two occasions, put in an extra ballot, he never said anything because he was sure that it would all catch up to him. At least that is what the Senator tried to tell himself.

When the contest was first cancelled, there was such an uproar over it, that it took it a lot for the Indian agent to get it restored. The order to cancel it came from a paper pusher in Ottawa. The Indian agent stressed that the Indians were restless. Rather than fight the Indians in the courts, it would cost less money to just keep them happy. It would be easier to have the program reinstated. So, for pragmatic reasons of this nature, the contest was restored.

There was a great deal of talk by everyone about what would happen next. People gossiped, or "shared news," as many people called it. Sharing news sounded more culturally grounded and more dignified than "gossiping." There was talk of how the competition was rigged by Cash's family. "It is all damn politics," an Old Timer said.

And with this came tighter rules and a promise

of tighter controls about how many ballots people could enter. There were others on the reserve who knew of Cash's attempt to fix the game in his favour. However, they were not as shy as the Senator in expressing their dislike for the fixing of the contest. They did not have the Senator's old fashioned faith in karma. Instead, they put their faith in the numbers and the odds.

Then the craziest thing happened. The Senator went home to tell his mother that he was indeed very excited by the contest, and shared it with Nadine – that the contest for the TV was being renewed. Nadine was very excited over this. She wanted to watch the programs which showed the latest fashions and latest trends from all over the world. Nadine was the most beautiful Cree women who had ever lived. She was so beautiful they say dough would form into bannock in her presence. When she danced they would say, "ê–mamâhtâwisimot." She dances with divinity. "The way she dances, she knows something that you will never know," Pacinîs would say to the Senator.

The Senator shared with her his plans to open a store. "Oh," she said, "it would be kind of like an ongoing garage sale."

"Tâpwê anima, nitotêm." He hesitated on the last word and had always secretly wished that she would think of him as more than a friend. Sometimes he thought she did seem to think of him that way and then other times he did not seem to be sure.

The Senator told his uncle, Pacinîs, that people would be bringing the TV in a special vehicle and that they would be coming later that day. Old Pacinîs, who always seemed to like getting dressed up for all occasions, protested for a bit and said he thought it all was a silly idea. However, once the Senator told him that a photographer for the Prince Albert Herald was also coming, he could not seem to stop thinking about the day when they would bring the TV

"I'll have to get ready," old Pacinîs said excitedly.

Pacinîs got giggly getting himself gussied up. He was always such a sucker for the crowds and for the stage. In fact, during the jousting fights of the 1940s he put on some plays for people. The scripts were all written in Cree syllabics, and it is said there is one complete set somewhere on the reserve. The people on Broken Elbow reserve said that they learned a lot of their craft from him, that they learned about showmanship, and relating to audiences and perhaps most of all they say they learned about being a performer, which he learned on his own terms. Buddy Bradley learned all this from him. Buddy Bradley was the Cree comedian who tried to break out of the confines of what people thought Indian performers should be.

Years ago, in the 1920s, there had been an anthropologist who had come out west from some fancy museum. He was interested in documenting the life ways and rituals of the Cree. He got permission from the Indian agent to be on the reserve, and to be there in order to interview people. He asked about the spiritual importance of bannock within Cree culture. Was it okay for cousins to marry each other? Was a three-legged dog considered to be sacred? And so on. However, where he seemed to go too far was when he started to ask people about their mating rituals. "Cha! What kind of fella is this who wants to work with us?" asked one old Cree woman. Paskwâw-Iskwêw bannock slapped him so hard when he asked her this question that he just sat there in silence for a long time. Some people said he was simply unable to move.

The old kohkom felt so bad that she brought him tea, but nothing else. The tea eventually got cold while the anthropologist sat there. So she made another fresh batch of tea, but nothing. Then she thought she would fry up some moose meat but nothing. She even went next door to borrow a môniyâw luxury, refined white sugar. Finally, it was getting dark, and she was worried that he would not leave. She certainly didn't want him to stay sitting at her table with his blank stare all night. So Pacinîs came by and pretended to be interested in telling the anthropologist something. He sat with him for a time, and looked to Nadine's ohkôma when the anthropologist was not looking. Pacinîs went on to tell the anthropologist all kinds of stories over a period of time. Over the winter, he told him many stories and the anthropologist filled many notebooks. Each day Pacinîs would take great care to dress up and wear his suit. He would wear his old mosôm hat. He was very dark but he did not have braids. Instead he liked his hair short, and in this way and in this manner, the anthropologist was somewhat disappointed. He wanted to record the "authentic Indian," not the shadow of an Indian that someone with short hair might seem to represent. While Pacinîs did not have long hair, what he did have going in his favour was his thorough command of the Cree language, and his thorough command of storytelling and Cree narrative lore.

Now with the coming of the TV, Pacinîs felt the stretch of stories in his mind again, and the stretch of the Cree language in the spaces of his mouth. Of course, he put on his suit and his mosôm hat. He was ready to talk and ready to tell stories. But perhaps more accurately, he was ready for stories. He was ready for the stories of the TV and of course he wanted to be in the Prince Albert Herald. The reporter was going to be there. Hopefully, the Senator would be able to translate his words properly – sometimes he was not quite able to translate some of the older words and some of the more difficult words. But he thought the ladies of Prince Albert would like and appreciate him.

Pâcinîs saw the blue truck pull up the long approach. The roads on the reserve were more like trails, rather than actual roads, but they seemed to be able able to do the trick for what people needed. The blue truck with the TV seemed to be moving along just fine.

The boys who were hired by the Department of Indian Affairs did their job. They did not say a lot but the

Senator could tell that the two men who were unloading the TV did not like Indians. The younger one with the strong blue eyes, carried the disdain more than the older one. The older one seemed to keep the younger one in check. The younger one was like a wiry young horse.

The Prince Albert Herald reporter arrived a bit later, but he was just in time for the Indian agent to announce Pacinîs as the winner of the TV The reporter took some shots of the TV once they had turned it on. Napoleon drove up and the Senator noticed that each time a vehicle drove past the TV, different patterns crossed the TV screen. The Prince Albert Herald Reporter asked Pacinîs if he thought that this was all progress, but Pacinîs just said, "only the future could tell." The reporter snapped a few more pictures of him with his new TV and then he went on his way.

THE FIRST TV ON THE RESERVE: PART THREE

The Senator and Pacinîs realized that they had to play around with wâposihtawakaya.[65] They kept trying to get the right reception. For the longest time they could only get the French station. There were all kinds of stories that were shared on the channel. But, for the most part, no one one at Broken Elbow could understand what was being said. Nonetheless, because they were telling stories, Pacinîs thought they should be honoured as storytellers, so he would make them tea and pour it into cups and put it by the TV for them when they would tell their stories. He would say "ahâw" even though he didn't completely understand what they meant in their little stories on the cikâstêpayihcikan.[66] But as a storyteller himself, he thought it was good to honour the other ones.

Then, old Moses Mostos, started to play around with reception, and eventually he was able to get the TV working well enough to get English channels. Pacinîs was able to understand a little bit more of the English channel but he still missed a good chunk of the words. Despite this, he still would make tea and bring it to the front of the TV for the people in the little box. Sometimes he would get fancy and make bannock and place it by the TV. When he finished watching the TV he would put grease on the bannock and give it to the dog, Not–Even. Not–Even was one of the three legged rez dogs. It seemed that there was some sort of gene which caused dogs in the area to have only three legs. They say that there was even a rock painting of a three legged dog.

Then they got Hockey Night in Canada when they played with the rabbit ears just right, and there was no looking back after that. At first it was only the Senator and Pacinîs that would watch the games, but then Napoleon

---

65   Rabbit ears
66   Television

started to come, and then Buddy Bradley would come. Buddy Bradley would come to study the techniques of the announcers, and apply those techniques to his comedy show. He practiced the dramatic reading, and the dramatic entry points, the hollers of narration that would get the crowd going. He did that a lot with the crowds that he would entertain. At first, they thought he was Italian, and occasionally he would be jeered with "Dance pow wow! Dance pow wow!" Some of the tricks that he learned from Hockey Night in Canada helped him around those tricky situations. Through all of these things, Pacinîs continued to put tea in front of the TV. At first, Napoleon thought this was bullshit, and he told the Senator what he thought this. But over time, he just accepted it as one of the numerous quirks of Pacinîs and like all things, he came to see it as a part of Pacinîs's quirky temperament. However, Napoleon was a pragmatic man, and when Pacinîs' wasn't looking, he would drink the tea. He would quietly tell Buddy Bradley that he thought it was goddamn bullshit to waste good tea.

Then Kihci Lars found out about Hockey Night in Canada and when he could he get away from his trapline, he would come down and watch the game.

"Hey," said one neechie, "are you going to Pacinîs' place tonight to watch the game?"

"Yes," said another. At first these conversations were spread out and thin. Then they became a bit more frequent and then before too long everyone was talking about the games on the flicker box. There were so many people who would come, they would have to gather outside to see who could get in. There was always a line up. In fact, Buddy Bradley put up a roped entrance to try to create excitement. He would only let in people who brought a gift. Some people would bring bannock. Some would bring frozen berries. Others would bring copies of Life magazine. Pacinîs liked this particularly well because he liked the pictures. He said that they were vibrant and full of details like a story. Then when the Senator's little house was full, they would auction off the seats in front of the bay window. They would jokingly call these the hand freeze seats, because their hands would get cold while they were watching game. The Senator got the idea that he may as well sell people snacks and stuff – so he sold Indian popcorn, kahkêwak,[67] chokecherry juice, and fried beaver tails, while they watched the game. He also rented moose hides to people who stood outside and watched through the windows so that they would keep warm. Mitoni kwayask ê–mah–miyo–sôniyakêt.[68]

All of this success was bound to attract the attention of others, including the Indian agent. The Indian agent wrote up citations and told people that they were going to be charged under section 123 of the Indian Act. When Buddy Bradley was on tour, he went to a library and looked up that section of the Indian Act, and realized that there was no such amendment to the Indian Act. They hired a lawyer to confront the Indian agent and the Indian agent backed down again. This all served to embolden the people on the reserve, so they sued the Indian agent for abusing his trust.

Another thing that the Senator started to do was take objects from people, give them some money, and after a certain period of time, they would give him the money back plus some extra for his trouble, and he would give them back their things. That was the beginning of the Third Hand Shop, and it all started during those hockey games.

---

67   dried meat
68   "Truly it was good to make lots of money."

THE THIRD HAND PAWN SHOP

The days at the Third Hand Pawn Shop folded into each, like an accordion, stretching and contracting. There was the ever-present wooden Indian in the front of the store which seemingly had a glow on ration day. Some of the old ones said that glow began to fade once ration days ceased to be of importance. There was also the familiar crackling of an AM radio, and the hovering about of the Senator. The year was 1962.

Society was opening up a great deal, and maybe the Age of the Rednecks was coming to an end. They would call it Redneckdämmering, "The Twilight of the Rednecks." Maybe he could get Nadine to sing in an opera about it. He loved the fact that she was in that German film all of those years ago which had screened at many Karl May festivals. Nadine had been the darling of the German press, and they had decreed it all as Bannockwüt, "the craze for the bannock." A wealthy industrialist from München had paid her a lot of money to act out one of the characters for a Karl May novel recreation. Nadine had used the money to help the Senator start the Third Hand Pawn Shop. She had then used her connections to get interesting objects for the pawn shop brought over from Germany. One of the greatest finds was a kaleidoscope that was crafted, some say, by Goethe himself. She had also helped the Senator set up his brisk overseas rabbit root mail order service.

There were people on the reserve who seemed to be jealous of the Senator's success. At first, people seemed to think that it was a bit of a novelty to have a pawn shop on the reserve. Some of the people, in fact most of the people, remembered a time when they would have to go to town on a horse. They remembered when it would take several hours to get to town. They would have to get permission from the Indian agent which, at times, was awkward and which, at times, would not always come. As time went on, and as the Senator's success grew, he seemed to engender more and more jealousy from the people on the reserve which he could not completely understand.

But it was really stories which fuelled the imagination of the Senator. His held the parts of many little stories, and in his moments of telling he would gather them together. It was often during the time that he was cleaning his shop he would think about all these stories. During these times of deep thought he would drag and push the broom over the entirety of the wood of the floor. When he was finished, he would think of a story that he wanted to tell. And throughout all of this, he would whistle along to the jingles that he heard jangling around in his head, and also on the AM radio that was always sending out sound in the shop.

The shop was full of many things, including the wooden Indian that greeted everyone as they came into the store. The old people jokingly called him atamiskâwikês.[69] The hand of the wooden Indian was raised up in the classic "how" gesture. The Senator was convinced that the pose of the hand of the wooden Indian might be an old Indian sign. He asked some of the kêhtê–ayak on the reserve to see if any of them could recognize the sign that the wooden Indian was making, if indeed any of them could sign. None of the old people really seemed to know Indian sign language anymore. The Senator felt disappointed by this. He wondered what else of the past that they did not know. He began to sweep the floor. He did this anytime that he became really nervous about something, or when he felt unsure

---

69   the greeter

about something. It was at this moment, like so many moments in the past, that he started to sweep the floor. He wondered about the future when young men would come and ask him about the past, about the glory and the meaning of the past. He wondered what he would tell the young people. What knowledge would he be able to share with them?

He did do a brisk volume of sales of old books. Not only did the folks on the reserve buy them, especially his constantly rotating stock of Louis L'Amour novels, but he also sold a lot to people from off the reserve. At first, many of them were unsure about so many people coming on to the reserve. Many of the people who were a little older remembered the "No Trespassing" signs.

One German named Helmut, who was from Düsseldorf and was an amateur botanist, came to the Third Hand Pawn Shop after ordering rabbit root from the Senator. Helmut had wondered what neechie meant. He wondered if it was Nietzsche the German philosopher. He wondered why all of the Indians greeted each other as this old German from the other century. He wondered why the Indians would be drawn to such a dark and sombre German philosopher.

Stories had a way of working on your soul, and a way of working on your mind. They were like medicine, like a bottle of Doctor Fowler's that would coat the lining of your stomach, and make you feel better. In fact, there were some of them, the good ones, that were like those bottles of medicine that those Watkin's salesmen would sell. They, like the stories, would go to work on making the sale and making you better.

There were stories about all kinds of things on the Broken Elbow Reserve. There were stories of past events, of past exploits, and of past adventures. The richness of the colours of these characters was vivid, like the crazy colours of the Village, leaving your mind shocked and torn in the same way the crazy multitude of colours that one would find in various houses on reserves would.

One focus of these stories was the wooden Indian in front of the store. Some people even said that Cash Williams, who wrote "Calijah," had been inspired by this wooden Indian. Others said that this wooden Indian had toured with Buffalo Bill. They said that Buffalo Bill would take the wooden Indian on tour with him – including to Venice, Italy. The one story was that Buffalo Bill had left the wooden Indian there after his tour had gone on for a bit. Eventually this wooden Indian ended up in the hands of an Italian Duke. Then, in the confusion of the fighting of the war, a Canadian soldier, who would become an Indian agent, took the wooden Indian back to Canada with him.

After the acâhkosi–otâpânâsk[70] incident, the Hockey Night in Canada snack sales and blanket rentals formed the economic basis of the Pawn Shop. It was to start something like a general store – although that morphed into more of a pawn shop. They would use the wooden Indian as a show piece and they would call it the Third Hand Pawn Shop because the Senator's hands would be the first ones to touch it since Buffalo Bill. The Indian agent was convinced that this would be a tourist draw, that many would come to the store, and that it would be a great success. The Indian agent had hoped that this would help him to get back in the good graces of the people at Indian Affairs. Nothing made bureaucrats feel better than a feel–good story about Indian economic success.

In the end, the Indian agent had to leave suddenly because of some sort of money scandal that the Senator could not completely remember anymore. But he did like

70   Space ship

that Indian agent at times, and generally, but not always, was kind to him. People could say a lot of things about the Senator but one thing that had to be said about him was that he was kind. The Indian agent had remembered that kindness and had gifted him the nêhiyawâhtik (wooden Indian).

The Third Hand Pawn Shop was not very busy so the Senator took the time to do some tidying up, and then he swept the floor. Once he was done that, he sat and he did some figuring in his books. And, when he was done that, he would polish the nêhiyawâhtik. Sometimes he was sure that when he moved the dust rag on the wooden Indian, when he polished him, he swore that he could hear the wooden Indian hum. He was not sure what that song was that he was humming. The Senator believed that strange things could happen. All of the old stories talked about this. In the end, he told himself that it was probably just the radio making the sounds. And that little story seemed to hold his imagination when the store was not busy– times like these.

ᐱᓄᑭᓂᐲ[71] WARMS UP

Sometimes the Senator also felt the statue get a little warmer, when he was around the wooden Indian. It gave off the same kind of warmth that a body would give off. He thought that was strange, that a wooden Indian would have the warmth of a human body. The Senator tried to tell himself that maybe it was the warm weather that had affected the wooden Indian. Or, perhaps it was the warmth within the pawn shop.

Nadine was coming by later to visit. She had not been back for a bit. She had lived out east in Toronto since she and Cash had broken up. Sometimes her son Jingles would live with her. Sometimes he stayed with the Senator as he was his adopted uncle.

The Senator wanted her to think he was the type of person who could keep his wigwam clean. He wanted to impress her as he was genuinely trying to convince her that in the future he would be a good mate. The bar was high with her after all. Her mother was featured in "Tomorrow's Teepees" which was a glory magazine produced by the department of Indian Affairs to demonstrate the great progress that Indians were making. The Senator's store, "The Third Hand" was featured as well. It was unusual for two people from the same reserve, namely the Broken Elbow Reserve, to be featured, yet they were. The old Indian agent had petitioned to get his pension reinstated because of the progress that the people of the reserve had made. There was some talk that he had been reinstated in the department – perhaps, some said, the head of a new unit which was committing old Indian stories to records with a local musician who was playing the flute to accompany the tracks. Some said that the tracks were quite uplifting. Some said that the tracks were quite objectifying. Some marvelled at the high tech spectacle of 8–tracks and

---

71   Pinokineechie

they wondered how their favourite stories would sound on this new medium.

The magazine "Tomorrow's Teepees" was widely read throughout the country, especially in Eastern Canada. Nadine was featured in the summer of 1961 edition, and her house, her modern teepee was noted as a great marvel, and was a demonstration of what Indian people could do if they set their mind to it. People applauded, especially the White folk. The Senator knew that if he was ever truly to find a home in Nadine's heart, he would have to have a clean shop. All day he was nervous for her to come for a visit, and kept watching the hands of the clock move closer to the position of 6 o'clock.

NADINE PÊ–KIYOKÊT[72]

Six o'clock finally came and the Senator was anxious. He felt his palms getting sweaty and his heart racing. He started to click his heels a bit, and he felt in all of the bones in his body that something big was going to happen. Nadine was going to be arriving at any minute. The Six O'Clock News was starting. He always got excited when he heard the opening jingle on CBC. Even though in the late 50s and early 60s most people on the reserve were getting very excited about television, he had always liked radios better. To the Senator, radios would always be closer to the old stories.

Nadine pulled up in her Chrysler. The seats of the Chrysler smelled of leather – she had paid the extra money to have leather. She had used the money from her bestselling novel. She had extra chrome, and her license plate said "MASINAHIKAN."[73] The colour of the car was a rich metallic maroon and it glimmered in the dusky light of the sun that was not quite day, nor had the sun faded into night. There were hints in the sky of a rich and heavy blue. The maroon of the car was glistening with the metallic stretch of paint, looking like a beautiful northern lake. The Senator could imagine loons making lonely calls on it. With this mind, he thought that placing the loon on a shiny coin would be a good idea. Not only would it be a beautiful image, but it would help with his vending machines. Nadine's mom could have little pieces of bannock that she put in little bags that would be vended. He wrote this idea to his local MP and never did hear back.

Nadine was smiling as she got out of her car. She had an intelligence in her eyes, and a gentle, beautiful

72 Nadine comes to visit
73 book

66

grace. Her long black hair stood still in the air, and she smiled. Her smile was slow at first, until it stretched across her face, like the sun stretches across the sky.

They say that her ôhkoma, Paskwâw–Iskwêw, made the best bannock north of the Rio Grande river. Everyone from far away came to eat her bannock. One time, for a book launch that Nadine had in Stockholm, her publisher had even flown the bannock in for a big party. Everyone in Sweden went crazy for it.

Nadine looked out straight with beautiful hazel eyes and said, "Hello Senator." She glowed when she said it.

"Hello, tânisi," the Senator responded, "mitoni ê–miyo–kîsikâk anohc," he said.

"It truly is." She understood Cree perfectly but often responded in English probably because of the long amount of time that she had lived off the reserve.

She approached the Senator and the Third Hand Pawn Shop.

"I have been cleaning the pawn shop, mahti pihtikwê."[74]

They entered and saw all of the things in all of their orderly lines. She marvelled at the store and at some of the new items. The item that particularly caught her attention was the wooden Indian.

"You know Senator," she said, "this wooden Indian is such a treasure. I am sure that one of my contacts in the European publishing industry, or even one of the German authors would love to buy it." She seemed to bounce as she said these words.

"Tâpwê anima," the Senator said. "The wooden Indian is truly a treasure," he paused, collecting his thoughts and in the process he remembered all of the

---

74   please come in

stories that went with it. "There have been many people who have passed through the store who have wanted to buy it. People from all over – locals, Germans, people from Montreal, people from other reserves, Americans – even someone from a museum in the Soviet Union."

"Did they offer you a good price?" Nadine said.

"Yes, I have been offered a lot of money, many times, but I have never accepted any offer, because if it wasn't for the wooden Indian, the store would not really have a name."

The Senator smiled and laughed. He thought of the way that the wooden Indian, nêhiyawâhtik, greeted everyone.

Nadine and the Senator talked for a bit longer, and the Senator thanked her again for the money that she had given him to help start the Third Hand Pawn Shop. They visited for a bit and drank tea. It started to rain, and the roads on the reserve would often get very muddy.

"Senator," Nadine said, "I am going to visit my mom later tonight, and since the roads are going to be bad, I am wondering if you could drive me over to see her?"

"Tâpwê," the Senator responded without hesitation.

They got in the Senator's old Ford truck. Then, as they were driving along listening to CCR on the radio, they heard a little bang from below the carriage of the car, and he laughed as if to cover up the worry in his voice. He could see the worry in her eye. But he could also see the way that she was still trying to smile through her worry.

"It must be hunters," the Senator said, trying to reassure Nadine, but they both knew that it wasn't that. Then there was another loud bang, and this time the truck actually shook. He had been meaning to get it fixed, but he was hoping that it would hold together. There was no reason why he didn't fix it, after all the till was full. Maybe it was just plain laziness that held him back. It was a shame, the Senator thought, that he was never able to really learn how to fix things like engines. Then another loud bang, and the truck bucked like a rodeo horse, and the truck moved forward, and then back again. With this, hot wet tea spilled all over Nadine's fancy dress.

Concern spread across her face and she said, "Senator, pull over please!" Rain continued to fall hard on the windshield. The windshield wipers strained to push the water off the windshield.

The Senator pulled over. The truck banged again. He got out of the truck and tried to figure out what was causing that horrible banging sound. He had opened up the hood a hundred times before, and he couldn't before fix it– it did not really make sense that he would suddenly be able to fix it now. He opened the hood and tinkered a bit more. He wiped off the rain that was falling on his face.

After what seemed like a long time, a couple of headlights approached them. The Senator squinted his eyes, putting his hands over them like he was scouting out into the distance. The hood of the truck fell down, narrowly missing his head, but caught his jacket, and he heard it rip apart. In the background, he could hear Nadine calling for help, her voice grateful yet slightly panicked. He tried to ask Nadine for help, but he was pretty sure that she did not hear him, and at this point, he wondered if she did hear him, if she would even care. He tried to wave for help, but it was difficult because his coat was jammed under the hood, and the fabric was wedged in there real tight. He tried to squirm around to get loose, but he couldn't get loose. The fabric must be doubled over and caught in the truck. He thought he must look like a rabbit caught in a noose.

The headlights came up closer, and they also became brighter. Even through the fabric the Senator felt the heat of the light on his skin. Under the glare of the light, he felt like a hot buffet item or someone about to be abducted by aliens. He tried to wipe the sweat from his brow but then remembered that his arm was caught. With his back facing the headlights, he really felt vulnerable. But, being a neechie, he could not help but laugh.

The vehicle approached a bit closer, the light got a bit more intense, and the engine seemed to get louder. Finally, he heard the thud of the vehicle door and he heard footsteps approach. He was hoping to all hell that it wasn't some redneck, but then he heard that voice which was like scratching sandpaper, and he heard Cash say, "Senator, how are you this fine evening?"

There was a skip in Cash's walk, a swagger. The young guys liked him because Cash would never back down from a job in a fight. He had a lot of chains on him, he wore tight Wrangler jeans, wore flashy belt buckles, and was trim. He was straight–forward, and was not the kind of Indian than anthropologists or rednecks liked. Rednecks didn't like him because he never backed down, and anthropologists didn't like him because they couldn't neatly map out his being for their ethnographic charts.

Cash's mosôm name was Kâ–Kociskâwâstim. The name meant "Galloping Horse." He acquired the nickname of "Sôniyâw" because his horse would often win races on Treaty Day. When Cash was born, he was sent to live with his grandfather for a spell and became very close to him. Because of this close relationship, he was given the name "Cash" as a nickname and it just stuck. At this point in time, no one was sure anymore what his original name was, since everyone just called him Cash now. When he would travel around with his grandfather, older people would call him Kikwêmis (your little namesake).

As Cash swaggered to the truck, he could hear Nadine calling again for help.

"Nadine. Kiya cî?"[75] Cash itwêw.

"Yes, Cash," she said, once again trying to maintain her grace.

"Mitoni aspin kayâs," itwêw.[76]

"Yes, it has been a long time."

"Aya, kimiyosin,"[77] Cash said.

As they talked, answering each other like song birds in the morning, there was not much that the Senator could do. He was really stuck. It seemed that there was still a flicker of the former romance that had existed.

Cash could not help but laugh when he saw the Senator all caught up, "Senator it looks like you got some problems with your truck." Ever since they were kids, Cash always had the edge on the Senator.

Nadine looked at the Senator and saw his helpless position, and for several moments the heaviness of looking at him saddened her. In the end, it was like that feeling you felt when you saw someone being pulled over by the police, and that could have been you pulled over, so you kept driving, feeling sorry for the other person briefly but in the end feeling okay, because you realized that it was not you who was pulled over.

The Senator continued to struggle, his belly dancing with a fierce determination, like a Métis jigger cranked up on coffee, or a chicken struggling from the Colonel's grasp.

"Well, boss," the Cash smiled, "you know what they say. You can never have enough Cash." Nadine tried not to laugh and smile, because she did not want the Senator to feel bad. She wanted the Senator to be able to

---

75   "Is that you?" Cash said.

76   "It has been a long time," he said.

77   "But, you are beautiful."

leave the situation with some dignity. But she could not completely conceal the fact that she really was happier with Cash. She even liked how that sounded, "happier with Cash." She was hoping that the Senator would be able to see this, and would retreat out of the situation, although he was still stuck and it was impossible to see how he would find his way out of the situation. And Cash kept pushing him, not leaving him much room to retreat. The Senator was like a wounded deer who was being stalked by a very able and fast wolf.

The Senator struggled like a fish on a fishing line. He felt bad about the situation and, with the grace of an old Cree story, put aside his own ego in the hopes of trying to make things better for Nadine. He felt bad that he never did get his truck fixed but perhaps what made him feel worse was the fact that he could not imagine her sitting on the side of the road. While he hated to admit it, Cash at this moment in time had him beat. He would have to concede defeat.

There was a silence that surrounded the truck, a silence that moved around the Senator, and made the fabric of his coat dance about, the fabric slippery like the wind, like the wheat which would dance in the open prairie in fall. It was silence which ripped sound up like little pieces of paper, and pressed the ink on the paper, contorted it, pushing the words completely out of order to a point where they no longer made any sense. Silence of this kind, at this moment, was like words which were crumpled and completely out of their regular form.

Finally, the Senator broke out of his predicament, and got loose. The tearing of his jacket, however, was loud. The sound of the tear interrupted the previous exciting silence, adding form to words that had been hiding beneath the silence, like something that had been immersed below the water and was now being dragged to the surface.

"You should go with Cash." The Senator was sad, his heart was filled with a great deal of heaviness and he longed for things to be different. Nadine gave him a half smile and got into Cash's much newer truck. He wished he could shake a rattle like his grandfather and make everything better. He wished he had that sort of power. He thought about his grandfather and wondered if that was one of the reasons why he liked to have so many things in the pawn shop. He wanted to be surrounded by objects just like his grandfather was always surrounded by objects and by little songs that had been written over time, so that his grandfather could show with the history of the object. He could bring the object to life with a good story. That is really the life force of the Senator.

But as Cash's car pulled away he realized that he could not ever fully have those things in his life because they would never be. As he watched Cash's car go, he let out the loneliest and wildest how. The cry sent shivers up his spine. After, he shook his head, and waited by the truck. It would not be long before someone would come by to help him and boost his car.

MOOSE HUNTING AT THE ZOO

Everyone loved to gather at the Third Hand Pawn Shop. At night, especially in the winter, they would come to hear the Senator tell his stories. Sometimes in the telling of the stories, the Senator told them that they were like storytelling astronauts. They flew from their everyday thoughts to the stars of what they could be. Their spirits were stardust and the bodies became the blanket to hold the stardust in.

Sometimes those assembled at the shop would get so caught up in his stories that they would forget to eat. Then the story would bannock slap them when they were least expecting it. Sometimes the stories were so thrilling, and so full of detail that the Senator's experience as a bush pilot would kick in. He would make quick decisions in the middle of storytelling – just like when his plane was on the verge of crashing. One engine, a main character, would fall out of place, flames would come from the side of the wing, and the plane would begin to crash towards the ground. Then the Senator would take decisive action, raise the pitch of his voice, as if grabbing the throttle of a crashing plane. He would let out a little from the rear engine, and guide and move the plane slowly to the ground.

After a night of storytelling, the Senator smiled as his spoon clanked against his coffee cup. He smiled because he knew that Jingles was about to hunt a moose and become a man. Jingles was 13 years old, and it was time for him to cross the threshold into manhood. The rite of passage was important and it was often Kihci Lars who was asked to oversee it. It was in large part because he knew the bush so well, and because he spoke Cree so well. And, perhaps most practically, he had stayed out of politics.

All cultures had rites of passage for boys to pass into manhood. The passage into manhood was important because it would help provide a grounding for him – it would help him to remember where he came from. Other cultures marked things differently. For instance, the Wonder Bread eaters were rumoured to have a ritual which held that the young person would sit with a chartered accountant to figure out how they could retire at the age of 52.

Jingles was the son of Cash, but in many ways he was closer to the Senator. Jingles was not interested in power and money like his father, but rather was more interested in reading books. He also loved to thumb through the old Life magazines that were neatly stacked in one of the side rooms. In the room there was of chess board, which the Senator and Jingles would play sometimes. There were also fancy wooden chairs which were a slick sienna red – and they were shiny. There were also fancy maple lamps with rich red lampshades.

Many times Jingles would stay at the Third Hand Pawn shop for stretches at a time. It was as though Cash would forget about him. Some say that the Senator was extra kind to Jingles because Jingles was Nadine's son. Some say that his kindness to Jingles was just one way that he could express his love for Nadine.

Now the time had come for Jingles to find his place in the world. His father Cash was very busy and was on the road. He was away at political meetings. So, it became the task of the Senator to sit in for the boy, and to take him under his wing.

Jingles had been told to come the next day. The Senator told him that he should come around noon. That he should come with blankets, a gun, and some food. And that he should come with some kind of offering or gift.

The thing that the Senator always admired about

Buddy Bradley was his refusal to move beyond what people thought Indian people should be. Most of the people on the Broken Elbow reserve were like that. They spoke Cree fluently, with the exception of a couple of families. Very few of the men had long hair. That may have been because many of them had been in the military.

It was early morning; the Senator had fallen asleep in his Lazy Boy after being up all night, watching television. He had been watching French programs. The Senator would sometimes put on his beaver cap. Then he would pretend he was a coureur des bois, travelling into the future. After about one hour, he would fall asleep in his Lazy Boy with a little le pôkêt by his side. He would even be wearing a sash on his body. Then he would ê-mah-matwêhikêt iskwayikohk wâpan.[78] He was awoken by the knock on the door. It was Jingles. The Senator's snore stopped abruptly and his body flipped like a caught fish until he eventually fell out of his chair. Jingles had waited for a few minutes until he had unleashed a flurry of enthusiastic knocks upon the Senator's door, which was like a tired old road with tracks upon it.

As Jingles approached the house, he made sure that he had everything. He was so excited to give the Senator his gift. The Senator stumbled away from the floor, threw his beaver hat in the closet, and popped a breath mint in the hopes that it might be Nadine at the door. He knew that it was a long shot, but he always wanted to be prepared. It was his perpetual and somewhat naive optimism that some of the younger ones could not fully fathom. The Senator ran to his fridge, grabbed a little bit of bear grease and put it on his face. He always thought that a dab of bear grease made him look like a Hollywood movie star. When he felt the softness of that grease, it made him feel sexy. He knew, after seeing Dr. Charging Horse, and being through

---

78   He would knock on the door until dawn.

his seminar and workshop, knew that if he was ever to win Nadine over, he had to feel sexy. He knew that this was the only way. If he could feel sexy, then just maybe, he might finally get a place permanently in Nadine's heart.

He opened the door, only half expecting to see Nadine. It was Jingles. He had the same sparkle in his eye like his mom Nadine.

"Tânisi my boy," the Senator said with a warm smile.

"Good morning Senator," Jingles said. Jingles stood in front of the door, his face broad with a smile. He had his gun, all of his camping gear, loosely organized, and he had a special package which was a gift for the Senator.

"Pîhtikwê boy."[79] The Senator smiled so hard that it seemed like his smile might hurt his face.

"Okay Senator," he smiled with great triumph, "I am ready to go see Kihci Lars." He raced toward the coffee machine, prepped it, and looked at himself smile in the shiny mirror of the chrome. Then he turned on the radio program that played the oldies. The Senator went back to the shed getting the things that they needed – blankets, his moose caller whistle made from an old coffee tin, and, of course, the guns.

They were both happy as they sat at table. There was the familiar clank of the Senator's spoon on his cup, the low steady blow of the wind from the fans on the floor of the pawn shop. They sat at the table by the radio, eating a simple breakfast of cereal. For the milk, they used water downed evaporated milk. The radio announcer ran through the sports, the news, and other things. Then, there was a special bulletin.

"One of the train cars carrying animals for Circus Maximus has overturned. Two cheetahs have been released and are on the prowl, somewhere in the forests north

---

79   "Come in boy,"

and west of the city," he paused, for dramatic effect. "All hunters have been ordered to stay out of the area." Jingles looked at the Senator with shock. That's exactly where they were planning to go moose hunting. Now, the wardens had closed down the area.

"Senator," said Jingles in a mild voice, "do you think we could just wait until the next week or maybe even two when the cougars are found?" He paused, and tried to reassure himself that everything was going to be alright. "They should have found the cougars by then, right?"

The Senator wanted to tell him that everything was going to be okay, but he couldn't really do that. He knew that everything was not as easy as it could be, or as easy as it sounded, but at the same time, the Senator felt that he owed Jingles the truth. Jingles had always been a sensitive young man, and the Senator didn't want to tell him anything that would be seen as untrue.

"My boy," he paused and looked at him, scratching his head at the same time, "I am honoured when you asked me to be part of this. Part of your hunt. Part of this time when you become a man." He laughed when he started to remember his own quest to become a man, when he went out with old Pâcinîs to get his first moose. "We can't really change the date." He could see the frustration in Jingle's eyes, and noticed how his head seemed to lower a little. "That is the day that we told everyone that you would do it." He paused again, "It would be hard to back out of it now."

"Has the date ever been changed?"

The Senator thought about that for a bit and then gave Jimmy an answer that he knew he probably would not want to hear.

"Back in 1944, old man Pâcinîs tried to change the date, on account of war, and on account of a shortage of ammunition. But old Pâcinîs was told that he had to go out anyway. The bugger had no bullets, nothing but guts and determination. The young lad had gone out to the bush himself, and had wrestled a bull moose to the ground with his bare hands, and then, as the story goes, he stabbed the beast in the heart. And that was that."

They talked for a bit longer and then they drove out to the bush north of the reserve. Kihci Lars greeted them, and was not excessively talkative. Kihci Lars gathered his staff and his buffalo robe. The Senator and Jingles wanted to hear from Kihci Lars about what they were going to do in terms of the escaped cheetahs and the hunt. They stood by Lars' cabin, and they waited a bit. It was clear that Lars was deep in thought. Finally, he spoke: "It is not really safe to go to the forest." The Senator looked at Jingles with a raised eyebrow, and then looked to the ground again. "We will go to the zoo. We will get your moose there."

MOOSE HUNTING AT THE ZOO:
PART TWO

They knew that they had to try and get to the zoo as soon as possible as everyone was waiting for the feast. Everyone had been getting ready and they had been talking about it for some time. The Senator really didn't mind going to the zoo to get the moose. Now some of the more conservative of the people on the reserve may question that. They may even say that because the moose was not killed in the wild that the whole process was flawed. Some of the old time hunters may even say that it wouldn't really count because the moose did not have a fair chance to escape. The moose should have a fair chance to avoid being captured. If ol' Nap was still around, and had not gone to Paris to see his old flame from the war, he would probably say this. At the very least, the Senator could figure that he would not have approved of the "cheating way" that they got the moose.

They talked a bit about how hunting the moose at the zoo might be perceived as cheating. Then Lars added, "It is not going to be easy to get into that zoo. There will be security, and pulling that moose out there will not be an easy feat." The Senator asked what kind of plan Lars had.

Lars replied, "Okay my boy, tonight we are going to go to the zoo down south. We are going to go inside and hide in the washrooms until it is dark. Then when everyone leaves, we will get a moose."

"Can't wait."

"It's going to be a gooder."

While they spoke in the kitchen, the AM radio droned.

"There is one problem I was thinking of Senator."

"What is that my boy."

"Well, once we get the moose, how will we get it to

your truck?"

"That is a good point my boy." The Senator thought maybe they could quarter the moose right there in the zoo, and take it little by little to truck it. But as they talked about it, they thought that it would not be the smartest way to do it. They should just drag the whole moose to the truck, and then bring the moose back to the reserve to butcher it. There was a security guard so they realized that they would have to be extra sneaky about getting the moose out of the zoo. "Pretend the security guard is a Blackfoot warrior," the Senator said. That seemed to make the adventure all the more exciting for Jingles.

The year was 1964. There was a lot happening. The pass system had been over for four years, and now Indians were free to travel without a permit. Also the Beatles were just catching on and there seemed to be something in the air that the Senator could not completely place. His pawn shop business had grown, including his brisk mail order service for bannock dough kits and rabbit root. Someday the Senator hoped to turn the whole store over to his nephew and leave it with him. Surely bagging his own moose would be part of that journey for him to find his place in the community.

They planned to get there relatively close to the time of closing which they did. The zoo was to close at 6. So they went at 4. They mingled for a bit so that it would not be suspicious. They thought that it would be too suspicious if they went in at 5.30. Someone would say, "Sir, the zoo closes at 6. You really don't get your money's worth if you come in now. Come back tomorrow. That way you can get more value for your money." White people always seemed so worried about their money. "Value for your money." "Time is money." "Money makes the world go around." All of these little môniyâw aphorisms would run through the mind of the Senator whenever he ate Wonder Bread.

Sure, the Senator liked to make money as much as the next guy. But he didn't try to make money at the expense of everything else. Sometimes he might give someone a deal on some of his merchandise if he had a sense of what their price point might be. It was this philosophy, this underlying business shrewdness coupled with generosity that had helped build his business.

Once he, Lars, and Jingle got into the zoo, they tried to walk around the zoo. They had tried to park the truck close, but not too close, to the entrance so that they could escape relatively easily, but they didn't want to make it look too obvious. It was kind of like when Cree people would exaggerate how many people that they were related to, but at the same time, they would underplay that as well sometimes, so that if the time was right, they could try to get their snag on.

They decided to hide in the shed by gorillas. It was a shed close to the fence and not easy to get to. On the way, the Senator had tried to jump over the fence, but he got his pants caught and there was the sound a great tear. His buffalo was still in the coral, but that was mostly due to the shorts that he wore. But Jingles had seen those shorts on the clothes line and by the sweet beard of Nanabush, when those shorts fluttered in the wind, they looked like a parachute.

"Senator, did you fart?"

"Cha boy, no. We are at the zoo, and there are all kind of strange smells. Must be the musky smell of gorilla."

"Senator," said Jingles, "I think you probably blew a hole in your shortzes." Jingles tried his best to move away from him.

"So Kihci Lars, how am I actually going to kill the moose?"

"Good question, my boy." Kihci Lars paused when

he realized that he had not thought of this detail. He had
to think of an answer, "My boy," he said, "you will have to
fashion a spear. I brought my hunting knife." He paused
and tried to sound like he was being really epic. "Go
now, and find a stick, then bring it back here to fashion
into a spear. You can use my knife to make your spear."
Jingles took this to be very important task. He thought
of it as a very solemn ceremony,, and he tried his best to
sound humble and full of humility when he answered the
Senator.

Sure enough he went out and got his stick and he
whittled away at the wood for a long time until he had
made it into a spear. He kept sharpening and sharpening
it as ispi ê–âti–tipiskâk . Before too long he had something
that resembled a spear .

"Senator," Jingles said, "I hear someone coming."
He only called him when something was really serious.
Lars motioned for them to crouch down. They huddled
down between a couple of worn out barrels and the
Senator was heard to say "my hip, my hip!" He whispered.

The person who came into the gorilla shed had a
very heavy step, and was smoking. "Stinky gorilla," the
man with the husky voice said. He fumbled around for a
bit, and the left.

"Êkosi mâka?"

"Môy cêskwa," [80] said Kihci Lars as he clutched his
staff. "Let's wait for an apisîs more longer till we are sure
that everyone has cleared out."

After the man left, Jingles pulled out his map of the
zoo. He flipped it open and then, with great earnestness,
traced his finger across the map. "Lars," he said, "we have
to walk about 200 feet from here to where the moose are.
We have to walk right by the lions."

The Senator chuckled and said, "misi–pâkwâci–

---

80   "Not yet,"

pôsiwak."

"Then, it is about 150 feet to the truck from there. We will have to drag the moose that far, but really no different than someone pulling it through the bush."

They waited a bit longer – just to make sure that everyone had left the zoo. That way everything would go smoothly. They would go into the fenced area and Jingles would kill the moose with his spear.

They rose from their hiding spot and walked out of the gorilla shed. The Senator was sure he stepped in some gorilla poop and he tried to wipe off his loafers on the grass. He swore a little and tried to get ready for the big hunt. Kihci Lars kept focused and tried to help keep a look out.

"Okay my boy, we are close to the moose fenced in area," the Senator said, "we are almost there. Once we get there, you are on your own. I won't be able to intervene or help you in any way."

"Ahâw" Jingles said with solemnity.

The bull moose was sleeping and he was quite magnificent. He had wide and thick horns. Jingles edged up to the fence, jumped off, and entered the fenced in area. He landed on both feet and grabbed his spear. Then Kihci Lars made the moose call and with that Jingles was alone in the fenced area. He remembered an illustrated history of Rome book that he once read at the library and a picture of a gladiator in the Colosseum. He grabbed the spear, like that gladiator, and he made himself fierce so that he could face the furry beast.

Slowly, the moose woke up after Kihci Lars did the moose call. At that point, Lars motioned that he would be going. The moose got up, stretching as he rose. Once the moose had stood up, he looked at Jingles and snorted. The moose stamped his feet and charged.

As the moose charged towards him, Jingles grabbed

his spear and tried his best to stare down the moose, but the moose kept charging. Jingles tried to be brave and he wanted so badly to be a man, but he ended up dropping the spear. He bent over, his cisk facing the charging moose, as he tried to grab the spear, but he could not get it. The Senator wanted to yell to watch out, but he knew that he couldn't intervene.

Then, "BOOM!" The moose antlers hit Jingles' ass in a powerful way, and completely barrelled him over.

"awiya," Jingles yelled.

The Senator had to had to bite his lip so that he would not make a sound.

Jingles crawled around. They could hear the lion roar. The Senator's eye looked at the one giraffe and he imagined what kind of neck bone soup that long, long neck would make.

Then as the moose turned around to face him again, Jingles tried his best to grab his spear, but he dropped it again. The moose charged and narrowly missed him.

The thrill of everything was too much for Jingles and he dropped the spear for the third time. Then the craziest thing happened. The moose spun around again. But then the moose just stood there, looking at Jingles. He just kept looking at him, until finally the great beast of the forest, slowly walked towards him. Jingles was too nervous and scared to do anything. The moose kept coming towards him, slowly, slowly. Finally, the moose started licking Jingles' face. That big spongy tongue kept tracing and trickling on his face.

Jingles grabbed his spear, but the moose kept looking at him, with his big brown eyes. This went on for a bit, and there was nothing that Jingles could do. He couldn't bring himself to kill the moose.

MOOSE HUNTING AT THE ZOO: PART THREE

On the long road back to the reserve, they did not say much. Kihci Lars muttered a few things, like "You have to hunt as hard as the next guy, to eat beside the next guy" and finally asked Jingles what his favourite Beatles song was, and asked him other things.

They stopped at an all night truck stop, and Kihci Lars got a coffee and Jingles got himself a bottle of pop and a bag of chips. The Senator got coffee that he poured into his tall thermos. He poured some from his thermos into his long, tall ceramic cup. Just as he was clanking his spoon against the side of the cup. He heard Jingles yell, "Look out!"

Just then the truck hit a moose. There was blood all over the grill, and guts on the road. They looked at each other. They made an agreement with their eyes that they would not tell anyone what had happened – and more specifically how Jingles had hunted and bagged the moose. When they got to the reserve the Senator hammered out the dents on his truck, poured himself another cup of coffee, and then he and Jingles cleaned the "hunted moose." The feast went on as planned and people honoured Jingles for becoming a man.

ᐱᓄᑭᓂᐦᑎ BECOMES A MAN

The story of ᐱᓄᑭᓂᐦᑎ is one of the most important stories of the broken Elbow reserve. Sometimes a story, like the story of ᐱᓄᑭᓂᐦᑎ, is told so many times, and told by so many storytellers, that we forget the spark of the original story. It was the kind of story that was born in the fire and power of the first making of bannock.

ᐱᓄᑭᓂᐦᑎ was a cigar store Indian that had been in the Senator's Third Hand Pawn Shop since the 1960s but its creation date was unknown. That cigar store Indian had become an icon at the store, something that people would hang their stories on, and perhaps, in some small way, their hope. The old timers said that he was made out of chokecherry wood. The branches of those old chokecherry trees were formed into his body; they gave him home; they gave him life. There was a great forest near the Broken Elbow reserve and the old timers said that there were some old growth chokecherry trees in that forest. Those trees, they said, were planted by the Wahwâ–napêw himself when he was passing through the area. The old timers said that the branches that formed the body of the wooden Indian were the last that grew in that old time, kayâs ago way.

The Third Hand Pawn Shop had become a tourist destination since the Senator started it in 1962. The Senator had attracted tourists because of his mail order rabbit root sales. The Senator asked his uncle Pâcinîs to tell real old Indian Stories. Pâcinîs was a good storyteller and knew lots of stories. But he really wasn't into telling stories to the Germans. So, he would just read Louis L'Amour novels, and make up stories from those. The Germans seemed to like them and it kept the cash register of the pawn shop busy.

---

81   Pinokineechie

It was tricky sometimes for the Senator to run his pawn shop. Sometimes he would get people who would try to trade in moose meat to get their stuff back, and there were, of course, local artisans who were always trying to bring in their stuff. What really kept the shop going were the high end items that the Senator would get from Europe that he would sell to collectors – particularly from the United States. They would often drive up or phone to see what was new. Napoleon, until his health really failed, would go to Europe to get some things for him. However, despite the many offers, ᐱᓄᑭᓂᐢ was one thing that the Senator would never sell.

ᐱᓄᑭᓂᐢ would be brought out on special occasions on the Broken Elbow reserve. Special events like birthdays, celebrations of recent shack–ups, and shack–downs, and even celebrations of large bingo winnings in Kistapinānihk (or Prince Albert as the cowboys say).

The story of ᐱᓄᑭᓂᐢ begins one special night. People were excited about meeting this Prime Minister because he really seemed to listen to First Nations people. Not the kind of listening like when someone you love is trying to tell you how their day went but all you are thinking about is how the hockey game is going. So you listen in the hopes that if you give the impression that you are listening, then the story will finish and you can get back to watching the game. No, that is not how this Prime Minister listened. Môya,[82] he listened deeply – like everything depended on it. And, he could remember everyone's name. Names were important to Indians and maybe just maybe, that is one of the reasons why this Prime Minister was so popular with Indians. He listened so hard that his jowls shook, like clothes on a laundry line blown about by the wind. He was different from some of the other môniyâwak because he actually seemed to care.

82   No

The Senator used to talk about the time Napoleon was arrested back in the day. The police came down on him hard as soon as he left the reserve. They didn't throw the book at him, they threw a whole library at him.

Through this night, through all of the ensuing festivities, a series of events led to a strange shift in the bannock force of the universe.

At one point in the night, some of Paskwâw–Iskwêw's bannock dough fell on ᐱᓅᑭᓯᐢ. They say Paskwâw–Iskwêw had in her possession the original bannock recipe that was passed on from kôhkom to grand–daughter for hundreds of years. At another point, a drunk Hutterite thought it would be funny to put lard on the cheeks of ᐱᓅᑭᓯᐢ. Later, Buddy Bradley, the local comedian on the Broken Elbow reserve put his winning bingo card, still damp with the tears of the midnight bingo caller, in the hand of ᐱᓅᑭᓯᐢ. Finally, the Senator spilled some of the precious KFC gravy on ᐱᓅᑭᓯᐢ's feet.

The Senator didn't like things going wrong, didn't like doing things in a mâmâsîs[83] way. The Senator often told Jingles, "You shouldn't tell a story in the wrong way. Just like you shouldn't have eyes on your cousin's old lady even though she might be hotter than kôhkom's bannock."

The night of the bush party when the Senator and his friends poured all of those ingredients on the wooden cigar Indian, the boys had shared a bucket of Co–op vanilla ice cream. This was back when Indians first started eating ice cream. The thing is that they really didn't know ice cream could mess up a neechie's cisk situation. As they laughed on their way into the bush, they started to fart from all of the ice cream. Pâcinîs said, "wahwâ sîsîp–tâkwan!"[84] They sounded like a jazz band, trumpeting from their frisky ciskies.

83   poorly done way
84   "Wow, it sounds like a duck!"

Old Pâcinîs brought the old cigar store Indian along. He dragged it along with some special rope that he had tied to his waist. Someone had gotten it in their heads that if they brought the old cigar store Indian with them, it would bring them good luck. They thought that the luck from the cigar store Indian would make them invincible and the Indian agent would not be able to see them.

"Pâcinîs," the Senator itwêw, "you dropped something. Something fell out of your pocket." Pâcinîs stopped moving, and so did the Cigar Store Indian which he was pulling. He looked down and he said, "nug–gah–cha, that is my winning bingo card from last night. I won $100! I was just so proud of it. Even the bingo caller was so happy he splashed his tears on it." He laughed.

The Senator wanted to keep moving to the bush. "Wâpahta ôma Pâcinîs.[85] I'll just tuck it in this spot here."

"Miywâsin ôma," Pâcinîs itwêw.

The Senator tucked the winning bingo ticket in a little nook in the sculpture. Buddy Bradley, the local Indian comedian, lit a cigarette while he waited. As soon as the tear–splashed, slightly crumpled, bingo card touched the body of the cigar store Indian, it sent a shock wave through the Senator which caused him to pee a tinkle and fart a little at the same time.

"Stakâc[86] Senator," Buddy paused to take a drag of his cigarette and he pulled his body back, and he did his best James Dean, "no more ice cream for you."

The Senator laughed nervously and wondered what had just happened.

They kept going and the three old friends found their favourite spot in the bush. While they were resting, the wooden cigar store Indian brushed against Old Pâcinîs' jacket, which got tangled up on something, and a little

85   "Look at this Pâcinîs"
86   "holy smokes"

bit of the special chokecherry wine he was carrying fell on the cigar store Indian. Right at the moment when that happened, the wooden Indian flashed and glowed. Pâcinîs got so startled he fumbled the bottle and it fell and broke on the cigar store Indian. It started pulsating vigorously and shone very brightly. They all heard Not–Even, the nomadic three legged rez dog, howl in the distance.

Buddy Bradley tugged on this cigarette, "Holy smokerinos boys. What the heck just happened."

Pâcinîs itwêw, "that cigar store Indian is very bright."

"Cha," said the Senator. "I don't know what the heck it is, but it made me a pee a little in my pantz." They all laughed.

Pâcinîs approached the cigar store Indian. "Holeh, our own little Calijah here is very warm." They could still hear Not–Even howling in the distance, but it seemed like the howl was getting louder and closer.

"You know," itwêw Buddy, "I am hungry. I have some bannock here. But it is kind of cold. I'll just put it on the wooden Indian."

The Senator also had a hankering for something to eat. "You know, I have a little of that secret sauce that Colonel guy from down south gave me. I'll put it on our little wooden Indian." They both put it on at the same time. Unknown to the trio, they had placed four mystical elements on the wooden Indian made from rare chokecherry wood. The four mystical elements were: KFC gravy, chokecherry wine brewed under a full moon, the tears of a midnight bingo caller, and bannock made from the original bannock recipe. By putting all of the four primordial neechie elements together, they helped bring forward a series of events that would soon spiral out of control.

A big flash happened. Lights shot out of the

wooden Indian in such a dazzling array that a couple of people on the reserve went blind. However, thankfully they received special glasses from Indian Affairs, which allowed them to see again. The second that the KFC gravy hit the wooden Indian, as the legend is sung by the bards throughout Creedom, Not–Even, the three legged rez dog, after licking the very warm gravy from the wooden indian, howled the spookiest howl the world has ever heard. They say when he was done howlin', all of the skin on the fried chicken within a ten–mile radius evaporated into the air. With that, the wooden Indian ê–nâpêwipayit,[87] and ᐱᔪᐱᓂᕐ began to take human form.

At first, when he took human form, he could not speak. He just looked at everyone with a great intensity. The old people tried to speak different languages to him – Cree, Saulteaux – but he did not respond to anything. The Senator took him back to the Third Hand Pawn Shop and made sure he was safe and warm, and had fresh bannock in his belly. When word got out, people began to visit the spot where the wooden Indian had turned into a man. A truck load of Crees, even from Rocky Boy Montana, came.

---

87   he becomes a man

MISSING THE WOODEN INDIAN

At first, the Senator was not sure about ᐱᑎᑯᓂ. It seemed weird to have him now, walking around like a person rather than having him standing at the entrance of the pawn shop, greeting customers.

The Senator paused and looked at the spot where ᐱᑎᑯᓂ used to stand. There was an emptiness that he felt. The spaces around were different. The colours looked different. Even the way the light filled the room was different. As time went on it was not just the spaces around him which were different, so too were the spaces of the reserve, so too were the spaces of the roads, so too were the spaces of the trees and also the spaces of days. After he became the Chief nothing was the same – nothing would ever be the same.

After the Senator spoke to ᐱᑎᑯᓂ, he noticed that things had shifted, that things would not be the same. He remembered the time he would take cleaning him as someone would wash a child. Now that child had grown up, he no longer needed him.

The Senator always tried his best to get along with people from the reserve. He always tried to be kind to people. He always took the time to talk to old people. He would take time to drive them to town after they would get their cheques. Some of the Old People were visionaries, they thought that maybe one day they could have their money transferred through smoke signals, instead of old fashioned paper.

As the Senator drove down the road, the dust blew up and around the truck, scattering the light of the day as it filtered through. All the Senator had thought and had done was like light scattered through dust.

The roads of the reserve held all kinds of stories. And the nuances of all of those old voices. Each of these stories formed patterns. The Senator would retrace these with the movement of his truck. The spinning tires cut in the gravel like little paths.

MISSING THE WOODEN INDIAN: PART TWO

At last, after being away from the Third Hand Pawn Shop, ᐱᓄᑭᓂᕽ came to talk to the Senator. "Senator, can I talk to you?" said ᐱᓄᑭᓂᕽ.

"Ahâw mâka. sure come in."

He smiled as he walked in. "Remember Senator, when I used to stand here?"

"Yes, I do my boy. I remember." The Senator did that laugh – where he would rub his belly and let out a laugh which was like a wild horse.

"You know Senator," he said, "I still have vague memories of my other life. My life as the wooden Indian. I remember I used to feel so trapped within the wood. I felt like I could not breathe."

"It is okay, my boy." The Senator said as he got up. "Let me fix you some tea, and let's talk a little."

CHICKEN BUCKET PROPHECIES

As ᐱᓄᐯᕐ took human form, the murmurs of the reserve people grew louder and louder, and people kept talking more and more. Finally, the Senator decided to take him to old Pâcinîs. The Senator, after touching base with the local band council, decided that he would take ᐱᓄᐯᕐ.

Throughout human history, there have been many ways in which people could interpret the future. The ancient Greeks had an oracle of Delphi. Old Cree hunters would interpret moose guts and they would throw them on the ground and try to see the patterns, and from those patterns try to understand the future. The Senator had hunted with some of these old time hunters, and as it became harder and harder to get moose guts, he turned his attention to new forms. When the fella on the reserve got an economic development grant after the White Paper, the people on the rez got an economic development grant to start a fried chicken company.

On his way to take ᐱᓄᐯᕐ to see Pâcinîs, the Senator rolled a cigarette. He always used drum tobacco. He was pretty good at rolling and he could even roll while he was riding a horse. There was something so delicious about the taste of tobacco in his mouth, gliding and landing in all of the various places. He thought that tobacco was a lot like an amplifier. It took the taste, and just made it so much more intense. That is probably why all of the old fellas always talked about the joy of tasting tobacco in their mouth after a good meal.

ᐱᓄᐯᕐ was still finding his way into his skin. He still felt a bit stunned and had that early–morning–before–coffee look. He stumbled a little when he walked, being uneasy in his movements. He moved around like a newly born colt sometimes, the Senator thought.

As they edged towards Pâcinîs', the Senator tried to

tell a few jokes to limber up his mind. ᐱᑭᓂᐢ got some of the jokes, but some of them flew over him like a bunch of balloons. Okay, maybe a really fast metal bird.

They knocked on the door and waited for a bit. The Senator knew that the old man was probably watching an rerun of "Sanford and Son" and maybe even "Gunsmoke." Sure, it was 1975 now, and it had been 17 years since the first television came to the reserve, but he still would put tea on top of the television. It was like he was giving an offering, a gift, to the story tellers on the flicker box. Whenever the Senator came to see old Pâcinîs, he would also bring him tea. He went to fancy hippie stores in the city and got fancy tea there sometimes.

Finally, Pâcinîs came to the door.

"Tânisi," itêw The Senator.

"Tânisi my nephew. Pê–pihtikwê. Tawâw."[88] He paused for a minute and continued in English for the benefit of ᐱᑭᓂᐢ who was only slowly beginning to understand Cree. It was like his knowledge of Cree was like someone taking blind stabs in the dark at something, and they weren't really sure where it was. "We are here to have this man's future read."

Pâcinîs nodded quietly and motioned for them to come in. He had fashioned a rocking chair into a neechie lazy boy. He even had fashioned a little area underneath for where he could keep stuff like snacks and magazines. He especially like LIFE magazine which gave him a real look into the world without having to struggle his way through the English language.

ᐱᑭᓂᐢ was slowly gaining his wits, and looked less wide–eyed than before. He seemed to be more in his body.

They all shook hands with one another and they sat down.

"Kinôhtêkatân cî?"[89]

---

88   "Come in my nephew. There is room."
89   "Are you hungry?"

"Ahâw,"the Senator replied.

"Ahâw," itêw kisêyisis. "Mêtoni tâkahki–kîkway ôma. This is truly a great thing that you have here."

ᐱᓯᑭᓂᐢ nodded, and then astounded everyone when he said, "kinanâskomitin." He spoke the words flawlessly and crisply.

Pâcinîs lifted up the bucket, and said the following words, "hâw mâka, I shake my bingo balls in all directions, and lend money to all my relations." The Senator then tapped him on the shoulder and slipped him a fiver.

Then he motioned for ᐱᓯᑭᓂᐢ to show his hands and then lowered them into the bucket of grease. "Now roll them in the bucket."

And then ᐱᓯᑭᓂᐢ did that. He put his hands in the bucket of grease. And he even lathered them together. The Senator told him, "Okay, don't over do it. You aren't choking a chicken."

"Ahâw," he said with a great deal of enthusiasm. His colour was becoming more like a human and less like the colour that he was when he had been a wooden Indian.

"Now nôsim,"[90] the kisêyinîs Pâcinîs said, "rub your hands in the bucket." He paused again and then continued. "Imagine," he said, "that you are drawing your own very soul."

They could hear the lathering of his hands and the sound of his hand hitting the bucket.

"Êkosi mâka."[91] Then the Senator went and got a picture of Colonel Sanders and put it in front of the bucket. Then they all held up the bucket together and said in unison, "I shake my bingo balls in all directions, and lend money to all my relations." With that they tapped each other and money was exchanged all around their little circle.

"Hâw, let us love it." The Senator then put a cup of tea by the Colonel's picture and began to interpret the lines

90   my grandson
91   "Alright, then."

that ᐱᔪᑭᓂᕆ had left in the inside of the bucket.

The Senator and ᐱᔪᑭᓂᕆ waited with great anticipation for what Pâcinîs would say about the markings in the bucket. He closed his eyes and searched the landscape of all that he was for the answer.

"I see you being a star, a great star." With those words gravy started to drip from the picture of the Colonel. "The gravy marks are only seen when there is great power present when one is interpreting the contents of the bucket. You are going to change the way everything is done on this reserve. Nothing will be the same."

ᐱᔪᑭᓂᕆ could not contain himself anymore. "I feel every cell in my body move. I feel so alive. I feel like I could do anything now."

The Senator continued, "with this great gift you have, my boy, the bannock in all the universe is shaking and I'm afraid that there's going to be great change." They all looked at each other with great excitement and also great anticipation.

THE SENATOR TAKES ᐱᓱᐱᓯᒡ TO GET HIS TREATY CARD

At first when ᐱᓱᐱᓯᒡ took human form, everyone was quite excited. They realized that something quite extraordinary had occurred. "Mêtoni mamâhtâwipayik, itwêcik kêhte ayâk." There was time for a bit of marvelling, time for people to be entertained by the greatness of the story, and time for the events to be taken into people's minds and to be processed. Now the honeymoon of the experience was over and it was time to get back to the daily pulse and rhythm of reserve life.

Old Pacînîs ê–kî–âcimikot: "awa kiskisototawacâhkwêw, êkwa poko kawîcihânaw, ka–miskâsot, ka–pimâtisit kwayask."[92] As usual Pâcinîs was poetic in his storytelling, he was a master at the art of telling a story, but also of kinwâcimopicikêwin, the art of elongating a story. Some might call that bullshitting, some people may call it lying, but that is a narrow conception. The process of elongating a story, kinwâcimopicikêwin,[93] was the art of discerning an audience and reaching out to that audience. It was the way of filling in the space between the audience and story.

Finally, the time came for the marvel to become practical. It was time to get him new clothes. It was time to get him lodging. The Senator, with support of the band council, said that it would be fine for him to keep living there. In fact, everyone agreed that it would be odd if he didn't live there. After all, as a wooden Indian he had lived there – if you could call being a wooden Indian living—for many years. But his days of being a nêhiyawâhtik were over. Now, he was a real Indian.

Part of being a real Indian was hanging out with

---

92   he spoke of him, "This one is trying to remember his soul, and we must help him, to find himself, and to live well."

93   to elongate a story

older relatives. Since the Senator had adopted him, all of the Senator's relatives were now ∧ᗊᑭ᛬ᓐᕐ's relatives. ∧ᗊᑭ᛬ᓐᕐ affectionately called him nôhcâwîs which meant "my little father." He would get the Senator to tell him stories into the wee hours of the night. He would get him to share what he knew, and he asked the Senator to trace the old words onto his soul. Slowly, slowly, he was remembering things. He was remembering things with his soul.

One day as they were having breakfast in the yellowy, light of new dawn, the crackle of frying eggs and the toasting smell of Nadine's mother's bannock, which had been heralded the best bannock north of the Rio Grande River, ∧ᗊᑭ᛬ᓐᕐ looked Senator straight on with the seriousness of a midnight bingo caller and said, "nôhcâwîs môy kiyâpic ê–nêhiyawâhtikoyân."[94]

The Senator responded, "tâpwê anima."

But with a look of frustration mixed with a dash of frustration mixed with a dash of disappointment, ∧ᗊᑭ᛬ᓐᕐ added, "well, there are a few things that I need to become a real man."

The Senator looked at him with that look that relatives give when the other person clearly does not know what the hell they are talking about. "Kîkwây ê–isiyan?"[95] said the Senator.

He sat up in his seat and tried his very best to project his voice clearly so that his voice would sound clearly to the Senator. "Well, I mean, I need to kill my first moose."

The ∧ᗊᑭ᛬ᓐᕐ was clearly disappointed but he did his best to conceal it. He really wanted to be a real Indian. He wanted to be accepted by the people of the community. He wanted to be accepted by the people of the Broken Elbow reserve. He really thought in order to be accepted he had to go through the various rights of passage such as moose hunting. As best as he could figure, the first hunt and the feast was the key.

---

94   "Uncle, I am no longer a wooden Indian."
95   "What did you say to me?"

The Senator leaned into him and tapped him on the shoulder. "My boy," he smiled. "I know sometimes things are hard for you. I know that it has been hard for you to take human form."

"Tâpwê ayimân ôma," said ᐱᓄᐯᓂᐟ.

"My boy," the Senator smiled again, and gave him that mosôm smile that he gave when he tried to tell himself and others that everything was going to be okay. It was the same look that he gave Nadine when his truck broke down and Cash had come to pick her up. "It is okay that you never hunted. It is okay that you never promised game for everyone." Once again ᐱᓄᐯᓂᐟ looked puzzled as if to say, "how the heck can that be possible?"

The Senator let the mind catch up to his words, "With all that you have done with the chicken, opening up all of the branches of the Chief's Fried Chicken, you have more than feasted the community." With that the Senator felt as though his fear had been dealt with to some extent. He felt as though everything was going to be miywâsin. That everything was going to be okay. With that they continued to eat their mouth watering breakfast.

Another day, ᐱᓄᐯᓂᐟ who was very inquisitive and curious, liked to talk things out. He was by nature a conversationalist. The Senator certainly was that too, but at a certain point the Senator did hold back on his words. He tried to make ᐱᓄᐯᓂᐟ feel welcome in the space of the conversations. Often these conversations would occur while the two were cruising around the roads of the reserve, or cruising to town.

The open wind of the parklands of the northern prairies had a way of not only shaking one's hair around, but it also had a way of shaking one's mind up and so, as they cruised around, ᐱᓄᐯᓂᐟ opened his mind and let out his words.

"Nôhcâwîs," itwêw awa, "kiyâpic ê–mâmitoniyihtamân ôma kâkî– ispayik."[96]

---

96   "Uncle," he said, "I am still thinking about what happened."

The Senator smiled and with his hands on the dials of the radio, he tried to find some good music until he finally found something that seemed to resonate with him. It was a track being played of Johnny Cash.

"You know, Senator, I keep thinking. I keep wondering kîspin tâpwê niya tâpwê ê-nêhiyawêyân?"

"Look at your brown skin boy, you are definitely an Indian." There could be no mistaking that. ᐱᔨᐠᓯᐣ certainly was of a darker complexion.

"But I mean Senator," and these words were hard for him to get his mind around, "sometimes..." He wanted to continue but it was as though he was choking on his words. "Sometimes I feel my whole being get cold and I remember being nêhiyawâhtik. I remember being the wooden Indian."

The Senator did that look which indicated that he hoped that he could make things better. It was half a look of confidence, but also a look which had an understated sense of panic embedded in it. It was a look which indicated that he was trying to find his way through a situation, but he really wasn't sure how it was going to go.

"Mahti wihtamawin ôma.⁹⁷ It is better to talk it out rather than to hold it all in, my boy."

"Nôhcâwis," ᐱᔨᐠᓯᐣ said and with that he began to tremble a little bit.

The Senator could see that it was hard for him to push through the words. He could see that ᐱᔨᐠᓯᐣ was having a hard time to try and figure out where to take his words in the space of his conversations.

"I feel like I can see the quiet spaces of the Third Hand Pawn Shop. It is night and I can see the mice scurrying across the floor. I can hear the tick tock of the old clock by the workshop. It is so intense that I just want to scream. I feel like I am this being trapped inside this wooden frame."

The Senator tried to calm him down and reminded him of what old Pacinîs had said would happen. He had

97   "Please tell me this."

warned that he would get confused once he took human form. The more he felt the panic, the closer he was to turning back to a wooden Indian.

ᐱᓄᐳᖮᒉ kept observing the world around him. He was a careful learner, but he was also a fast learner. He watched the coming and going of people from the reserve. He noticed the coming and going from people's stories, and the coming and going from people's wallets. He saw birthdays and, sadly, a few funerals.

He saw the passing of some of the old timers – most of them were Pâcinîs' generation. These were the ones that had been particularly difficult to lose. But, of course the most difficult one to lose of all was Pâcinîs. People from all over the world came to his funeral. The Prime Minister even sent a handwritten letter to the Senator, telling him stories of the times that he would sit at that café on Central Avenue in Prince Albert. He would sit there with old timers and he would talk to them. Languages were not really his thing. Just as the Quebeçois would wince and smile when he would speak French, the Cree old timers would wince and smile at him. They didn't want to hurt his feelings despite his poor efforts. They could hardly believe that a môniyâw, especially the Prime Minister of Canada would talk to them. Not only did the passing of Pâcinîs mean that the information of those old timers was potentially lost, but it also meant that whenever people like the Prime Minister remembered these things, people made a point of honouring that memory, and so his letter was read out loud at the wake. While the letter was read, they seemed to clip along at a rate of about 1 minute or so of the English words, and then 1 minute of the translation.

The light of the fridge was open, streaming onto the floor of the kitchen, blocked in patches by ᐱᓄᐳᖮᒉ's body. He was putting on the four Indian elements to keep his human form: the bannock from the original recipe, KFC gravy, chokecherry wine cured under a full moon, and the tears of a midnight bingo caller. He knocked the cup which contained his teeth and then proceeded to step on them with his heavy foot. He was conscious not to yell because he believed there was a burglar in the house. In fact, the Senator imagined a cat burglar burgling around like a sneaky teepee creeper. He put his glasses on but he accidentally put them on upside down and his focus was somewhat lopsided. As he moved out towards the kitchen to take a peek out the window, he saw the light of the fridge opening and closing, and he could make out a form: "It's a cat burglar," he thought. It really was and he did his best to move slowly.

ᐱᖃᑭᖕᒦ, on the other hand, was equally startled because he was having a snack, but at the same time he was putting the four elements on himself. He remembered that the Senator had warned him that it would be best if other people did not see him do this. It would be hard to explain to people.

He tried to conceal what he was doing but the Senator moved up towards him and then grabbed him and squeezed him like he was squeezing toothpaste out of a tube. ᐱᖃᑭᖕᒦ was in bit of a weakened form because he had only administered three of the Indian elements to his body. The Senator was twisting and turning and finally his glasses fell off completely. As their feet stomped around the room, they eventually smashed his Indian Affairs special – the black heavy framed glasses that many of the people on the reserve had. Not just the everyday neechies but also the neechies on TV Eventually, in the melee, and the ê-pihtikwêhk sound of their encounter, the Senator slipped again on the glasses and fell flat on the glasses with his flat cisk. He grabbed his hip, and could feel sharp pains, shooting down his right leg: "awiya! awiya! the Senator yelped. ᐱᖃᑭᖕᒦ, after having encountered the roughness of the initial part of the melee and the initial shock of being grabbed, now could see the Senator in his one–piece flannel pyjamas, and started to laugh, "nôhcâwîs," he paused, "I am your nephew." With that all the Senator could muster at the moment was "cha!"

THE SENATOR TAKES ᐱᓄᑭᑌᓂᐲ TO GET HIS TREATY CARD: PART TWO

The Senator couldn't see at all without his glasses. He tried duct taping them together but that did not seem to work very well. The right side was crushed so bad that when he tried to look through everything looked like a kaleidoscope. The cracks in the glasses made it look like there were little TV sets. The light was fractured and the Senator had to laugh. It reminded him of the first television on the reserve. For a second, the Senator considered putting little rabbit ears on his head but then he laughed so hard because he realized how absurd the idea was. But the Senator was full of such crazy ideas.

"My boy," said the Senator, "kiwî–itôhtênânaw ôtênahk."[98]

"Tânêhki nôhcâwis?"[99]

"Well, my boy I have to go into Indian Affairs. I need to get approval for new glasses and new dentures."

They got into the Senator's truck – the cold orange truck. The other people on the reserve affectionately referred to it as the môsâpêw–otâpânask.[100]

The môsapêw–otâpânask had heavy thick mud flaps that fluttered in the wind. He had a factory 8–track player which was used to amplify CCR through prairies.

As they drove, the Senator kept looking at ᐱᓄᑭᑌᓂᐲ while he drove. After each glance ᐱᓄᑭᑌᓂᐲ would sneak a look back. Finally, ᐱᓄᑭᑌᓂᐲ broke the successive chain of glances.

He said, "Nôhcâwîs kîkwây ê–mâmitonêyihtaman?"[101]

"I am thinking boy that you really don't have any

---

98   "We are going to town."

99   "Why uncle?"

100   the bachelor vehicle

101   "Uncle what are you thinking?"

ID," he paused. "Maybe you shouldn't drive."

"Cha. Senator. Who is going to drive now? You can't even see. You look like Mr. Magoo." And with that he laughed.

"Good point, but you know it all gets me thinking." He looked out the window, searching for his thoughts in the shifting landscape outside. Despite his best efforts all he could see was the over–saturated light that was passing by him and through his line of sight – mitoni wâh – wâskotêyihtam. His thoughts were full of light.

"You know, my boy, I think that it would be good to go get you some ID," the Senator itêw.

"How could I get it?"

"Well, the band could pass a Band Council Resolution giving you the basic documentation that you will need."

ᐱᒪᑎᓯ WANTS TO SEE THE WORLD

Since he took human form, ᐱᒪᑎᓯ felt the blood in his veins flowing, and his cells dividing, and his awareness of the world growing. He knew that he wanted to see more of the world. He wanted to see the place where all of the big wigs in Ottawa made their decisions, he wanted to go to Detroit to see rez cars, before they were rezified, and of course he wanted to go to Las Vegas.

People knew that ᐱᒪᑎᓯ was different. He had more charisma than the other leaders, and he had a way with the ladies, a way that would make them chuckle under their breath. They say he even had special powers. Each neechie telling their story would list different powers that he had, depending on the storyteller, and depending on the story being told. Everyone liked him. He chatted up the old people – he knew the value of the small chit chat that the old timers liked. He would get them their mail in town, and he would take special orders for things that they wanted in town. He would never ask for money and seemed to do it all from the bottom of his heart.

While ᐱᒪᑎᓯ was wildly popular, what really made him popular was the fact the he was humble. He knew that he had something different about him from the time that he became a man. From the time that the four Indian elements joined together to give him a piece of the divine, êkwa mîna mêtoni ê–mamâhtâwisit. But during these first stages of him being a man, he felt kind and did not want to stand out from others. He just wanted to be a regular Indian Act neechie. Nothing out of the ordinary – nothing special. Just another blueberry in a blueberry patch. But deep down, ê–môsihtâhk, ê–kiskêyihtahk[102] that this would not be possible. Still, he wanted to believe in this myth, just like people who believed Santa, or people who believed in the albino bingo caller. He wanted to believe even though he knew the illusion would only last a

---

102   he felt, he knew

little while. It was kind of like when people would believe in election results, only to have the results of the election contested, and then to have it appealed. There was a brief moment when everything was good and when everyone believed it was so, and he was in that moment right now.

In order to make himself seem like "one of the guys," he took the job as the "honey truck" driver on the reserve. People thought that he really humbled himself, that despite having his powers, he would take the "honey" from the septic tanks. When he would go around like a bee, gathering the honey, he would stop to visit old people. He would have tea with them and sometimes he would smoke, but with they had to be careful with the smoking because a strange flame could ignite the methane fumes from the honey wagon and cause a great explosion. These were the sort of fireworks that you didn't want to see on a reserve.

Sometimes, some of the old kohkom's would invite him in for lemon meringue pie. Sometimes they would whip some whipping cream and give it to him on fancy jello with fruit cocktail. They would sit and tell the stories of old. Sometimes they would listen to Buck Owens and the Buckaroos. They would laugh and tap their toes.

Sometimes when he got back he would go to the Senator's house. Sometimes the Senator would pull out his harmonica and reminisce about his days as a high stakes bingo caller in Europe in the early 1960s. This was after the pass system was reworked so neechies could leave the reserve without restriction. Also there was the story about how the Senator got the upper hand against the Indian agent, but that is another story for another time. The point is that the Senator had seen the world, and had stories of what he had seen.

ᐱᓄᐯᐅᓰ wanted to see the world too. He wanted to tell stories of the world like the Senator.

ᐱᑕᑭ WANTS TO SEE THE WORLD: PART TWO

ᐱᑕᑭ saw the reserve each and every day. The same roads, the same people, the same waves on the road. Of course, there was the wave which was almost a salute, then there was the quick index poke, and then of course the wave that was vicious and friendly at the same time. The older people would wave back but usually in a more restrained fashion. Then there was the "lazy Al" wave. What they did was keep the right hand on the wheel. Then they would raise their index finger, and then they also raise their middle finger. Then there was the non–committal wave. People would just raise their hand in a disinterested fashion. It was out of obligation – no passion.

After the original blast of light, those around him had their memories scrambled by the Bannarchists, the secret society to protect the original bannock recipe. How the Senator became a Bannarchist is a story for later. The Senator and the other Bannarchists had decided the best thing would be to say that ᐱᑕᑭ was the Senator's nephew. They told everyone that he had been away for awhile and had just come back home. Some people understood "being away from home for awhile" in a different way. Some understood that he had been away to one of those residential schools. Others had said that he had been a bush pilot like his uncle the Senator. Others understood this curious, quizzical statement to mean that he had been away to the city. That he had got mixed up with the wrong crowd, and that he had been lost. Now he was working at the Senator's Third Hand Pawn Shop. This way he had something of a cover to conceal his true identity.

He looked out the window, he looked out for the truth, and he wondered about all of the places beyond his sight, and he grew more restless.

"You know, Senator, I hear them talking sometimes when they don't think I am listening." He paused.

The Senator looked at him, like older relatives often look at us when they are disgusted with our city ways, or our lack of bannock making skills, "tâpwê, you are special. You are my boy. You help me out a lot."

ᐱᔪᐲᓂᕈ replied, "Senator, thanks for saying all of that." He paused. "I really appreciate that but I have to ask. When I was cleaning up earlier, I couldn't find the cleaning agents."

The Senator laughed, that old man kind of chuckle, and said, "Cha boy! When do you think that Indian agents could clean? You are on your own boy."

"No, Senator," ᐱᔪᐲᓂᕈ laughed, "I mean the stuff you clean with – you know like cleaning soap."

"Soap? you mean to clean your colon – too much chicken, cî?"

ᐱᔪᐲᓂᕈ no longer felt completely mixed up—he figured he was ½ as alert as the Senator so things could not be that bad. "No so–ap. Rhymes with dope."

"You mean you want to smoke that hippie grass?" the Senator asked very disappointedly. He looked down and didn't say anything. ᐱᔪᐲᓂᕈ realized that the Senator was like a Minotaur lost in the maze of the English language, and that there was really no reasoning with him. He just accepted at this moment he would have to figure out for himself where the stuff was. The Senator was a proud man and didn't want to admit that he was lost in the English language, so he changed the topic. He remembered how Câmes Dean would tug on his smoke and look serious.

"You know my boy," the Senator said, "that you started out as a cigar store Indian. You know that something special happened that night that you came into being. All of the Indian elements came together, and you are the living embodiment of those elements – all coming together, like a recipe forming in a mixing bowl – that is you. You are kind of like a magic, walking bannock recipe, nipôyêm?. It was Nadine's mom's bannock that really got everything in motion. It was the spark that started the brush fire."

After the Senator said this, ᐱᔪᑭᓯᐢ thought that it was an odd way to say it. It was like saying that he was a brush fire – something out of control. He felt everything was going well. The Senator just smiled at him in that uncle kind of way, without realizing what he had said. ᐱᔪᑭᓯᐢ didn't want to hurt the Senator's feelings, so he just muttered something back. The Senator was after all, the man who had taken him in as kin and made him feel at home. ᐱᔪᑭᓯᐢ vowed at that moment that no matter what happened in his attempt to see the world, he would always be loyal to the Senator, he would always take care of him. Feelings overwhelmed him, and he rushed over to the Senator, and gave him the biggest bear hug a neechie ever got.

"Holeh Smokerinoes," the Senator laughed, his somewhat overweight body trying to absorb the movement of ᐱᔪᑭᓯᐢ toward him. He felt a little awkward, so he started to laugh, but it was an uneasy kind of laugh. ᐱᔪᑭᓯᐢ was simply overcome with emotion and he just started to cry. The Senator felt a little awkward, and started to pat him on his back, kind of like how you would pat a baby on the back, but not really, but kind of.

GOOD DREAMS

ᐱᓄᑭᓂᐦ had the best sleep of his life. In all of the time, that ê–kî–pimôhtêt askihk[103] He had never slept so well. Not even the time when he and the Senator went out and bought the extended family meal from Cash's Fried Chicken. He and the Senator did not have a huge family, and the extended family meal was for when you expected van load upon van load of relatives jumping off and coming into the house and everyone jumping, and getting crazy for the chicken. It was a hell of a lot chicken for two people. Afterward, both ᐱᓄᑭᓂᐦ and the Senator drifted outside of their bodies and they saw the world. And ᐱᓄᑭᓂᐦ dreamt of a lot of things. He wanted to see all of the parts of the world that he had not seen yet, and with that he set off to see the world. He packed the biggest lunch box of bologna sammiches and he marched right out the door.

---

103   He walked the earth

THE HEART OF WHITENESS

The Wahwâ–man saw everything and he saw nothing. He could hear the sound of one hand making bannock, and he could feel the surge of the bannock force throughout the whole universe. He kept floating through various mystical realms. His body did not fully form in any particular time or place. His eyes and mind were heavy but his soul and being were very light, wrapped up in radiance – an orange radiance. The Wahwâ–man felt like he was flying, like he was flying to the bottom of all, all that was, and all that ever would be. He felt the winds of time and space blow against him, and against his well–styled hair which was soaked with an intoxicating cocktail of masko-pimiy[104] and brill cream.

But then after a great old time, he became restless. He knew that he wanted to come back to the world of things, ê–nôhtê–pimohtêyân askîhk kîhtwâm. [105] He felt his body moving away from stone form and a lightness return.

The Wahwâ–man saw things that he could not fully understand right away. It took time for him to centre himself, to find his place in the world again. But, he began to feel comfortable in his human form again and he slowly returned to his old thoughts and dreams.

As he drifted back into his body, he drifted into the matrix of time and space, journeying to the heart of whiteness. He knew that the Bannarchists would be weaker in the future. It seems that there had been rips in the fabric of the bannock force. At first, they were small little rips. They were small tiny frays in the cloth of the cosmic bannock force. He looked down upon the earth and saw the people called the "Wonder Bread" Eaters.

He thought long and hard about the strange bannock called "Wonder Bread." He could not see the

---

104   bear grease
105   I want to walk on the earth again.

wonder in it. For this reason, the Wahwâ–man thought that this bread could be called "konita–pahkwêsikan" – the bread of no purpose.

However, the Wahwâ–man did have one purpose for being on the earth. He wanted to bestow upon the Senator the title of "bannarchist." The Bannarchists had been a quiet force in history. They had been a secret society, passing their secrets, and their secret responsibility, through the ages since the time of the Egyptian pharaohs. They were guardians of truth and had intervened many times in history to protect the secrets of the original bannock recipe, and to shepherd the bannock force. Many times they had put their lives on the line. Many times they had risked everything to try to keep balance in the bannock force. As the ultimate manifestation of the bannock force, the Wahwâ–man was to make contact with the Senator. He had to make sure that the Senator would shepherd the bannock. With the rise of the Wonder Bread eaters, the bannock force was under threat.

Over the years, as the ultimate manifestation of the bannock force, the Wahwâ–man had done many crazy things. Because of these deeds, at times he became tired. He had decided that if the bannock force was to survive in the modern times, he had guide and teach the Senator. But, just as important, the Wahwâ–man had to enter the heart of whiteness, to get to the essence of what the Wonder Bread Eaters were really about, in order to fully understand the threat.

He had learned that his dreams were a portal to get to the heart of whiteness. They were an entry point. He dreamed about the bread. Sometimes in his dreams he could almost taste it on his tongue. He dreamed of a house, and white picket fences. He dreamed that in order to settle down, he had to be like a settler. He would have a great job. Life would be ordered, regular, and convenient. He would have a new suit, complete with a great pair of fancy slacks.

The Wahwâ-man said out loud to himself as he was walking, "I have pulled some fast ones in my time. Now, that I am about to enter the land of Wonder Bread Eaters, I can't help but think about the stretch of my whole life. I can't help but think about what my life means. While I was out burning my cisk and whipping the heck out of trees, big changes were happening in our land. I mean here I was being crazy, living life big like a fully patched member of Creedence Clearwater Revival.

"But the Wonder Bread Eaters," he paused, "seem so hard working, taking everything slowly, step by step. But what have I been doing? Throwing my eyeballs in the air, and tricking my little brothers and sisters to dance. Meanwhile, the English are building forts and marching in orderly lines. I should have protected the animals and the land. Maybe by going into the heart of whiteness, into the centre of the Wonder Bread dough itself, I could maybe bring balance back to the force of the bannock. And maybe, just maybe, make it up to my little brothers and sisters for all of the stunts that I have performed over the years."

He shook his head again thinking of these things. He had demonstrated that he could live without Indian Affairs glasses by taking his eyes out of their sockets and throwing them into the air. But he was trying to put all of this aside now. He had a scar on his cisk, and he had to squint once in awhile because of the eye ball episode, but he sure had some good stories.

Now, he wanted to put it all behind him: get a bungalow, get a mortgage, have a white picket fence, pay taxes and get ahead. He was going to play it straight, walk a straight line, no matter what obstacles he would face. He knew that the key to everything was a mortgage. Instead of wandering around all of the time, he would settle down, and be in one place most of the time. He would get a job at Indian Affairs and everything would be swell.

THE WAHWÂ–MAN AND
INDIAN AFFAIRS

Time had passed and the Wahwâ–man had now been amongst the Wonder Bread Eaters for some time. He looked back at those early days when he had first landed his job at Indian Affairs. He remembered when meeting the district manager. The district manager of Indian Affairs was overweight, with his excess fat hanging over his belt. The overlap of the fat looked like the domed part of a cupcake. He had a balding head which he tried to compensate for with a comb–over. Still, his bald head opened up large areas of pink on his head. Light from his office window caught the surface of these spots and made his bald head shine. The manager's handshake was firm and a bit rough and he looked straight into the other person's eyes when he did it. He had glasses which were big enough to have their own postal code. However, the arms of the glasses were crunched into his chubby head. His own arms were like chubby sausages and were very hairy. Behind the manager were pictures of various things: the manager with his Shriner friends, a picture of him holding up a big fish, a picture of him bowling with his swell bowling slacks. He also had one of those phones that had little red cubes that would flicker when a call was coming in. His name was embossed on one of those name plates with a fancy gold trim that sat on his desk. He also had one of those fancy watches that people get after years of service to their companies.

"So this is the land of the Wonder Bread Eaters!" the Wahwâ–man thought. He felt excited, and he could feel his heart beat like a pow wow drum.

After they exchanged a few words and a handshake, the Indian Affairs manager said, "Sit down, young man, I am so glad that you are part of the team."

"Glad to hear that sir," the Wahwâ–man said, trying to use his words like a Wonder Bread Eater. Ê–

kakwê–môniyâwêpinikêt.[106]

"Listen," the manager said, taking a puff of his cigar. He crunched up his chubby nose and pushed the glasses back on his chubby face. He then put his cigar down and looked down at the file folder. "It says here that you are fresh off the reservation."

He paused, "Is that true?"

"Yes, that is, sir."

The manager looked at him very seriously and took a long drag of his cigar. "Well, this is a different kind of rodeo here boy, as you know." He paused again and butted out his cigar a bit more. He continued, "No more living pay cheque to pay cheque. Now you have a pension plan and real shot at a future."

He paused, and then looked at the Wahwâ–man. As sober as a midnight bingo caller, he looked the Wahwâ–man straight in the eye and said, "Boy, do you like pow wow?"

"Well sir, I like the visiting. I like the colourful garb and food."

"Look boy, I am going to give it to you straight. You work for the Department of Indian Affairs now. We don't need one of those hippy Indians who wants to save the world and his people, who wears chokers to work, and who has a name that no one can say."

The manager continued, "Just stay away from those pow wows, those Indian shin digs, and everything will be fine."

The Wahwâ–man nodded, and looked at him big-eyed.

The manager then looked serious and leaned in towards the Wahwâ–man and said, "I've got something to tell you," his voice was somewhat quieter, but his eyes became more focused. "I want to tell you something," he said, like he was telling the Wahwâ–man a secret or something. Then he pulled his body back to where he had been sitting, and he raised his voice.

The manager seemed to get a bit more excited and

---

106   "He pitches things with a white accent."

said, "This is the 70s and disco is where it is at, baby! Can you look at me straight in the eye, boy, and tell me you can do the goddamn hustle?"

The Wahwâ–man looked at him quizzically and said, "What is this hustle? Is it a dance amongst your people? And what does it mean?"

The district manager let out a raucous loud laugh which he controlled as he brought the laugh back to words.

"Son, it is more than a dance. It is a lifestyle choice. It is a dance for hard working folks like me and you who need to blow off some steam."

"Tell me more."

"I will in time, but we need to get you more adapted to the white world. As soon as we do, I will take you down to Central Avenue and get you a leisure suit."

The manager added one more thing, "You have a weird name. Can I just call you Wally?" He said it in a quick and to–the–point way. And the way he said it, it was like the Wahwâ man could taste and smell every cigar that the manager had smoked over the years, and all of that smoke seemed to linger in his throat.

"Okay," the Wahwâ–man said without really thinking.

"Okay, Wally. One more thing. Cut your hair. Then get that survey of the needs of rez dogs done and we will all be happy." He smiled and added, "Remember kid, I like you. Don't give me a reason not to."

Another time, after spending the afternoon with the manager looking for a suit, Wally practiced walking in his new leisure suit. He practiced his disco strut. He was trying to show the sheen of his leisure suit pants in the open light of the day. It was times like this that Wally was really starting to feel the wonder of the land of the Wonder Bread Eaters.

Wally was trying so hard to fit in, he would often stand around the water cooler at work and talk to people about various events and things that were going on in the area.

Then one day he found a folder labeled "TOP SECRET" by the water cooler. Someone must have accidentally left it behind. It was a detailed plan of how Indian Affairs was going to issue large glasses with their coverage. They thought that they would make neechies less attractive by issuing ridiculously large glasses. Some of the finest minds in the Department of Indian Affairs had gotten together, and had determined that if the glasses that Indians wore were clunky and funny looking, then the neechies would be less attractive. With that, with the evaporation of their attractiveness, it was felt that they would be less sexy, which in turn meant that there would be less teepee creeping. To put it into Indian Affairs parlance, there would be "a slowing of the Indian population." This, coupled with more Indians moving to the land of the Wonder Bread Eaters, and with some working for the Department of Indian Affairs, would bring about a quick assimilation.

The Wahwâ–man was really getting into the rhythm of living in the land of the Wonder Bread eaters. The Wahwâ–man would have Wonder Bread for his toast in the morning. The Wahwâ–man would have Wonder Bread for his processed meat sandwiches for lunch, and sometimes when he would make a beautiful bird in the oven, and invite the gang from the Department over for drinks, he would make the dressing for the bird out of Wonder Bread. To make Wonder Bread even more amazing, he would top it off with mayonnaise.

Forget about pow wow, forget about round dances, and make way for the square dance and a little do–si–do. Saving money, instead of helping a needy friend, was his life now.

One of the beauties of living in the land of the Wonder Bread Eaters was that he no longer spent all of his time on storytelling and wandering. Wally had enough money to buy TV dinners. He was saving so much that he was making regular pension contributions. He thought in horror that in the time of all his wanderings, he never did have a pension plan.

His first task while working at Indian Affairs was to do a survey and study of the needs of reserve dogs in the district. When he kept working on it, he thought about the Senator's three legged dog called "Not–Even." He tried to think of how this dog could have a normal life.

Sometimes he began to miss his old life but he could not just leave his post at Indian Affairs. The money was pretty good, at least better than any the money he made wandering the earth. He had made many financial commitments and he could not walk away from these commitments. He could not walk away from his payments. He knew that above all things, he could not walk away from his mortgage. That would be a violation of one of the most important rules of the Wonder Bread eaters. Indians would move from their camps from river to valley, valley to river, bush to bush, and brush to brush. Not the Wonder Bread Eaters. They liked security. They were like farmers and liked to plant their roots deep in one place. It was in their mortgage payments and, of course, in their fine lawns, that the Wonder Bread Eaters found their centre. Now as he tried to make sense of the life that he had chosen, he tried to find the place where he would build the lodge of his soul – namely his bungalow.

The Wahwâ–man missed being called the Wahwâ–man, but was slowly getting used to being called Wally. He reasoned that a change in name was the price that he would have to pay for economic security. Sure some of those other neechies had more freedom, sure some of those other neechies had better hair and longer hair, but the Wahwâ–man had security. He had a permanent teepee crazy glued into the earth – his bungalow. Wally had come to the fatal realization sometime in the 1890s that the buffalo were not going to come back. Ever since then, he had been looking for something to anchor him down, something else to help guide him, something else to help him find his way. And now, he seemed to have found that through his bungalow and also his Wonder Bread.

WHEN CASH STARTED CHIEF'S FRIED CHICKEN

By 1970, the mood on the reserve was really changing. You could see it in how people walked, you could see it in how people smiled at each other, and greeted each other, the way young people would meet each other in the streets, and their eyes would twinkle at each other as if they knew something, as if the twinkle indicated that they believed that there was, indeed, hope. Even the rez dogs were wagging their tails a bit more often. The intense wagging seemed to indicate some measure of hope, and by–the–sweet–beard–of–Nanabush, if even rez dogs could hope then any being, be they two–legged, four–legged, or seventeen–legged, could hope. The sôniyâw had been like a wîhtikow – sucking out the hope.

No one could really say when things went completely wrong. Perhaps it was the Blackfoot motivational speaker who had come around. He had inspired and moved people. He had shaken them from their slumber and had shown them that they didn't have to dance Powwow for the white man anymore. He taught them that they could dance for themselves, feel the hoka for themselves, and dance like no colonizer was watching them. Dance in such a way that they could let their hair down, loosen the hair from their tight braids, and really let it rip.

The dark times is what all of the old people remembered. They remembered when everything had changed so greatly for all of those people of the long ago time. They spoke of how the Indian Act had really done a number on them trying to be Indians. They spoke of the grim days of the schools and everything that went along with it. They spoke of how their children were not able to speak Cree, but others kept speaking. It was tricky to see what the difference was in terms of who spoke it and who didn't. The Senator was sure that some egghead would probably write something on this. Some egghead would try to figure it out. For the old time Indian it was considered a great compliment because of the important role that chickens played in Indian culture.

Neechie hustle was the the flow of the times. Neechies were strutting around again like they were back in the 1860s. Neechies were wearing their hair in long braids and they were expected to be in the best of everything. Indians were going to pow wows, bannock was cool again, and children were refusing the wonder bread sandwiches at the lunch program that Indian Affairs sponsored at the school. It was around this time that the Wahwâ–man was working hard, trying to work his way up at Indian Affairs.

Times were changing and they were changing fast. It was like the years when the buffalo, kôkâwîwak, were entering the earth, but this time only the reverse. This time it was like the buffalo were coming back. This time everything was on its head, and this time everything seemed to be going in the favour of Indians. This was a good time to be an Indian, and it was also a good time to be an Indian who was in business. At one time the nêhiyaw were lords of the prairies. At one time Cree was the dominant language of business. Nêhiyawak were fast talkers and had certainly learned to maximize their potential and economic positions so that they could maximize their profits. But this was done not for their own gains – not to make themselves more wealthy but rather so that they could provide more food for their families and other people.

After the White Paper was widely rejected by Indian people, the government scrambled to try to figure out what they should do next. There was no way that they would legislate their way out of this one, so the only way was to try to win the Indians over. It was the same sort of thing that happens when a mihkwâyâw[107] makes a horrible racist

107   redneck

joke without their knowing that you are in fact an Indian. Then to try and cover their tracks they will say, "Well, you know that some of my best friends are Indians."

It was a way of almost trying to justify their position. The White Paper was kind of like that. It was like a bad racist joke, and when the people didn't laugh – when the Indians didn't go for it, the government scrambled to try and make it look like it was doing the right thing for Indians. The government faked a smile, and then slapped the backs of Indians. The country then slipped them envelopes of bills with which they could start their businesses and organizations. That is when the idea of "economic development" really got underway. It was also the beginning of the neechie mafia. It was at this time a new cadre of neechies began to arise. They were intent on cashing in on years of oppression. They were intent on cashing in all of that oppression so that perhaps even in a small way they could live better lives. This new class of neechies was different from the older leaders, but they were also different from the grassroots movement, which gave them their power.

Now, when thought of in a certain way, it did make some sense, at least that is what the Wahwâ–man thought. To be honest, he was tired of wandering the earth and he wanted to settle down. He had to– he really had no choice. He had worn out so many moccasins walking that he didn't know where he would ever get another pair. There were so few people who made the moccasins in the old–fashioned way. Those were the type of moccasins that would take you across the tundra, the type that could take you through the spaces of many deep and dark forests. But here he was working at Indian Affairs, and he really wanted to make a good impression on his boss – who was of Eastern European ancestry. He had met the father of his boss once, and that old Eastern European would talk in a thick European accent. It was difficult to tell what was being said.

But, at any rate, the Wahwâ–man knew that he

had to try to leave a good impression on his boss – that was the very least he could do. In fact, he wasn't just trying to present a good impression, he was trying to work really hard so that he would get a promotion, and move his way up the Indian Affairs ladder. He changed his name to an English name. He also made sure that he bought a bungalow and by–the–sweet–beard–of–Nanabush he said the word "swell" a lot. Once the White Paper was defeated on the 8–track plane of reality and, in turn, on the plane of reality as well, that was when the Wahwâ–man was in charge of implementing a new economic project. He was in charge of implementing the new economic program which everyone in the department of Indian Affairs said would help everything blow over, at least that was their hope. It was funny, the Wahwâ man thought, how money was thought to make things better but in the end seemed to only make things worse. The Senator had thought that the influx of new dollars from Indian Affairs would be the new fur traders – but he was not sure how it would work. That is the reason why he didn't take the money for economic development.

The Wahwâ–man was decked out in all of his finest môniyâw finery. He had his jumpsuit and by–the–sweet–flute–of–Nanabush, he sure looked swell in it. In fact, he looked so swell that he made everything in the room look swell. In fact, there was such a vibe of swellness that Cash could not but feel that he was part of the vibe.

The Wahwâ–man greeted Cash as he strode into the office.

"Hello," the Wahwâ–man said as he extended his arm with great enthusiasm.

"Tânisi," Cash said, as he slightly lowered his cowboy hat, and tugged on it as though he was creating a bit of a salute.

"Hello," the Wahwâ–man said again, as though he was trying to skate over the linguistic bravado of Cash speaking Cree. Cash got the hint of this linguistic play, and perhaps under other circumstances he would have said something, but given the circumstances, given the fact that he needed the money for his business idea he decided to hold his horses and just wait for the next opening. Cash thought that he would try to make a joke to keep that swell vibe going.

"Like your suit," Cash smiled and tugged on his hat again.

The Wahwâ-man, through all of his journeys in life, wanted to find his way, in that good way, in that special way. One could not underestimate the effect of flattery upon this process. Throughout time and space, the animal had always known that flattery was a key way to reach into the small places in his heart.

"Why thank you," the Wahwâ-man was warming up to this chief. He pulled out his jar of jelly beans and offered him some. For some reason he thought that a fella should have jelly beans on hand, in his office.

"Please," the Wahwâ-man said.

"Don't mind if I do," Cash said, surprising himself with his newly acquired môniyâwêwin,[108] his newly acquired môniyâw accent. He felt guilt about it, but not for too long. Cash had paid his dues, and it was about time that he was able to cash in a bit. He had worked hard and wanted his portion. Cash figured it was going to be guys like him who would be able to cash in, leaving behind older fellas like the Senator and some of those radical hippie types. The old fellas were so far out that they would never play the game, and the hippies were so far out that they didn't really understand what the game was. If you didn't understand the rules of the game how could you play it?

Their conversation continued, the Wahwâ-man loosened his tie and continued to speak, "Look boss," some could tell immediately that Cash really liked being called that, "as we all know, times are changing. And there are going to be those who get their share and there are going

---

108   white language

to be those who are left behind." There was almost a knowing wink between them but their eyes did not quite make the gesture, even though they almost seemed able to psychologically communicate to each other the situation that was going on.

"Mr. Wally, if," he paused briefly, "if I can call you that, I like your style, and I like the way you think."

The Wahwâ-man could tell that the meeting was going very well, and he was sure that he would get a promotion out of this, and maybe even work his way up to district manager. "Here is the deal boss...." As he said this Cash leaned in. "I've got some donors, some gold, some sôniyaw."[109]

"Keep talking there, pilgrim." For a second there Cash thought that he was John Wayne, and he had to shake his head to snap out of it. "I really want to hear what you got going on in that noggin of yours."

The Wahwâ-man leaned into the centre of the space of their conversation. "As you know, a lot of the young fellas are making a lot of noise, getting their clothes all in a knot, and I am not really sure what can be done about it all."

"I've been thinking the same thing about the young people. I just don't see where they are going with it all, I just don't get it."

"Go on..."

"Well, they are all talking about treaties, and how those treaties are important. I agree with that much, but I think your old boy Trudeau is on to something when he says that they have to be modernized."

"I couldn't agree more with you."

"I mean, the buffalo are long gone, and it does matter how loud I play CCR on my 8-track, they simply are not going to come back. We need a new buffalo." It was then that Cash's eyes got a little narrower, and the Wahwâ man drew in the seriousness of it. "I know the buffalo

---

109   môniyâw

aren't going to save us – so we need something new."

"What do you have in mind?"

"With a little bit of help, I think that I could get things off the ground. I think that with just a little start-up capital I could get a business going."

"Well, I just happen to have some money."

"I was thinking maybe 500,000."

"500,000 is too much my friend. Sorry. As much as it hurts me, I just can't put that much bannock in the oven. I could set you up with 100,000. I know that is not much, but I hope that it could be some needed money – get you started like.

Cash kêtahtawê ê–kî–mahkicâpipayit.[110] His eyes became very large indeed. He found the words of this Indian agent quite astonishing. How the hell did he get that lucky? Despite his disbelief that that Indian Affairs was offering sôniyâw instead of offering him a study of what was wrong, he tried to be calm. He didn't want to seem too enthusiastic. "100,000 would be just fine, I think. What I really want is to start to sell chicken. That is what I really want to do. Now here is what I have observed over the last while. There are a lot of neechies around here on this reserve that must have, you know that Colonel Sanders angle."

"Yes, I know of the chickens."

"My theory is that I think I should host a modern day shut eye dance. Wally, can I call you Wally?"

"Sure boss. We gotta call each other friend names since we are going to be working together a lot. That is how I would like it."

"Miywâsin, I think that maybe we should talk about some of the details of the deal."

"I agree," Wally paused and looked at him with a look more serious than a midnight bingo caller. "So, what do you got? What is your pitch?"

"Okay, I brought a few sketches to give you the

---

110   Cash suddenly had big eyes.

vision I had." He paused and handed him the stuff. "I got them, but in laminate, real fancy–like," Cash said.

"Impressive!" he raised his eyebrow and smiled. "I like a state–of–the–art presentation."

He paused and looked at the goods. The Wally man smiled and nodded, congratulating Cash. They were progressive Indians and they both knew it. They wanted progress, they were both tired of wandering around, and tired of wandering stories. Economic development was the way to go, and was the way that everything was panning out. There were even fancy brochures in the Indian Affairs office to this effect – trying to help people get out of the economic hole that they found themselves in. The way of hunting and trapping and the buffalo was so 1880s. If Indians wanted to just survive they could keep doing what they had done. But, if they wanted to do more than survive they would try to find a new way of making money. That is what they were talking about right now in this office. That is what was giving them hope.

It wasn't like the Wahwâ–man and Cash were against the old stories. It wasn't like they were against speaking Cree, quite the contrary actually. Cash was one of the finest speakers around. But the thing was this – they knew that if they wanted to survive into the next time that they would have to start doing things that they hadn't done before. No one wanted to be dependent on the government for anything. They wanted to be Cree, they didn't want the government to give them anything. They didn't want "rations." Cash remembered how his ohkoma – his grandmother wouldn't take rations from the Indian agent. She would rather go hunt in the bush to try to get food to provide for her family. It had always been that way with ohkoma. A lot of those old women were very powerful, very strong, and fiercely independent. Even though Cash was all about progress, he respected the hell out of all of the old ladies who held the culture together. Without them, none of the Cree would exist, and the whole talk that he was having with Wally from Indian Affairs wouldn't even make any sense, because the space for it to occur would just not happen; it just wouldn't be possible.

Cash and the Wahwâ-man went through all of the laminated purple stuff, and photos. Cash explained that they weren't really purple, it was just that was the only colour that the Gestetner graph could make. He also, with some measure of embarrassment, said that is why he had purple hands. They laughed, "serves me right for trying to be a môniyâw and use this fancy technology."

What Cash was proposing was truly epic, and would change the whole nature of the way everything was. He wanted to start a chain of chicken restaurants and he wanted to serve fried chicken. Since the mid-1960s fried chicken had been a huge hit on many reserves and he wanted it to be a hit on his reserve of Broken Elbow. He was going to put forward something innovative – he was going to have an "extended family meal." He had worked out how all of the math would work and he had prepared some very shiny ads to this effect. He was going to start off with the reserves in the district, and then expand from there. He would get some of the sôniyâw that Indian Affairs had left over from previous projects – housing projects.

Cash knew that if the opening was to make a splash, he would need some rock and roll, some shake and bake. He would need some jelly on the bannock. Where it would all go from there, he was not completely sure. All he knew was that he wanted to make some money, he wanted to get some of the young people on the reserve working, and he wanted to offer the people of the reserve some modern food. Many people of Cash's generation had lived through a lot of hard times and they did not romanticize things. Rather, people like him tended to take a hard, grim look at reality and always thought of what they had to do in order to survive.

"We will call it 'Chief's Fried Chicken.'"

"That is a damn fine idea," the Wahwâ man said after Cash's rather long presentation. "When do you think you can have this ready to go?"

"Well, it is going to take a while. I am going to hire this old Swede to share his recipe for fried chicken. He made the best fried chicken that I have ever had. If we get him on board, we will have a hit."

"But how do we get him on our side, boss? What do we have to do to get him on board?"

"Well, we get him some furniture from this weird Swedish store called Ikea, and a real fancy dog sled. That crazy guy."

"You know a lot of those fellas, those Swede Ikea–fellas, they like to trap and hunt like us Indians."

"Ain't that the damn truth," Cash said.

"Maybe that is the problem with so many of the young people today. They don't know how to hunt and shit like our ancestors." He paused. "How would you play this argument, boss? What would you say to the possibility that maybe, just maybe what we are doing is making it worse for young Indians of the reservation? I know that I am going to have some district manager busting my balls on that one."

"Keep on telling me what you are thinking," Cash adjusted his hat again. He did that whenever he was deep in thought.

"Well, if you are going to take young people off the land, away from hunting, how am I going to sell this to the tree–hugging hippies in the department?"

"Tâpwê it will be difficult if you frame it like that, but I think that there is another way to frame it," Cash paused. "That is what my nôhkom always taught me. She taught me that if you are trying to get someone to believe you, if you are trying to get someone on your side, you have to tell them a great story, and I know just the man who can tell us this story," he paused again. "Have you ever been to the Broken Elbow reserve?"

"I went there once as a child – I think I went to the sports dance on the reserve long ago."

"It has changed a lot since then, but I wouldn't want to get that suit of yours dirty." Cash slapped him on the back and laughed, and the Wahwâ-man replied with nervous laughter. "You probably got that fancy suit of yours at Simpson Sears, didn't you?"

"Why yes, I did."

"Listen, I have been Chief for a long time and I never did get a Treaty suit," he paused, "Now instead of getting one of those suits that would have been the rage in the 1800s and made all of the young maidens giggle at the fur trading, I want something more contemporary. Can you take me to Simpson Sears to get a fancy suit like yours?"

"Sure, but we'll have to keep the paper loose on this."

"I got you."

"And I got you, son."

Cash continued and thought that the Senator could tell the story of the great prairie chicken shirt to the people at the department. Cash knew that he would have to do something extraordinary to accomplish this, so he decided to head out to see the Senator the very next day.

He got into his truck and drove. Sure, there was a meeting in town that he was supposed to be going to, but he assumed he would be able to skip it. Getting the story to the Indian Affairs grant was of course the way to go. He got some of the motivational speaking 8-tracks of the Blackfoot guy who had been to the reserve a few weeks back. As he was getting ready to go, he told the Wahwâ-man that he would be back soon and that he would bring him everything that he thought that they would need in order to solidify the grant from Indian Affairs. It seemed the more he thought about it, the more paperwork and glossy Gestetner graph laminated drafts would appeal to the bureaucrats of Indian Affairs. But, if he was to win over the heart and soul of Indian Affairs, then it was time that he signed the paper. It was the ideal paper of môniyâwak which sought to destroy the Treaties.

There was another side of Trudeau which was warmer and which won him over to a lot of people. That was the whole part that the hippies liked. And, the topping that made Trudeau so hard to resist, even by the hardcore neechies, with their massive Buffalo Bill headdresses which reached for the sky, was the idea that everyone would have a second chance, and an equal chance. That idea of Trudeau's had a lot of sway and saved the day.

The next day Cash got into his truck and headed out to the reserve. Cash had stayed at a hotel that night in town – he liked the breakfast that he had. He liked the piles of pancakes and the real syrup from Quebec.

The road out to the reserve was very very bumpy. Cash hoped that if Cash's Fried Chicken really hit it big, that he would be able to make the roads better for his people. Even though Cash had known the Senator all of his life, there was still a lingering hostility between them.

The thing that maybe made Cash the angriest about the Senator was that he felt the Senator was always wandering around in the stories. He would find little place marks in the landscape of the story. These little landscapes would help him find his way home again.

Cash thought it was time to get out of the stories and into the world. He wondered how the Senator would take the news of what he was going to say to him about how the balance had been shifted for good. He knew that once he made the way to start the chicken chain, that he could never go back. But he also knew that too much had changed, to go back to a sturdy, stable fact that could hold down an anchor of memory, that could help someone stretch into the future.

When he got to the Senator's, the fierce, three-legged dog called Not–Even hopped on his legs. While the dog was fundamentally of a friendly disposition, he would still turn to this sudden anger. How he lost his one leg, no one could ever really say, but because he only had the three legs, that dog had something extra to prove. He threw the dog some of the choice Hutterite sausage that was so prized in these parts. It seemed a waste to give this beast the sausage, but it would have seemed like a bigger waste of an opportunity not to give it to him. The path to prosperity was through the Senator's stories and the way to get to the Senator was to change the balance of things, and to also get past this dog called Not-Even. So even though this piece of Hutterite sausage was of the highest quality, the price paid was relatively small, considering what the pay-off would be in the end.

He knocked on the door, and the house ate the sound that his hand was making. Not-Even came up to him, and he really barked at him. Dogs were strange in that way. They could sense things right away. They could tell what people were thinking– they could sense where someone's soul was at. Not-Even had sensed that there was something not quite right about Cash and how he related to the Senator.

Not-Even approached him with hackles raised, and head down. Cash tried to laugh because he thought there was something comical about seeing a three-legged dog moving towards him in an aggressive way. But perhaps out of respect for the Senator, and for the dog himself, he promised to never steal from a neechie who can't hunt, that is just a takay thing to do. He was never scared, and the dog nodded at him, and inched closer to him and he thought that the dog almost fell over. This went on for a bit, back and forth: feigning being scared and inching forward. Fear, movement; fear and movement. Finally, the old kisêyiniwatim, this old man dog was getting tired, and finally laid down. He feigned anger for a bit, showed his teeth, even though a few were missing. At the sight of a three-legged dog with many missing teeth, Cash could hold his laughter no longer and he laughed so hard that his belly hurt. Not-Even could sense this laughter – and it hurt his heart. He lowered his head, lowered it so low that the ground seemed to cover over him. Cash actually felt bad because there was something pitiful about him, and it was this pitifulness that reminded Cash of the Senator.

Cash knocked again and waited; there was still no sign of the Senator. He could hear the buzz of the television and the muffled voices talking in English. Cash wondered at that moment if that is how English sounded to his grandparents who really didn't speak English – to them maybe English sounded like this, a distant far–off sound, that seemed so far away. , that seemed so distant. He wondered if he seemed so strange to his grandparents, and that had always left a hole in his heart.

He waited a while, and still nothing. No Senator. He kept thinking and thinking. Well, he thought, I may as well wait. He looked again at Not–Even, and when he did look at him the dog then looked away. The dog wouldn't even look at him. Cash felt sorry for the old kisêyiniwâtim and he moved towards him. The kisêyiniwâtim accepted the petting. He sighed a deep sigh as dogs sometimes do, and he squinted tight, lifting his head to meet Cash's hand.

"There, there atim,"[111] Cash said as he petted the dog's head.

Cash kept thinking about a lot of things – flashes of his past life. He started to think about the old stories, the old places and the old language.

Cash started to slip into the land of the dream. In this dream land everything was so lightly threaded, and held the being together. There he saw the Senator floating above everything – above the community farm, above the church steeple, above all of the fields of their childhood. There was a great lightness to his being, he seemed free, like he had a freedom in the flying, in the movement in the sky. Below Cash saw himself with a large heavy lady, sinking into the ground. Heavy and falling into the earth. There seemed no way that he could reach the sky. It was at that moment that he realized what he had to do to release the heaviness from his being. And he hoped that the words that he would say to the Senator, and the power and being behind the words, would allow the Senator to reach those places in the deep of space where they had been so long ago.

Cash felt the warmth of Not–Even lick his face. He

---

111   dog

was not accustomed to being close to a dog, but the dog had opened himself up to him, so he thought that he may as well reciprocate. Maybe if the Senator came back in his truck and saw Cash petting his dog, perhaps he would be more open to him – more open to Cash – and more open to Cash's ideas and his dream for the future.

Finally, he heard the engine of the Senator's truck approaching. He could hear the familiar pattern of the knocks and bangs of the engine, and he could see the movement of the old orange truck. The orange had the tinge of rust, smouldering in little chunks of orange–brown throughout the stretch of the metal. The Senator had a funny way of bouncing in the seat of the truck just like he was riding a tractor. He wondered why he would sit down like that. He wondered why he did it, but it must have been because of all of those years of farming. All of those years of farming had caused him to have that habit.

The Senator had a driveway that moved into a circle and would take someone around the yard and then back out again. Cash was sitting in that middle area of land, relaxing, petting the dog. The Senator took a bit, raised his eyebrows slightly, and proceeded to spin around the circle. After he took the one look at him, Cash could tell that he was truly straining himself to see what was going on, but not too much.

The Senator got out of his truck with the truck facing away from Cash. Once he had gotten his groceries and his mail he turned around to face the house and Cash, and said, "tânisi."

Cash replied, "tânisi."

"Mêtoni ê–miyo–kîsikâk."[112]

Cash followed his Cree with more, "tâpwê anima."

The Senator kept moving towards the door of the house, "come and have some tea with me."

Cash entered the Senator's house and sat down on the older chair in the dining room. The Senator didn't

---

112   "It is a beautiful day."

say much, but got the water going and fiddled around in the kitchen. Old Crees were okay with silence. That was because of the time before texting and internet, people would spend time with their words. They were not as rushed as they are today.

Cash said, "Senator, there is something that I want." Right then the kettle whistled and Cash had to take a bit of time to prepare the tea. He gathered the rest of the stuff: honey, sugar, a tin of evaporated milk, and spoons. For the Senator, having tea was not simply passing through a window in a drive–through, but involved detail and patience.

After everything was at last out, in the midst of the ticking clock, Cash continued. "Senator there is something that I want to tell you."

The Senator then brought the cups, and poured the tea. He looked up slowly and said to Cash, "kîkwây ê–nôhtê–isiyin?"[113]

Cash said, "Well, I just want to say there was a time when we were very close."

The Senator said, "Yes, that is true."

Cash said, "Well Senator, I want to tell you that I have decided to give up on Nadine. I don't want to get in your way with her anymore."

The Senator didn't say much at first and kept going with the little tea ritual that he had designed. After a few seconds the Senator simply said, "kah."

"Now is our time to make our impression upon the world," said Cash. "With Chief's Fried Chicken, we can make the world speak Cree."

The Senator paused, his spoon jingling, and said as sober as a midnight bingo caller, "I heard that you are planning to open a big chicken store, a big place where you are going to sell chicken. Cha! Are you going to be the next colonel?" They both laughed, and Cash said, "aya, môy

---

113   "What did you want to say to me?"

tâpiskôc colonel, aya niya piko."[114]

"Well, I think you will do pretty well at that," the Senator paused. There was a warmth in his voice, a way of remembering when they had been friends. They had been friends so long, but too long had passed since they couldn't be friends. The Senator continued, "You know, I have always admired you, and what you do. You were making money when a lot of other people had just given up. I think it was because our people had stood up in 1885."

"Aha tâpwê. My mosôm had always taught me to be strong and to hold some one."

The Senator paused. He went over to the wall and took down that old picture. He brought it over. "Here is your one grandfather, he was in the heat of the battle."

"Êkwa mîna kimosômipân,"[115] said Cash. "This is true."

The Senator poured tea for Cash, and then asked if there was anything he could do to help. Cash told him that he was going to pitch the economic plan to the fella at Indian Affairs, that the Indian Affairs man was game to support him, that he was going to give him a grant to help in the assistance of the establishment of Chief's Fried Chicken. The Senator nodded and said that was what the reserve needed. He knew that the young people needed hope, that they needed something to believe. The Senator even suggested that they put syllabics on the buckets. He figured they could get some cultural money for that. He knew that the French were getting money for their language. Surely, by–the–sweet–bingo–balls–of–Nanabush they could do the same thing for the Indians and their languages.

Cash continued, "Okay, here is the deal. We need a slogan."

Senator: "You mean like when they protest?"

---

114   "Not like the Colonel, I am just me."

115   "And your late mosôm"

Cash: "cha," he said it more gently, he let the cha slide more, like the sound that a crane a would make as it slowly glided into the stream.

Senator: "Slogan. You mean like like a fancy jingle for ads."

Cash: "Yes, that is what I am talking about."

Senator: "Well you want to make the bucket the centre, because if you tell them about the bucket, you will sell more chicken. You don't want to just sell individual pieces of chicken, you want to sell as much chicken as you can."

Cash: "Okay, so what do you get then, nîci-kâhkêwahk."

Senator: "Here is a good one, why not call it 'Pow Wow in a Bucket'?"

Cash: "I like that. Miywâsin ôma."

Senator: "Yeah it is a goodie." He paused. "Okay, here is the deal. I know why you are being nice to me. I know what you are aiming for here. All that stuff about Nadine and everything. I know what you really need is me to go to the department of Indian Affairs."

Cash: "I kind of figured you would know what I was coming here for."

Senator: "I know that you want me to go tell the shut–eye dance but make it sound like it is an old Indian story so that they will think chicken is part of our culture. That is what you want?"

Cash: "Yes, that is what I would like. Do you think that you can help me? You are the one Indian on this reserve besides myself that understands the business world, and the one Indian who has the old–fashioned neechie hustle that our mosôms had."

The Senator paused and smiled, and sipped his tea. They heard Not–Even bark at something outside. They knew that a rez rocket must be passing by and that was the reason that the old kiseyiniwâtim was barking. The Senator went and got the pot and put more water in it. While he was waiting for it to whistle, he kept looking at that picture of their grandfathers on the wall. He looked at it for a long time until the whistle of the kettle came again. He went and got the water and poured the water into cups with fresh tea bags. Then there was the familiar clack of his spoons against the side of the cup.

The Senator continued, "okay, I will help you, but I want a cut."

Cash nodded slowly to show his agreement, "hâw mâka."

Senator added, "Not too much, but enough."

"Okay, what else?"

"Well, as you know, I have plans to send my rabbit root to Germany as a love remedy. I need some sôniyaw to get it started." The Senator spoke in a clear way to make his points. It was as though he was almost over-articulating his words.

Cash replied, "Okay. Sounds good, but I need 12 months to give you the kind of money that you need. I know that those tourists will eat this shit up."

Senator, "Okay, sounds good."

Cash agreed, "hâw mâka." Cash had an annoying habit of shifting to Cree whenever he wanted to sound more cultural. It kind of annoyed the Senator, but this was the deal that could make everything right. He knew that with all of the German tourists that came to the pawn shop every summer, he could make a killing in Germany. He wanted to give a lecture tour like that Blackfoot doctor.

THE BUNGALOW

The District Manager of Indian Affairs had set up the Wahwâ-man with a realtor. At first the Wahwâ-man did not really understand. He was so used to someone in the band office controlling the housing situation. He remembered how he had tried extra hard to be nice to everyone in the hopes that it would help him get a good house. The idea that everyone would be in charge of their own funding seemed strange to the Wahwâ-man. He realized that if everyone could buy their own house in the land of the Wonder Bread Eaters then maybe they were all their own chiefs, all in their own little way.

He went to the realtor's office and he certainly felt grand walking into that office. He felt like a chief. The realtor had a moustache and had very wavy hair. He had big thick glasses. He chewed gum and had a quick beat in the way that he talked to the Wahwâ-man.

"Okay boss," he said snapping his gum, his lips like the head of a snapping turtle moving in and out, "Here's how I see it shaking down." Wally nodded with enthusiasm. "We are going to get you a fine bungalow"

"Sounds good," Wally said smiling.

Wally listened with great interest and focus to the realtor who was describing the house.

Eventually, he found his bungalow, and he really liked his house and he really liked the features of his house. The bungalow had all of the things that were essential in the land of the Wonder Bread Eaters. He had a white picket fence, a great lawn and a hedge.

The place really was perfect. There was even a spot on the deck for a huge barbecue. Wally had heard the Wonder Bread Eaters were very enthusiastic about barbecuing. In fact, he heard that barbecuing was the môniyâw equivalent of the buffalo hunt. In fact, the smoke from the barbecue, was seen as a kind of môniyâw smudge.

Wally was so excited that he could not sleep. He tossed and turned, and turned and tossed. He even tried to sleep in different positions and on the floor. He did fall asleep finally.

In the morning, he thought about how to sleep better next time. He knew that he had to cut down on the amount of rabbit root tea that he drank during the day. It was hard to give up this tea which had brought him so much merriment and joy over the years. But, he knew that if he were to fit into the land of the Wonder Bread Eaters, that he would have to put away this sweet elixir for a bit. The medicine was too powerful, and the house of his body, which had become made of Wonder Bread straw, could only hold so much funk. He realized that to survive and succeed in the land of the Wonder Bread Eaters he had to slow things down a bit. He had to slow down the funk, and square up his dance.

After Wally had settled in, he had a little chat with his new neighbour Bob. Bob was in good shape, muscular, former infantry, but he had a bit of a belly. He always wore fancy slacks and a fancy shirt. He offered his muscular arm and hand to shake Wally's.

"Put it here partner!" Wally was a bit taken aback, but he did shake the hand. "My name is Bob. Welcome to the neighbourhood."

"Why, thank you. Everything looks really good here in Wonder Bread Lane, and I think that life is going to be just grand."

"Life is grand here," said Bob. "Looks like we're going to have a little colour in the Wonder Bread."

He laughed nervously and Wally thought for a moment and then looked at him. Bob looked at him with a twinkle in his eye and asks him, "You are kind of dark? Are you Italian? Or French? Or something like that?"

The Wahwâ–man looked at Bob a bit dumfounded said, "No."

Bob looked at him again, in a direct but still a pleasant voice. "Well, are you some kind of Mexican? You know how to make burritos? Can you put them on the barbie? I can speak for everyone on this lane, and say we would love to eat them here. Maybe we can go to the supermarket and stroll down the ethnic aisle and you can show me some good eats."

"The kind of bread that I can make is bannock," Wally said.

"Bannock?"

Wally laughed, but was not completely sure why. He genuinely liked Bob, but he knew that with a guy like Bob you had to be straight forward and shoot from the hip.

"I am an Indian," Wally said. Bob was surprised at first because he said that he thought he was too fair to be an Indian, and that his cheekbones were not high enough. Wally assured him that he was indeed an Indian and even showed him his Treaty card. Bob did not really seem to mind that he was an Indian, but seemed more worried as to what Wally could really offer to the community cook outs.

Wally just kept doing what he was doing, and kept bringing home a steady pay cheque. He was fixed to one spot, and his mortgage was the anchor to keep him there. Wally kept working at Indian Affairs. He kept working on his reporting on the needs of rez dogs in the district. But, he didn't mind some travel. In fact, it was that travel that helped him break out of some of the monotony that he was feeling in the land of Wonder Bread eaters.

BECOMING A WONDER BREAD EATER

Slowly, Wally was settling into the suburbs and his life with the Wonder Bread Eaters. One fine Saturday, Wally was outside, enjoying his yard. He stood by the fence which separated his yard from the yard of Bob. Bob was outside tinkering with something.

"Wally, by gosh, I like you a lot. You are a goddamn swell neighbour."

"You are a pretty fine neighbour as well. You are pretty swell, and you always help me when I need help. Helping me figure out things in the land of the Wonder Bread Eaters."

"But Wally, I gotta ask you. Where is the lil Missus?"

"You mean do I have lady friend?"

"Or a wife?"

"No, not yet."

"So are you a bachelor?"

"Why yes, I am."

Bob slapped Wally on the back. Bob laughed, "We need to change that."

They paused here for a moment and talked about their plans for the day. Bob broke the flow and said, "You know that old man from Broken Elbow reserve."

"Which one?"

"The guy who runs the pawn shop."

"Oh," Wally said, "do you mean the Senator?"

"Yes," Bob said. "He is the one. He is the one that kind of reminds me of you."

Wally laughed a little. After a while, they continued their discussion of their plans for the day.

As Wally sat in his comfortable lazy boy chair, he began to survey his mind and began to think of all of the good that could be done after his study of the needs of the rez dogs was concluded. Maybe he could even recommend a fake leg for the Senator's dog Not-Even. There were so many things to be done.

143

THE LAWN

The Wahwâ–man continued to work hard on his report for the Department of Indian Affairs, surveying the needs of the reserve dogs who lived on the reserves in the district. Not only was the report going to be in English, but it was going to be in Cree syllabics so that the older people in the district could read it.

While he was working on the report, he heard stories of strange events that were happening on the nearby Broken Elbow reserve. He heard fantastical tales of the nêhiyawâhtik[116] who had been in the Senator's pawnshop and how this being had become a man. Old men and young bingo callers were asked to come to break bannock and to try to interpret the random grease marks of used KFC chicken buckets. They were asked to try to figure out what it could mean. How could a wooden Indian just suddenly become a person?

What could it all mean? Neechies gathered around campfires to try to discern the significance of what had happened. Could it signal the emergence of a new power which would give them all hope? Could the emergence of the man, who had been a wooden Indian, give them all hope?

At first, the Wahwâ–man had wanted to go to investigate and write a report for the local Indian Affairs office, but he was told by his boss not to worry about it. He was told that someone else had been put in charge of that investigation and not to worry about it. Since he had been amongst the Wonder Bread Eaters, the Wahwâ–man, or Wally, as he became known, also stopped believing in miracles. In the land of the Wonder Bread eaters, everything was predictable and settled. There was no mysterious place where miracles could rest and hide. Even the plants had this order, this constant array of patterns. They seemed to grow in a fixed pattern; everything was predicable.

116   Wooden–Indian

At first, when the Wahwâ–man moved into the neighbourhood, he thought that he was supposed to have some sort of ceremony for the grass plants which were all around his bungalow. He was ready to contact some grass dancers from the Broken Elbow reserve. He was going to ask four to five to make the ground sacred. However, Wahwâ–nâpêw was disappointed when he learned that the Wonder Bread eaters had no songs for the grass.

In the land of the Wonder Bread Eaters, things were of course much different than in the lands of the Bannock Eaters. The Wahwâ–man despaired that there were no miracles amongst the Wonder Bread Eaters, but then he realized that it was not a matter of miracles, but a matter of convenience. Wonder Bread itself epitomized this way of life. The new bread was a great culinary convenience, a little culinary miracle. When a Wonder Bread Eater wanted a sammich he could just get down to the business of making a sammich. One didn't have to make a big fire, and get little Jimmy to go out and get more wood so that little Jimmy could put it on the fire – to make the fire bigger. Once those flames started to lick the sky, then the sammich makers could start to lick their lips, but it would still be maybe two more hours before the bannock would be ready. Then there was the practical problem of having to share with relatives and wayward travellers. By the time everyone had their share, maybe there would be nothing left. Then, how the heck would one have the sammich that they had originally wanted? One would have to keep shelling out money, paying little Jimmy to get more wood, and would have to buy the flour again, and one would never get bannock for the sammich. There would be no money to put towards the pension after all of these transactions.

The more he thought about it the more he realized the desperate plight of the rez dogs and he realized what a precarious existence that they, in fact, lived. Wally wanted to make their lives easier and more convenient. In the heart of whiteness, the thing that helped move everything along was the regularity of things, such as regular lawn work. Lawn work was the key to order, order was the key to happiness. It was through lawn work that time integration could occur. It was through the lawn work that so many môniyâw prided themselves on, that true integration could occur. It was in fact something that could be accomplished where the Indian Act had previously failed. The glorious green order was the key to the order, to the maple leaf and the beaver on the nickels. Progress would come in small things like lawn work, and wonder bread. It was a bread that didn't need fire, or relatives, or little Jimmy for that matter. It also came pre-sliced and it was so convenient. It was made for modern living, and modern people.

The old Crees had songs that when you sang them really hard, they could bring things into being. One singer would start and another singer would later join in. They would echo each other in their singing. The same thing happened in the land of the Wonder Bread Eaters. On a warm spring or summer day, the lawn mowers would call out in succession to each other like old Cree singers would call out to each other in succession, answering each other with their metallic hum. There was a unity in their metallic hum. Mêtoni mâmawi-pîwâpiskowêpicikêhk.[117] The nâpêwak,[118] heads high in the air, a sense of pageantry, nay a sense of regality, as they carried themselves with dignity in that good way. One time, and the Wahwâ-man couldn't remember where he heard it from, but there was a story that the Indian at the end of the trail painting was actually a môniyâw who was living in a bungalow and was no longer able to cut his lawn anymore because of a bad hip. Because he was so forlorn, he just sat there on the tractor unable to move. His head down. The story went that an artist from around Sante Fe had seen this poignant scene and then he just re-interpreted it – instead of a môniyâw

---

117   Truly, there was a unison of sounding metal.
118   the men

on his metal horse it was a neechie on his horse.

The Wahwâ–man was settling in to his job at Indian Affairs, and he was getting a lot of guidance from his neighbour in terms of how to weave everything together. Bob was like his teacher. He was his white soothsayer, if you will.

Bob had encouraged him in his new life. Bob would say, "You've got a good solid life and there is a lot that others could learn from you. You are good people. Just think, not too long ago, your people were hunting buffalo; now you are hunting the dream of good living. Bob took Wally to a hardware store so that he could get a really good lawn tractor.

After looking around the hardware store, he finally found a shiny red lawn tractor that he really liked. Bob flagged down one of the people on the floor, and when they hesitated, Bob made a bitter scene and proclaimed, "This slow service better not be because this boy is an Indian!" He paused as he got madder, as though he was summoning all of his strength.

"This fella pays taxes like the rest of you!" When the store clerk tried to note that he was dealing with another customer, Bob kept at him until he finally relented.

Bob smiled to the Wahwâ–man after bullying the sales person and gave an approving nod to the Wahwâ–man to get on the lawn tractor. The Wahwâ–man saddled the mower and knew that this one would be his. He wondered if the môniyâw folks had a special dance or something to honour the lawn tractor in a collective spirit. But what Bob said next surprised the Wahwâ–man, or Wally – his sacred Wonder Bread name.

"Son," Bob said, as he ran his hand through his whitening hair, "I've seen a lot of things in my life and one thing I will say is that everyone is really for himself, in this dog eat dog world."

The Wahwâ–man paused and smiled then looked at Bob and asked him, "What do you mean?"

"Well, don't try to kid yourself that lawn work is about making the whole neighbourhood look good. Quite the contrary – it is about making each property look good, making each property owner feel good."

Wally just kind of stared at him for a bit until Bob said it in a more blunt and direct way, "Son, it is like a goddamn competition. This lawn mower could put you on top of that pile and make you the top dog."

Wally got off of his lawn tractor. While he did, he remembered the time kayâs ago, when he was known as mahikan–wayân[119] and he had the finest buffalo runner horse in the whole encampment. Now, he grabbed the reins of his lawn tractor, and moved through a stretch of his lawn. He was settling into the neighbourhood just like he was settling into his lawn mower seat.

Sometimes Wally really thought about the land of the Wonder Bread Eaters, and at times he had doubts about his new home, at least flickers. Sometimes the Wahwâ–man really thought deeply about where he lived—the land of the Wonder Bread Eaters.

For instance, he thought about a Wonder Bread slap. A Wonder Bread slap just didn't sound very deadly. It sounded weak. A Wonder Bread slap sounded like something that someone would do with a velvet glove – and a smile. A Wonder Bread slap would tickle more than it would hurt.

A bannock slap however was something different. A bannock slap was something that would sting, and it would be greasy. You would feel the grease of the slap soak into the core of your skin, and move into each cell. It would sink so deep that your ancestors would feel it.

At first, Wally felt glorious in the warmth of the early morning sun. The yellow of the sun stretched across the lawn, glistening in yellow pockets.

As the day fell upon the field, old deep thoughts began to awaken in the Wahwâ–man, as he looked upon

---

119   wolf hide

the yellow of the field. He realized that this was a yellow flowered enemy, an enemy that was as determined and focused as any Blackfoot warrior. In the cover of the night, the not so dandy, the dandy himself, with a plant body of a thousand parts had spread out, all over this lawn destroying the hard work and pride in ownership that he had invested his being into.

Before the day had fully dawned into being, and before his neighbour had fully woken up, he got his lawn mower, and charged into the yellow plague of dandelions. He cut down all of the dandelions, their yellow bodies falling on all sides of him. Their lifeless bodies strewn across the greenness of the lawn. One of his neighbours across the street yelled out, "Hey buddy. Can you shut down your little lawn pow wow?" Bob heard the commotion and marched over to the neighbour across the street and said, "There's going to be no goddamn redneckery on my street and on my watch." The neighbour backed down even though Bob was older. Bob had a crew cut, a few tattoos, and had been in the 101 Airborne. He didn't take shit from anyone.

The season of the dandelions was upon them. The seas of yellow shifted and stirred the greenness of the fields. During this time a man's worth seemed to be assured by how often he cut his lawn. Every time Wally did cut his lawn, Bob would smile at him and yell, "That's my boy." Other people in the neighbourhood marvelled at his industry and hard work. One even remarked at work while he was standing at the water cooler, "That lad is one hell of a lad. Shows you what those Natives can do once they put their minds to it." One group of kids even came on a school tour. It was recorded by a newspaper and showed the modern Native at work. There was much fanfare throughout all of this: except from that one neighbour across the street. He still had his doubts and would look disapprovingly whenever the Wahwâ–man would cut his grass. He would go to look at the lawn when the Wahwâ–

man was at work. But he could never find anything wrong with the way in which the Wahwâ–man did his lawn. In fact, when no one was looking, he took a notebook, and scribbled down some notes so that he could improve his lawn cutting technique. There was not a yellow mark to be found on the Wahwâ–man's lawn. It was a perfectly ordered pattern of green, cut in a perfect pattern.

But then the Wahwâ–man took things too far. He put on his after market kimowan–kîskisikan, rain cutter. It was a special blade that cut the dandelions even when it rained. He even made a dandelion song which he would sing before he would go out on his mower. Then he had another cutter which used a stealth motor, so he could go out and ambush the dandelions in the middle of the night.

Bob was one of those men who was always on the lookout. He was constantly vigilant. He saw Wally outside fooling around, thought that he was a burglar and phoned the police. First there were the sirens, the taking of the statement, and then the sit down. "Wally, you've gone too far this time." The Wahwâ–man's grass cutting ceremonies were who he was. They were the heart of whiteness, and he would not put them aside. He kept doing them more and more, and with greater intensity.

Despite pulling him aside a few more times, and despite having tried to talk to him, Bob finally had to distance himself from Wally. Others built higher fences and the Wahwâ–man felt alone. He felt truly alone.

Finally, it was just too much. It was too much for the Wahwâ–man to hold in. Finally, the Wahwâ–man just kinda snapped. He was not used to so much order, and then when he achieved order, the môniyâw ordered him to slow down his Wonder Bread regularity.

He was not used to such order, and so many orders. He had been a wanderer, and had, despite all of his follies, ê–tipêyimisot.[120] He had been a wanderer, but now he was making camp, settling down, in the heart of whiteness.

---

120   he governed himself

He was like a lawn Santa light decoration that was being pumped with too much electricity. Sooner or later the wires overheat.

The order. The order. It reminded him of the time that the British came marching in neat little rows of soldiers, and then gridded the map with iron fences and new names for places.

Finally, the wires of the Wahwâ–man did in fact overheat, and he went to the back of his yard. He gathered a bucket full of freshly cut yellow petals of the dandelions, and crushed them, and mixed bacon grease with them, and made a paint. He covered himself with the yellow and went to the fancy grass, the lawn, wearing only his gitch. He laid there all night and remembered all of the things and all of the songs that gave him strength. He went into the deep quiet, places of his soul. He started tapping his leg, getting a beat, which was like his drum. He heard Bob yelling at him, "Put some clothes on you damn hippie." But kiyâm.[121] The Wahwâ–man drifted above the earth and was transported through a grease worm hole.

He sang his favorite CCR song, which gave him power, and it was so strong that there was a twisting wind of song that tore through the bannock grease wormholes. A space was opened up for him. He felt his mind and body become light, and before too long he awoke, covered in bannock grease, laying in the ditch on the road to the band office of Broken Elbow reserve.

Not–Even hopped over and licked his face. He saw a pick up full of neechies honking and waving at him with an old mosôm in the back with long hair, and cool sunglasses.

"Not–Even," a boy from an approaching group of kids yelled.

"âstam ôtê,"[122] said a girl with piercing eyes that held the deep intelligence of old oceans and ancestral

---

121   whatever

122   "Come here"

stars.

"Tânisi. We saw you fall from the sky. You must be magic or sumtin. Are you the man they call Reveen?"

"Môya.[123] Nisîmis. No, my little sister. I am just simply a neechie who could really use some bannock right now. My lips have only tasted Wonder Bread for some time. And the wonder of it has left me."

"Kîkwây ôma [124] Wonder Bread?"

"Something that you never want to taste kid. Something you never want to taste."

"Nîcîwâkan,"[125] said another. "Why are you so greasy? Looks like you are covered in bear grease." He paused. "Are you some kind of medicine man or something?"

"Môya. I am just simply an Indian looking for some bannock."

"Well, the chief is having a big party for Chief's Fried Chicken, just yonder over there. He is handing out bannock – Nadine's mom's bannock."

"kinanâskomitinâwâw,"[126] itêw.[127] He gave the kids all of his money and made his way to the bannock. It was good to be with the Bannock Eaters again. It was good to be home.

---

123   "No"
124   "What is it?"
125   "My companion"
126   "I thank you"
127   he said

A DOG CALLED KONITA

It was morning, early morning, just on the other side of dawn's calling. It was that point of the morning when the dusty star light filled the dark line of the sky.

The Senator did not know where he was. At first, he was afraid to open his eyes. What if he had ended up at a redneck rodeo? What if he had ended up at a Shriner's convention and had passed out on the ballroom floor? Or maybe he had been captured by an Indian Affairs person, who was going to do some experiment on him. He heard no banjo music so he nudged out the possibility he'd woken up in the middle of a redneck lair.

Whatever it was around him, he thought he would do things in stages. He decided to open his eyes quickly and then close them quickly. He thought that it would be a good way to get a sense if there was anything around him. Plus, it was a way of taking the edge of his fear away. He did this, but it was too quick for him to really see anything. The only bit of information that really registered with him was that there was sunlight. But that is all that he got.

Then he felt a heavy breath over him – and the breath was not that great. It was a strange cocktail of a variety of tastes. Whatever the next scent was that was lingering over him, he really had to open his eyes and see. So, with that, he opened his eyes to see. êkwa mîna he saw an item. He fumbled around for his Indian Affairs glasses and looked again. Sure enough, it was a dog.

"Argh!" the Senator said as the dog continued to try to lick his face. "It was you I was worried about." He laughed, and pet the dog. "Konita about konita," he said quietly as he laughed again, petting the dog. It was funny because konita meant that there was no purpose for something, and so it seemed that there was no purpose for his fear. He was a nomadic dog, that would move from place to place, from household to household, where he would be fed and given shelter, and other things. If he had been a dog amongst the white folk, he would have been considered a nuisance, and he probably would have been caught and captured. He would then be taken to a place and locked out of the way, and taken out of the sight of concerned citizens, and then everything would return to some sense of normalcy. But amongst the neechies in the stretch of neechiedom, with all of its comforts, this dog was admired for his survival skills, his toughness, and his ability to survive despite the odds. He gave neechies hope, because they said, "if this dog can survive then by–the–beard–of–Nanabush, I can survive." In fact, there were many ballads singing his praises. Ironically, the dog named Konita helped shaped their lives with purpose and for that, above all else, he was respected. When people would see him on the road, they would put down food for him. In fact, the expression "putting food down" had become an expression on the Broken Elbow Reserve, and was used for whenever someone was trying to show that they really respected something.

"Tânisi êkwa kiya?"[128] he said. "How are you this fine morning?" The multicoloured dog with a fit sturdy form tapped him on the chest with a paw. He tapped four times. The Senator muttered "âhaw," and nuzzled and scratched his cheek more, thinking that it was some kind of sign. "Kah!" he said as he continued to think about what the tapping could possibly mean.

The old time Indians always spoke of things having a purpose. They also spoke of times in their lives when things in the field of their experience would forever be changed. They would open their eyes wide when they would talk of such moments and would feel compelled to feed everyone who had listened to their stories. They

128   "How are you?"

called it "kwêskî" moment. Those were the times when they would have visions, or see little miracles in the world around them. This "kwêskî" moment would forever shape their perceptions of things. They would not experience the world the same way after. Forever after, their experiences of everything in their lives would be influenced by these events. This "kwêskî" would be a filter for everything that would flow after. They would suddenly see things in a way that made sense to them. Everyone had moments like this, but some neechies were more open to these insights than others. While the Senator wore plaid and not buckskin, and while the Senator rode in a car and not on a horse, he held these old time stories close to his heart.

The simple and shy Konita licking his face changed him. Sometimes the Senator felt the pain of never being able to find a true love. A true love who he could live with, and grow old with. He realized that eating at a buffet was probably never going to fill his being. No, if he ate that much he might as well just get himself a wîhtikow bucket from Chief's Fried Chicken. The simple lick from the dog reminded him that above all else, he had to survive. Above all, he had to keep moving, and to find his place in the world again.

He pet the dog then went to the truck to get him a bit of kahkêwak[129] and he would cut it into small portions for him. That is how Konita liked to nibble on his food – just like how he liked to experience the world all around him – in small pieces.

Konita wagged his tail, as the Senator continued to give him attention. Konita knew that with the Senator he would get this attention for the Senator was generally regarded as a kind being. Dogs could sense things like that.

The people on the reserve had many stories about Konita and they would often share them at community

---

129   dried meat

events. One of the stories that had a great deal of circulation was that Konita was half wolf. But you could never be sure about stories like this. Sometimes the Senator would look at him, and be able to see the wolf paws, other times not. Other times, the Senator would see the wolf nose, but other times he would not. So, the Senator himself was unsure of the story. Sometimes stories would pass and go in so many directions, and with so many it was hard to find and decide what the threads of the original story had been.

Sometimes a story was like a song that you just felt the need to sing. It was kind of like how the Senator felt when CCR would blast on the radio. He would call out, singing, which was almost shouting in response to John Fogerty's lonesome crying. The songs of CCR – just like Nadine's voice – seemed to make him sad and whole at the same time. The Senator thought that John Fogerty had to have had his heart broken to be able to sing that way.

The Senator got in his car and decided to drive. He often thought that to sing like that John Fogerty must have some Cree blood in there somewhere. The Senator thought that John Fogerty must have, at least, a Cree heart. He also thought that maybe he had some French blood in him on account of those fierce sideburns. Maybe one of his grandfathers was an old French fur trader. Sometimes the Senator even agonized that if John Fogerty closed his eyes, and sang to the true depth of his heart, that maybe, just maybe, he could sing the land back whole again.

Then the Senator thought maybe, just maybe, John Fogerty could not sing the land back whole again, but maybe he could sing the truck back into being. The Senator then turned on the radio, the old AM radio, with its scratchy twang that somehow the Senator found soothing. Fogerty continued to sing again, and the dog tapped the seat of the car four times, and the Senator once again was sure that what was coming through the radio, that song of Fogerty, was a sacred song, with a sacred message. And a sacred power in it. He felt a bolt of energy and the whole car suddenly jolted. Then he felt a flash of energy move through him and he stretched his mind and being to embrace it. However, it was too much for the Senator. Of late, he was not keeping up with his jumping–jacks, and he felt his body collapse a bit.

It took a while, but he came back to consciousness. He listened to the radio with great interest. There was something truly magical about the crackle of the AM radio; it seemed to be like a vessel which contained all kinds of sound. There was a call–in show, a show where people would phone in to try and sell things. Then there was a little bit of honky tonk, a song that was beautiful, then a funky song that had the strangest beat that the Senator had heard in a long time. Then there was some old time gospel music from the United States. That preacher had a powerful voice. He talked funny, almost as funny as a redneck singing Cree songs. The Senator really couldn't understand who the hell the guy was talking about, but he did like the singing. The Senator was driving along with the windows open. Konita's face was outside the window, letting the wind splash against his face, like water against a shore. Then the dog put his paw close to the Senator and tapped it four times. The Senator thought, "Wahwâ mêtoni mamâhtâwastim awa."[130]

---

130   "Wow, this dog is truly a powerful being."

REX ROVER: REDNECK RADIO

Konita looked at the Senator again with that sideways look that dogs sometimes do. That look that dogs give us when it is clear that they want to tell us something but they don't know how to put it in the right bark. Then the dog looked at the radio and looked back at him, and looked at the radio, and back again at the Senator. The Senator, taking this as a sign, turned the dial of the radio and got a new channel, one that he had missed previously. It was some kind of interview. The scratchy texture of the AM radio gave a certain gravelly quality to the voice of the speaker.

The Senator realized that it was the familiar voice of Prince Albert radio. It was Rex Rover.

"Well, listeners to CBKI we have a special guest in our studio today. A special guest who is shaking things up in our district. Someone who is sure to change things." There was a pause, "We live in a time of change. Who could forget what happened at Woodstock? Who could forget Martin Luther King? Who could forget the way we flew to the moon and the rocket ship?" He paused. "There are changes happening in our Indian communities. Changes that are shaking things up.

"That is exactly the stuff I am fighting against, Rex Rover," the guest said. The guest had a discernible Indian accent, and this was interesting to the Senator for a variety of reasons.

The host, Rex Rover tried to fake a laugh, tried through this to make it seem like he was in charge of everything. He wanted to give the impression that he was still in charge. "You hang up Chief," Rex laughed. "It sounds like you are going to have a little pow wow right here on my show."

"Listen, you redneck..." There were some beeps. "I am not going to stay on this program if you are going to talk to me in this fashion."

"Looks like we got ourselves an Indian right off the reservation!"

"I want all the Indian people out there to hear this. This redneck (bleep) is the reason why you have to come to my seminar tonight." They continued on for a bit. The banter was very lively and the Senator realized that the guest was Dr. Charging Horse. He was a noted psychologist and he was coming to the reserve that night to do an empowerment workshop. Dr. Charging Horse spoke of how the White man was always trying to silence the Indian. One of the key things that the Senator remembered Dr. Charging Horse saying about the seminars past: "They are about empowerment. They are about trying to find your place, trying to find your voice."

DR. CHARGING HORSE

The Senator also heard Dr. Charging Horse say
that he had his talks on 8–track tapes. Finally, the Senator
could remember that the empowerment seminar was going
to take place on the Broken Elbow Reserve that night at
7:30. He would charge $200 for each person who wanted
therapy that night. Charging Horse wanted to help every
Indian find their inner papoose. Finding the inner papoose,
he said, was the best way to find freedom and to also get
revenge against the Wonder Bread people. The Senator was
not really clear what Dr. Charging Horse meant by that, but
he remembered a pick up line that one of the older people
from the reserve used at the community hall. He said,
to a môniyâw–iskwêw,[131] "You know your lips look like
yummy Wonder Bread and, baby, my lips have only known
bannock. Could you be my little wonder woman tonight?"

The Senator really couldn't understand that line,
but by golly, it seemed to work. The Senator realized that
she would go with that. The Senator laughed to himself.
He knew that he had to find his inner papoose, he had to
find that quiet centre, that quiet place where he could be a
better man.

He often thought about Nadine and the many
stories that she would tell and write. Nadine was a woman
that men from all over the world had been entranced by.
Nadine was the kind of woman who was forever etched
in your mind. Someone who you could not forget. She left
a print on your soul in the same way that those painted
beings were left imprinted on those rocks. The Senator
could never forget her.

He wanted to go see Dr. Charging Horse's seminar.
He flipped around the AM dial and put on some old
country. He smiled to himself and decided to go get a new
pair of slacks. If he was going to hear this man speak, then
by–the–sweet–breath–of–baby–Nanabush he was going

131   white woman

to have to look the part.

The Senator sat in the truck listening to the radio. He was trying to figure out where he stood in relation to Nadine, where he stood in relation to life, where he stood in relation to other people, where he stood in relation to the ancestors, and where he stood in relation to his possibilities. It was around 7:30 now, and all things, all of these threads of being were beginning to set in, and wrap around him. There were still traces of the sun in the sky, and the remaining light had gathered in places of shadows. A good pair of slacks could really carry someone far.

The parking lot already glistened with the light from the metal of the cars. This was especially so with the cars that had metallic paint on them. Most of the band seemed to be here. There were even a couple of tractors parked at the far end of the field which was functioning as a make-shift parking lot. Even a couple of horses were hitched at locations off the way to the other side of the tractors. This really seemed to be a big deal. Also, maybe more than half of the vehicles were from neighbouring reserves. This motivational speaker really seemed to have attracted a large number of people from all over. The Senator figured that this was like the camp of another time when the buffalo were numerous on the prairies. A time when the neechies would gather for summer ceremonies, and also for a time of general visiting. Some of the cars were wrecks on wheels. Others had evidence of more elbow grease. The Senator tried to park as close as he could to the entrance of the place but, it was tricky because there were so many people. He could see people smiling and giggling as they walked up to the door. He could hear little bits of Cree conversations. They all kind of blended together to form a dull murmur. As he weaved around the pockets of metal, open spaces, and smiling faces, he waved several times at people and muttered, "tânisi." He would raise his fingers from the steering wheel, and he thought that the whole thing was funny but it was how people would say "tânisi" when driving. Maybe, the Senator thought, it was like sign language.

The light from the door of the rec centre seemed to be slightly amplified – maybe by the lingering light of the summer sky. He got out of the truck and he began to strut towards the entrance off of the rec centre. There were few things that could cause someone to strut with such intensity. One thing was a stylish pair of store–bought slacks. A smart pair of slacks were like little wings that caused him to flutter in the sky. He felt like a chubby little neechie angel. He laughed, and said to himself, "Cha, as if I am some kind of neechie cupid. As if."

He kept strutting. He knew that he was strutting for peace, for freedom, indeed for love – if not Nadine's hand, then the hand of someone he had not met yet. He swore that he heard a ringing in his ears, of the sweet trumpets of Câhkâpîs, and he could feel his ancestors patting him on the back and giving him strength. If only Nadine could see him now, see him with his new found power. He was strutting to his own inner rhythm, trying to find his inner voice, his inner papoose. This indeed was the message of Dr. Charging Horse.

As he paraded into the rec centre, he could not get over how full it was. People wore bright coloured shirts, the lights of the room caught the glasses, the Indian Affairs glasses, of people sitting throughout the room. Some people were standing. They seemed to be unable to sit down. Children ran around playing games of Indian agent and Indians – it always seemed to be the bossiest kid who became the Indian agent. Mosôms laughed and Kohkoms giggled. It was a good place to be, a good vibe, a strong vibe.

There were cameras all over the place. There was also special lighting set up. People were running around frantically with clip boards, production assistants helping assistants. It was a bingo hall hopped up on bush coffee. A slick môniyâw producer, fast talking as the flow of the

Saskatchewan river said, "That one. I want that one!" An assistant hurried over to where the producer was pointing. The Senator looked around like a gopher looking out from a hole on the prairie. He looked again at the slick môniyâw – he looked slick like those poodles that those blue-haired môniyâw women had.

As the Senator was thinking this, someone was carrying some kind of powdering trunk. Someone else was bringing a comb and blow dryer. They were moving quickly, right towards him – like wolves moving towards their kills. They had a couple of smiles as cheap as Wonder Bread promises.

They were slick producer types like the ones who worked on CBKIs talent show. One of them walked up to the Senator, he was wearing a sweater vest and, pointing at the Senator, said, "I love those slacks! I want the nation to see those slacks."

Before the Senator could properly react, the makeup brush hit his face, before the Senator could protest, the hair blower was giving him a blow job. He was then gussied up after a few more fixing moves. Another producer, maybe an intern, yelled, "Bring him over here."

The Senator felt a rush. A rush like the time they took the rocket ship from the top of the hill before they knew that it was going to crash into the legion in the town. He was so excited to be part of the show, and he knew that maybe this might help him get back with Nadine.

The producer said, "Bring him to Chair 2." The young woman who looked like a librarian or an Indian Affairs junior clerk, guided the Senator over again. The producer, who kind of looked like a poodle, gave more orders, yelling out like a camp caller, smiled at the Senator. "We need some shots of the crowd," he said. "Get that old Kohkom over there." He paused briefly, "Keep it tight!"

The Senator could feel the pulsing excitement in the room. He felt giggly and he actually giggled out loud. He could feel and hear the countless conversations moving about the room. He felt the hum and the vibrations of laughter moving through his skin like waves hitting the shoreline of the beach. He imagined that Nadine was somewhere in the crowd admiring his star–like status. Surely–to–Nanabush she must have liked his smart looking slacks. When the Senator put on the slacks, he knew in his heart that he would probably never be able to wear buckskin again.

Then the Dr. charged up the podium like a horse and rose to the stage. He looked sharper than a hunting knife. The Dr. had dyed his buckskin jacket purple and had embedded rhinestones in it. In fact, as he got up on stage, the song "Rhinestone Cowboy" began to play. When Glen Campbell hit the high note, the Dr. raised both of his fists in a power salute, and with that, the crowd cheered each time. Even the Kohkoms looked giggly. Everyone was going crazy, just like a pow wow.

The Senator could feel the lights of the camera on his face. He certainly felt like a buffet item now. Like those buffets in the big city, with all kinds of items. The Senator always thought that the Chinese must be very intelligent to have so many vegetables for buffet items. He imagined that there must be some great garden in China somewhere. He also thought that to have such a garden, and to make such tasty food, that those sêkipâcawâsak[132] must be pretty good little gardeners. The Senator had often wondered what would have happened if these Chinese gardeners would have been the farm instructors. Maybe things would have turned out differently, cî?

The Senator looked across the great space of the rec centre, he could feel the energy, and hope of the crowd. It was like all of that energy was passing through him. The song, "Rhinestone Cowboy" kept playing in the background, the energy of the crowd kept increasing, and Dr. Charging Horse kept pumping his hands in the air and the crowd mimicked this. There was a frenzy, a madness

132   Chinese people

that was spreading across the room. The energy was like one of those bush foxes that went crazy and went out of control on the reserve. The Senator could feel warmth on his cheek, like a warm bit of gravy.

The Senator looked at the other people in the chairs beside him. He could see and feel the same bewilderment that he felt in himself in them. There was one older kohkom, old Mrs. Anderson, with her kerchief, and kohkom rubber boots, over her moccasins. The Senator always liked that look. It reminded him of an older time. It reminded him of a time when people were still close to the land.

There were two others sitting in the chairs, in chairs one and three. The one, he didn't recognize. This one, to the left of him, also had rhinestones like the good doctor.

Dr. Charging Horse let out a spontaneous roar, "Can I hear a 'hoka!" Everyone yelled back in a strong, uniform almost monastic chant "'hoka!" at the top of their lungs, as if the chant came from a deep place in their soul. The Dr. continued, "Can I hear a 'hoka hey!" Everyone sang the chant back to him. Their sound was a tight sound with vibrating small little echoes in it, and it projected through the room with the boom of an old time bingo caller. The sound and the vibrations caused goose bumps to pucker up and kiss the surface of his skin. Just when he felt that his soul could hold no more, the Dr. grabbed the mic and began to speak.

"My brothers. My sis–tahs. My neechies." Two of the cameras were on him. One of them was a close–up, the other was a long shot. A third camera was systematically moving through the crowd.

The Senator was a bit overwhelmed but also excited because it looked like only a few of the people in the rec centre were actually going to be selected to be on the show.

"We need some shots of the crowd. Try to get shots! Take the shots tight, take the shots tight."

The Senator could now really feel the excitement

of the room. He could feel the hush and hum, the waves of laughter lapping lightly on his skin like water hitting the shoreline of a beach. He knew that this was his existence and he thought that maybe Nadine would be attracted to the star status. Maybe now, finally they could be a couple. Everyone was going crazy, just like a pow wow, and it seemed as though it was time that they would all remember. The Senator looked across the great space of the rec centre and he could see the excitement in the crowd and sense of the possibility of liberation. The song "Rhinestone Cowboy" kept blaring away, and the Dr. kept pumping his fists in the air, and each time the crowd cheered. The Senator wondered if they even knew why they were going wild anymore. It seemed like a brush fire on the reserve that had started out small and now burned so bright that no one now could remember why it burnt. All that mattered was that the fire of the crowd was burning, and the Senator could feel it on his cheeks. Dr. broke out into a simultaneous roar, "Can I hear a 'hoka!" Everyone yelled back "hoka!" at the top of their lungs. He continued, "Can I hear a hoka hey," everyone yelled back "hoka hey!" Then, just when he didn't think he could stand it anymore the Dr. grabbed the mic and began to speak.

"My brothers, my sisters, my neechies." Two of the cameras were on him. The other camera was systematically panning through the crowd. As the camera passed by, the neechies all grinned, with grins as wide as the prairies. All of those neechies wanted their little bits of fame.

"We have gathered here tonight," the Dr. continued, "to witness a rebirth. To allow all of you to be empowered, to feel the power!" Some yelled "hoka" in the crowd. There was a general stage of amazement and awe in the crowd. Just as the doctor was about to continue, a little kid ran up to the kôhkom the Senator did not recognize at first. It was actually Sylvia, old Teddy and Gertrude's daughter. She had left so long ago it was weird to see her here after all of those years. The child whispered in her ear.

She arched her body to hear the words of the child.

Dr. Charging Horse noticed this and swooped down off the stage towards them, and motioned for one of the cameras to zero in on them. "Little Jimmy," the Dr. said, "Little Jimmy – can I call you that?"

The boy was obviously paralyzed by the sudden attention – the camera was right on him. The boy froze and was wide-eyed. He didn't move. Sensing that this was not good for the cameras, the Dr. motioned for one of the assistants to put a microphone in the Kohkom's hand.

"Tânisi Kohkom."

The Kohkom was still surprised to be on the "show", she held back a little in her light retort. "Cha! How do you speak Cree? I thought you were Blackfoot..."

"To honour the people of this territory I thought I would learn a few words."

"Well gosh, that is very kind of you," she said.

A burly, chubby man from the crowd got up. He looked real pissed off and looked like he needed to get something off his chest. Instead of being threatened, the Dr. pulled him in and roped him like a rodeo daredevil.

"Give the man a mic!" he motioned to one of his assistants and one of the cameras zeroed in on the chubby man. Another was panning the crowd.

"My friends, our people have been pulled down too long." Someone from the audience yelled, "hoka! We should not be silent any longer." "Hoka hey" one voice erupted in response. "Hoka hey" trumpeted again, in scattered voices hustling their way up through the pathway of sound to the front of the room.

"What do you have to say bro-ther?" the Dr. said. The chubby man shifted his weight back and forth.

"Look, you are a damn Blackfoot! My grandfathers fought yours!" A few of the older men cheered, but a lot of the younger people along with the kohkoms gasped.

The Doctor rotated his hand in a semi-circle, as though he was cracking joints inside of him. "My brother, my friend. While your words sting me like an arrow, my love protects me." Then the Rhinestone Cowboy music kicks in again. Everyone waited for what he would say next.

"You say you are Cree and I must agree, my good friend, that is for sure a good thing. But so is being a Blackfoot."

The chubby–sturdy man replied by saying, "What the hell do you mean you looked up fool?"

A few of the older guys laughed again at this but this time their laughs were less numerous and less bold, like the punches of a tired boxer who was losing the match.

"How many of you love being a neechie?" He raised his fist again in the air and opened it up like he was throwing gold to the sky. With that the crowd went wild. Everyone went crazy. An eruption of "Hoka heys" filled and joined together in a loud chorus. It's like the whole room was shaking. It was like a great herd of buffalo was passing through the rec centre.

"Blackfoot. Cree. The white man has taught that these words should run into each like the horns of two rutting bulls." "Hoka," someone yelled. "But why," he said in his preacher–like voice, "why must we be put in these boxes?"

"Hoka," someone yelled.

"Let's throw away the boxes. Let's throw away these shackles of the white man and move towards something new."

The preacher Dr. continued, "How many of you love your horses?" At that, even the disgruntled older man put up his hand and smiled. The cameras kept rolling, and the grins kept coming. The crowd was loving this guy. Even one neechie who had taken off his cowboy hat earlier, put it back on in pride.

"The white man has also taught us that there is a difference between cowboys and Indians. But I ask you how many of you are rodeo riders?" A lot of the men got up, and the preacher doctor saluted them. Then everyone saluted them.

"There is no longer cowboy. There is no longer Indian. There just is."

"And with this, my brothers and sisters, I bring you liberation from the shackles of colonialism."

The doctor raised his hands like an old time preacher. And the crowd cheered again. "What a lovely pair of slacks." Everyone cheered. Even the Senator's brother–in–law couldn't help but cheer because by god they were a handsome pair of slacks.

"This is why we are here tonight, to talk about things that give us a sense of power. That give you a sense that you can do anything."

"Hoka yeah," yelled someone in the audience.

The Senator got up into the area where the doctor was and then he started to twirl around, "tâpwê, those pants truly fit me well The camera pawed him up like a frisky, hungry bear. He tried so hard not to laugh but it was very hard. He kept thinking that he looked like one of those modelling girls on the Price is Right. He wondered how his friends would take it. He wondered if they would still welcome him to their table in the morning for coffee or if they would just laugh at him. He wondered if they would quit taking him seriously, which could happen easily enough.

Everybody cheered, clapped, the cameras were rolling and everyone was loving it. The four people in the front started to tell their stories. They were really going out of their way to make themselves vulnerable. The good Dr. said that was part of empowerment and was what they were all about. Then things began to go wrong and they went gradually wrong as often does in a neechie story. Kinda like when a brush fire gets out of hand. It starts off unnoticeably enough, but then as time goes on, things get very crazy, and what started off as a little fire, becomes a huge raging inferno, consuming everything in its path.

ENTER THE MOSS BAG

The cameras stopped for a bit. Then there was a word from the sponsors: Chief Fried Chicken. It was part of the chief's economic diversification plan. He thought that the future rested in fried chicken. He had said on many occasions that he genuinely felt that it was going to be fried chicken that would change the position of Indigenous peoples.

The Senator kept smiling, and the slick producer had the cameras on him. The cameras captured every movement of the Senator. They also captured the large moss bags which were being brought out. There were four. One was brought closer to the Senator. The doctor explained to everyone that what the Senator was about was significant for neechies, as were the first steps of Neil Armstrong on the moon. The Doctor yelled to the crowd's delight. "This will be one step for neechies and one great leap for neechiekind." With that, the crowd went wild. Some of the old kohkoms even fainted they were so excited. And with that, the Rhinestone Cowboy song with the lyrics changed to "Rhinestone Indian" blasted through the rec centre.

The Senator took a step into the giant moss bag that had been brought out on stage. The Doctor told him that he was now going to begin to do some inner papoose work. It was time for him, the Doctor said, to let go of all of his inhibitions. He said the Senator should feel safe in the giant moss bag. It made him sure of how much he loved Nadine.

This is where the little brush fire became a crazy brush fire that got completely out of control. Just as the Senator got into the giant moss bag it was taped shut. The power in the rec centre went out. The police came shortly, yelling out that the Dr. was to blame, that he was in violation of various tax laws and that he was charged with tax evasion. With that, the Doctor fled, and the crowd was on the run. For a few moments, the Senator thought that one of the assistants would help him but the assistants just fled.

The crowd cleared, but one of the cops, who was an Indian cop, charged the Senator for a violation of fire regulations. Even though he was an Indian cop he seemed to be angrier and meaner than the other cops. Maybe it was because he felt that he had something to prove. The reason the Senator was deemed a fire hazard was because of all of the moss he wore. The Senator told them that was bullshit, but they kept at him with the false charges. The Senator tried to talk to the one officer, but the officer was a rookie with a hard brush cut who told the Senator that he was also going to be charged with resisting arrest.

When the Senator argued and said that he could not have resisted arrest because he was taped inside the moss bag, he was slapped with another fine. Eventually Jingles came and paid him up and they went back to the Senator's pawn shop and had a nice dinner of macaroni. The Blackfoot Doctor was never to be seen or heard from again. The people had pride in being neechie that no one could take away. Every time the Senator wore those slacks he remembered that inner papoose work he did, and Nadine remembered him and thanked him for getting her a television. Those slacks were like medicine, and he wore them almost every day for a year afterwards.

THE PRIME MINISTER COMES TO THE RESERVE

People always have a desire to believe in something. The Senator knew this perhaps more than anyone. He was always banking on the hope of people. He banked on the hopes of the people who brought their stuff to his store to try to get money – just like in the old days when people would bring in their buffalo hides to the trading posts. They would throw down the hides on the counter, and try to get the best price for what they had brought into the fort. The Senator was aware that people had that same kind of hope and faith when they bought things at the pawnshop.

There was a môniyâw Chief sometime ago that would take the time to talk to neechies and even have coffee with them. He would sit down and share stories with them. They would break bannock so to speak. He talked about Indian people in his speeches and he tried to make things better for neechies. Older neechies had his picture in their homes, often with themselves in the picture. The Prime Minister did go to reserves across the country. Then one day, he came to the Broken Elbow reserve again.

People were lined up in long rows to the see the Prime Minister. There was a rope which was attached to a few poles and then it was stretched down about 50 feet. There wasn't a red carpet but some of the kohkomak put embroidered star quilts down on the road, close to where the Prime Minister was going to walk. Everyone felt good when they knew that his feet would not touch the ground, but rather that he would be walking in the stars.

The black Oldsmobile stopped by the rope which led to the band office. The Prince Albert Herald reporter had taken a few pictures. Buddy Bradley was there snapping pictures as well, and he had planned to put them in the reserve newsletter. He made his copies on a mimeograph. The old fellas on the reserve called his newsletter an âcimowâsinahikanis.[133] Along the rope where the Prime Minister was walking along shaking hands, there were people screaming as they tried to stand closer to the rope. His fame as a lawyer propelled him into near rockstar status for he had represented many neechies in court. He was wearing a flashy and dashing blue suit. He had a thin moustache, and for a man in his mid 50s he was in good shape. He was slightly shorter than most. He had wiry arms, and had also been a bush pilot before the war. He had flown through many blizzards, and many people had been taken to a hospital and had their lives saved because of his heroism. There was one man who almost had his appendix burst, but due to the calm nerves of the Prime Minister, he was able to fly through the storm and the man was saved. There was another story that he was flying and a woman who was about to give birth was on board but the baby came a bit more quickly than anyone expected, so the Prime Minister had to land and actually deliver a baby. The mother actually named the baby after the pilot.

In World War II, he was a fighter pilot and in the last days of the war, he faced an advanced German fighter jet one on one. His piloting skills were supposed to be so good that he was able to outfight the jet which was technologically much more advanced than the air plane that he had. Some of the old Cree Anglicans said he was kind of like David who had fought Goliath. He had stared him straight down, and won. They say the advanced and powerful weapons do not always win when the person facing them has an advanced and powerful

133   the little book of stories

heart. They say that the Prime Minister was completely out of ammunition and all he had was his pistol. They say that he had to fly close enough to shoot the pilot with his pistol.

When he came home the Crees on the Broken Elbow reserve sang an honour song for him. Napoleon would often speak of the Prime Minister's bravery and said his valour was not unlike the valour of many of their grandfathers when they had fought against the Blackfoot. Napoleon also reminded them that it was the Prime Minister who was the one who stood up for him when Napoleon was denied entry into the Legion Hall.

The Prime Minister got up on a stage to speak to the crowd. There was a genuine frenzy in the room. Some of the younger kohkoms were screaming and they had tears in their eyes. They were screaming. One was even holding an old newspaper article which documented his World War Two heroism, and another had a newspaper article which had a picture of both the Senator and Napoleon smiling. Another kohkom got so excited she fainted. There were a couple of men in black suits who were standing beside him. They had sunglasses on, and were simply standing by without any emotion watching the crowd.

The Prime Minister said, "Tânisi nitotêmak. kitatamiskatinâwâw."[134] Everyone gasped. Another kohkom fainted as the Prime Minister spoke these words in Cree. He continued, "I have a program to announce." People sat tight in their seats. Even the older people in the crowd seemed excited as the Prime Minister spoke, "You have waited a long time for the buffalo to come back. You have waited a long time." A few of the older people said, "ahâw."

The Prime Minister continued, "Now I want to

---

134   "Hello my friends, I greet you."

bring the buffalo back to you through this new program. Chief Cash smiled because he knew that something historical was happening. He also knew that perhaps there might be some kind of infusion of cash into the reserve. This was important to his plans to expand the chicken company.

The Prime Minister continued with the vision of his new program. "The program is called the Buffalo Bus, and it will be a bus that will travel across the country and young people will share stories of where they come from. The buffalo will come back through the stories." With that everyone cheered. The Prime Minister continued to describe the program and noted that people would be chosen from every community. He announced that Buddy Bradley's son, Clifford, was chosen from the Broken Elbow reserve to be on the tour.

CLIFFORD BRADLEY IS CHOOSEN TO BE PART OF THE BUFFALO BUS

Clifford, Buddy Bradley's son, was excited to be one of the people chosen to go on the Buffalo Bus. Before he left he spent a couple of weeks with the Senator gathering stories and getting the Senator to tell him the narrative lore of the reserve.

On the day he was to leave, his kohkom packed him a lunch and Buddy Bradley, his father, got him a good sleeping bag, and pulled him aside and told him what to expect while he was on the road, "You know son, there are going to be people who will expect certain things from you as you are on the road. They will expect certain things from you because you are an Indian. Some will think that you have certain powers – like you can talk to animals. Others will be surprised when you speak English well."

"I know dad. I remember when you told me about when you would go on the road and people would have certain expectations of you just because you were an Indian."

"That is right my son. They were not used to the idea that an Indian could be a stand–up comedian at that time."

"What would they do dad, when you got up and started to tell jokes?"

"They would just yell out 'Dance pow wow! Dance pow wow!'"

"Cha, didn't they know that not all Indians are pow wow dancers."

"Son, it was a different time."

Clifford was happy to be on the bus, on the buffalo bus, which was going to ride through the country, and try to find places to stop where people could get out and tell their stories. They stopped at different reserves near the Broken Elbow reserve. Clifford could feel the bump and jingle of the road. "Mitoni mâyâtan mêskanâhk,"[135] he thought. The bounce and jingle of the road reminded him of when he would plow the fields with his father's tractors. Like most of the youth of his age, he was familiar with farm machinery. After they left the Broken Elbow reserve they stopped at a couple of other reserves in the district to pick up what people were calling the "buffalo runners." At one point, after they stopped at a truck stop, he even spilled coffee on his leg. "awiya!" he yelled.

A young woman from a nearby reserve sat a few seats down from where Clifford was sitting. She was smiling as she drank Coke from a bottle with a straw. If he could remember right, she was a distant cousin, but the pathway of cousinhood involved a couple of marriages and also a couple of ex–cousins–in–law which made Clifford think that if they were distant cousins they had enough different things in their bannock dough which would make them at least able to kiss, and even respectfully court in front of their kohkoms. In the circles of family historians, and keepers of family trees, nay family forests, one would think that it was okay. It would be considered with the margin of cousin error.

"Clifford," she said as she sipped from her straw.

"Yes," he said.

"Did you get the new Deep Purple 8–track?"

"Yeah. I really like it. I want to sing 'Smoke on the Water' with my handdrum."

"Aren't 8–tracks the greatest thing?" she said. She paused for a bit, and then looked at him as soberly as a midnite bingo caller and said, "You know, if you grew out your hair a bit longer, you could look like a darker version of the lead singer." He smiled and laughed. He pulled out his handdrum and played a version of "Smoke on the Water" which she seemed to like.

They kept driving, picking up other young people.

---

135   "The road is very bad."

The young people share their stories on the buffalo bus as they would stop in different towns along the way. Throughout the journey, Clifford would sing with his hand drum and the others on the bus seemed to really like his singing. Sometimes they would drive through the night making restroom breaks, as needed, other times they would pull over at a camp site. About every third day they would get motel rooms, and then they would have showers, just like at some of the camp sites. They tried to be as economical as they could, but they always seemed to have enough. They often made their own sammiches and did not need to eat at restaurants very often. Next they even started to stay in some motor hotels. They started to wonder where all of the extra resources were coming from. Then someone told them that it was Chief Cash – he was sending them money because he wanted the young people to be able to ride in class. Cash was funneling sôniyâw from the chicken sales into the buffalo bus. He even had the bus put a Chief's Fried Chicken logo on the side. He also had a CB radio put in for the driver for when they would get bored on the road. You could say that the CB was either a really advanced form of smoke signals or a very early and primitive form of the internet.

THEY COME TO THE REDNECK TOWN

Then in the middle of the day they were passing through a very small town. They had run out of sammiches and needed to get some food at a café as the diners were commonly called on the prairies. It was a quiet town. There was a bar that happened to have some pickups outside of it. There was a Legion Hall and a Co-op store. There were a few people walking around and a group of people who seemed to be standing in front of what appeared to be a café. The bus pulled close and Arnie the bus driver said, "I don't know about this. The restaurant is Kountry Kitchen Kafe."

One of the kids from the northern reach of the Prince Albert district said, "Well it sounds like we will get some good old fashioned cooking."

"No takay. Look again. Each word of the restaurant has a K in it."

"êkwa. . . ?"[136]

"That means KKK!"

"Holey shit," said Clifford. "We better be careful."

"We need to get some sammiches or something to eat. It might be better if we have one volunteer who might be willing to go in there and get us some food."

To go in there meant going through a group of rather tough looking men who were outside smoking. One of them even banged on the window of the bus. Arnie opened the window and the rough looking man looked at him and smiled, smoking. He was wearing farm boots, jeans and a white T-shirt – the other guys wore button up shirts. There were a few of them, including what appeared to be the leader who was knocking on the window. Arnie had been nervous as he moved to open the window in order to talk to the redneck.

"You folks passing through?" he said, his blond hair catching errant rays of the sun. His blue eyes

136   And ...?

179

were squinting. He tugged on his cigarette and seemed determined to smoke it to the bone. Arnie tried to conceal the fact that he was nervous. It was difficult for him because he stuttered and even on the reserve, and even in Cree, people had a hard time not to tease him a bit. He did have a brush cut which betrayed the fact the he was a little older than some of the neechies who preferred to have long hair. He just didn't have that let's stick–it–to–the–man mentality. He tried to respond, but all he could do was stutter. The redneck said, "What's wrong? The cat got your tongue?" The rest of the young men with him just stood around laughing.

Another one walked up to the window and said, "I don't think we're going to have a pow wow in this town today."

Arnie stammered and said, "We–we juh–just wah–waah–na get some food and . . . Wee. Wee . . .

The redneck said, "Sorry Chief. I don't speak Indian. Any of you boys speak Indian?" he said, looking at the others in his group. They all shook their heads, no.

The redneck laughed, "Seems like you have a pretty fancy van here. Why don't you let us take your fancy little van here for a spin? We promise we won't damage it."

Arnie stuttered and said, "I cah–cah–can't let you."

They laughed again and walked around to board the bus.

One of the kids asked, "Well, is someone going to do something?"

Another said, "I have to get off. I really have to pee."

"You goh–goh–gonna have to wait," said Arnie. Then Clarence, who was something of a nerd, got up. He had the whole glasses thing, and was handy with radios. He got up and said, "This is bullshit. I am not going to take this." He got up. One of the young women tried to get him to sit down but that didn't work. Then another person tried to get him to sit down, but he just kept moving towards the front of the bus. No one could stop him. The more the rednecks banged on the door of the bus, the more determined Clarence seemed to make it to the front of the bus to confront them. Arnie tried at the last minute to prevent him from confronting the rednecks. He stuck his arm out blocking Clarence's path. Clarence just looked at him through his thick glasses, and said, "This is something that I have to do." Arnie, with reluctance, opened the door of the bus.

Clarence went down the stairs with a focus that caught not only Arnie off guard, but also the rednecks who were outside the door. Even the others who were on the bus were a bit taken a back. The rednecks spread out once he got off the bus. He looked at the redneck leader straight in the eye. At first, the redneck was a bit taken aback, but then slowly the redneck fell back into the pattern of his hate, and moved back into the space of his hate and his arrogant confidence.

"Hey, looks like we got ourselves a little redskin nerd."

"Why I'll teach you to talk to me like that!" Clarence took a swing at the redneck and missed. The redneck laughed heartily with his friends. He had turned away, and when he turned back to Clarence he was clocked in the face. Blood started to trickle down his chin from his nose. He was shocked, and the laughter of the group was cut short. They looked at their leader to see what sort of reaction he would have. He wiped the blood from his face and said, "Not bad for a nerd. Especially an injun nerd." The rest of the rednecks started to laugh again and their necks seemed to get redder and redder. Arnie put his head in his hands and leaned into himself.

"Let me see," the redneck said. He grabbed Clarence's face and scrunched it up and said, "You look like a little fish." He knocked Clarence's glasses off and then the glasses fell to the ground. Then the redneck stepped on them. One of the kids in bus yelled, "Well, what are we going to do?" Another yelled out, "Poor Clarence. Can't one of you nâpêwak[137] go and help him."

Clarence said, without showing any fear, "You stupid asshole. I can't see." One of the other rednecks kicked Clarence in the stomach and with that Clarence fell to the ground.

Clifford got up, opened the compartment above him, calmly took out his bag, and from it he took out his drumstick and grabbed his hand drum which was on the neighbouring seat to him. He walked up to the front of the bus with his right hand holding the drumstick and his left hand holding the drum. He nodded to Arnie who smiled but nervously. "I really don't know what your hand drum is going to do against those boys out there, aya ..." Clifford nodded again, and Arnie opened the door. By this time some people had gathered around. A few of the local boys from the bar must have heard the commotion and were moving in on the scene.

The redneck said, "Looks like we have another injun who is going to put a little of their redskin red blood on our streets that our tax paying dollars will have to be used to pay to clean up."

"Clarence," Clifford said, "are you okay?" Clifford had thick braids and as he reached down to help Clarence, his braids swung a bit. When he offered his hand, Clarence kind of grimaced, and looked like he was going to push his hand away. But Clarence needed a hand, so he accepted it. "Mahti pasiko."[138]

"So," said the redneck."

"No, but I bead a little." The redneck didn't quite get the joke but Clarence did and he started to laugh.

"Looks like we got ourselves a goddamn comedian here."

"Actually," said Clifford, "My father was a

---

137   men

138   "Please get up."

comedian, and I believe he performed in that legion hall down the road."

The redneck looked at him, "Not possible. We have never had a goddamn pow wow in this town."

"Let the boy give us a bit of a show," said one of the local boys from across the street.

Clifford smiled and started to play his hand drum a bit.

"By god," said one of the men from across the street, "the boy is playing the song from duelling banjos."

"Yeah, but the beat is all messed up because of that damn drum. That damn drum kills the beat of most good songs."

"Listen boy, I don't know if you got the office memo, but you may as well put away your little drum, cuz we don't have those Indian shindigs or pow wows as you call 'em." At this moment Clarence looked the redneck fiercely in the eye and the redneck did not look away. He squinted because he could not really see right without his glasses.

"The problem with injun fellas is that you are always waiting and expecting the government to pay your bills." The redneck tugged on his cigarette and blew the smoke right in the face of Clifford. He made his mouth really wide when he blew the ring of smoke into his face. Clifford just smiled and started to sing a song. At first they just laughed at his song, "What the hell kind of bus is this anyway? You boys steal this bus from white folk?"

Another one said, "No, I don't think so. I don't think any white man would put a buffalo on the side of a bus."

The Chief mihkwâyâw[139] looked at him, and started to stare at him, clenching his fist. Clifford kept drumming and kept singing, smiling while he sung.

"Tânisi, tânisi, kâ–mihkwâyât!
mêtoni, mêtoni, miywâsin,

---

139   Redneck

ôma nikamowin."[140]

With that the Redneck's fist was no longer clenched.

"Mêtoni, mêtoni, miywâsin
ôma nikamowin,
kâ–mihkwâyât, hâw, a pow wow.
ahâw, ah hey."[141]

Without realizing what he was doing, the redneck began to dance, and it was like Clarence was controlling his actions with the song. Then the redneck started to move his hand up and down while Clifford was singing. One of the other rednecks said, "Clive, what the hell are you doing? It looks like this here Injun is using some kind of medsin on you." Then he looked around. "Eddy, go into the bar and tell Big Billy Bubba to bring his banjo out here as quick as he can. Tell him we need him now." Clifford kept singing,

"Mêtoni, mêtoni
miywâsin ôma
nikamowin."

Then the redneck started to move with even more force. He was moving his body around a great deal.

"Holeh shit Clive! This is real bad," said one of the rednecks. This is realbad." Clifford was using his singing power to make Clive the redneck pick his nose. "Well, I am a possum's uncle," the one redneck said, "Clive is picking his nose. This injun magic is pretty strong. Where the hell is Bubba?" Clifford kept singing and he made the redneck Clive give the finger to his friends. One of them got pissed off and slugged him. Another one of the rednecks said, "Why'd you do that, you stupid asshole. Clive can't control it. The injun is casting witchcraft spells." The others on the bus seemed to think it was safe to come out. Arnie opened the door but he seemed to have his cisk firmly planted on the seat of the bus.

---

140   hello, hello, redneck/ truly, truly, it is good, this song
141   truly, truly, it is good/ this song/ of the redneck

THE DUEL

Only after a few of the neechies had gotten off the
bus, Big Billy Bubba came barreling out of the bar. His belly
was exposed, showing his pale hairy skin to an unforgiving
sun, and to an even less forgiving crowd. He was wearing
a plaid shirt which was too hot for the summer weather.
Beads of sweat rested on his forehead. In a matter-of-fact
manner he walked up to Clifford and calmly said, "Well, I
guess we both know the rules." At that moment the sun hit
the metal places of his banjo. It glistened and was brilliant.
Clifford just stood there – the magic powers of the round
dance had put him into a stasis. Then Clifford looked
at his drum and the rest of the youth from the buffalo
bus were behind him with the exception of Arnie who
faithfully stayed in the bus. The rednecks and môniyâw
locals, including the original group of rednecks who had
been with Clive and the two or three folks who had been
watching from across the street. They gathered behind Billy
Bubba, and the duel began.

Clifford being the challenger, opened with his song:
"Tâpwê, tâpwê miywâsin
mêtoni, takahki-kîsikaw
mêtoni miywâsin
ta-ohci-nêhiyâwihk!"[142]

While he was singing the song, Clive the redneck starting
dancing pow wow. "What the is wrong with Clive?" said
one of the rednecks. "He is dancing pow wow!" At that
moment Clifford had to laugh. All he could think of now
was the way in which the red necks near this very site,
had yelled "Dance pow wow! Dance pow wow!" They had
yelled this to his father just down this very street. Down
yonder, Clifford thought, is the very place where my father
had tried to tell jokes, but the locals were not ready for

142   to be Cree

it. All that they wanted him to do was "Dance pow wow! Dance pow wow!" Clifford could hear their words clearly echoing through his mind as his father had told him this story over and over again and it seemed so vivid to him. Whenever Clifford thought of the story it was like a slow motion movie that would keep playing in his head over and over again. Now, he had to laugh. Now, it was a redneck himself, Clive, the redneck, who was dancing pow wow. He was dancing pow wow. He could not help but to dance pow wow.

Then it was the redneck's turn. Billy the redneck pulled out his banjo and all of the rednecks starting clapping and moving about like they were in a line dance. They all started clapping, and then Billy Bob started plucking with everything he was; everything that had mattered to him from the moment that he was conceived to the very moment that he plucked the strings of the banjo was manifested in that moment. His plucking of the strings was actually quite exquisite and made him feel as though his life had a great purpose. He plucked the strings of the banjo to play the song from "The Deliverance" sound track which was big in theatres that summer. When the redneck music was playing, Clive the redneck started to dance like a redneck. He started to move in such a way that the people around him recognized Clive. They started to do the square dance. They started to do the dosey–doe.

This went back and forth several times until finally one could say that the round dance was starting to get the edge over the square dance. Poor old Clive kept going back and forth between these two styles of dancing.

Then Clifford knew that he had to end it. He had to end the contest. He got his best song. The crowd waited in a hushed silence for what song that he could possibly choose. Then he started,

"Pahkwêsikan,[143] pahkwêsikan
gimme my gun,
pahkwêsikan, let's get this done
fool why did you bring
wonderbread to a pahkwêsikan fight.
I wonder, wonder
where's your head
Mr. Wonder Bread"

With that he put down his drum and clapped and said "ahâw" and the rednecks scattered. Everyone looked at Clifford for a bit, but they didn't say much. They just got back on the bus, and before too long the buffalo bus was on the way again.

---

143   bannock

AFTER ᐱᗑᑭᓂᔅ BECOMES A MAN

Mervin came again to the Senator at the kêhtê–ayakamik.[144] Clank, clank went the Senator's spoon on the side of the cup. "Nôsim," the Senator said, "I want to tell you about the time after ᐱᗑᑭᓂᔅ became a man."

After ᐱᗑᑭᓂᔅ became a man he was someone who loved to visit. He would visit everyone. One of the old mosôms was heard to say, "miywâsin ôma tâpiskôc ôki osk–ayâk ê–kî–wêpinahkik kiyôhkêwin.[145] Aya, moy awa." He became a favourite with the old people. He would plow the roads for old people, get water for them, take them to bingo and take them to town. He even took off for a spell of two weeks to go to Toronto to get them, those old ladies over der, to get them those fancy beads. He even got those really small shiny beads. Spending all of his time with the old ladies, he became a bit of an expert beader himself. In fact, he made a really realistic portrait of Elvis Aaron Presley. It was so vivid and realistic that people wondered if it was from another world; they wondered if it was another dimension. His high–quality beadwork added to his mythic aura.

It was said in quiet whispers that ᐱᗑᑭᓂᔅ could do things that other Indians could not do. There was much debate, in fact, as to whether or not he was actually even an Indian. Some people laughed at this talk, and then wondered what his origins really were. Others wondered what kind of power he possessed and they wondered if that power should in fact be feared.

Cash had been moving along quite well as Chief once the white paper was rejected. There was a lot of money that was flowing, and people like Cash were doing well from it. Ever since he got the grant for chicken, he was doing alright. He had Wrangler pants flown in from Calgary, he even had blueberries flown in from Quebec,

---

144   Old Folks home
145   "This is good because a lot of young people have seemingly thrown away visiting."

and he hired the ladies auxiliary to make pies and they would sell them to the tourists. There was really nothing that seemingly he couldn't do.

People are funny. Many times in many ways, there had been reports about the so-called Indian Problem and what could be done to help the problem of the Indians. Now, in the wake of the end of the 1960s, the hippie feel-good times in the days that followed Woodstock, a lot of old Indians started to believe, and their belief fuelled the energy of a lot of the young people. It was this feeling that really seemed to move them to action.

A lot of the old people were wondering why Cash never spent time with the old people anymore. "He is really pretending to be like a white person," they said, and some of them would say, "in the old days the people really stood beside their leaders." This is when the game started to get trickier. In the old days it was simple. The enemy was the Indian agent, but in this age, it was not really clear who the enemy was. While things were opening up, there was also a fuzziness, and a lack of clarity.

One day, which seemed like just any other day, ᐱᓄᑭᓂᕐ went to one of the old people's places. He was greeted with a warm smile and a warm cup of tea. He sat there with the old person and helped them translate a letter. He then told the old person that he would take them to town. While they were sitting there the old man started telling stories, which is something that old people were known to do.

"Tell me what you think. Do you think it is good when Indian people start to make our own money?"

ᐱᓄᑭᓂᕐ grabbed the cup and huddled, leaning into the table, and leaning into the words of the old man. He, ᐱᓄᑭᓂᕐ, was known for taking his time with his words, and would always think about what he was going to say before he would say it. That is one of the reasons why the old people liked him so much. He took his time with his words like an old person, like a buffalo chewing prairie grass slowly, not in a hurry to move, and not in a hurry to finish eating. That is how ᐱᓄᑭᓂᕐ talked and that is how he drank his tea. Tea was, as all of the old ones said, the backbone of storytelling. And the evaporated milk was like the fiddle music in the background. Just like you could have tea without putting in some evaporated milk, you could also have storytelling without fiddle music. Sure you could have it, but it wasn't the same.

"Nôsim," the old man said, "a lot of us old timers have been talking. In the kayâs ago days, the Cree people used to make a lot of money in the fur trade. Some of our mosôms could use one name at one post, and then use another name at another post. It is kind of like how some of those young people change their name to get Columbia House records."

"Aha," ᐱᓄᑭᓯᔅ said with great solemnity and ceremony.

ᐱᓄᑭᓯᔅ heard a lot of the old stories, and this old story rested deep in his bones. It was this story that he would wrap himself with in the spaces of his dreams.

"And then the Indian agent came along with the Indian Act, and the môniyâw really started to act up. There were lots of restrictions and it was hard to make a living. And then in more modern times, fellas like the Senator could really make a good living. But one thing that they always had when they were making this money was generosity. Sure those fellas made some serious money, but they would share it, like when someone wins at bingo, or has a good day out hunting, they share with everyone. The more you earned, the more you would share."

"Aha."

"You see, after Cash got this money with the Senator's help, he got rich, that Cash. But he didn't really share it with anyone. He left the Senator in the dust. A lot of us people, especially us older folks, don't think much of this."

"Aha."

"We realize that we need a leader who cares for the people." ᐱᓄᑭᓯᔅ made a point of looking down on the floor humble-like.

"We have been talking and we feel that you could

and should be our leader." With that, the clock seemed to tick louder and more slowly.

"Môya," ᐱᓄᑭᓯᐢ said, "niya piko oskinîkîs.[146] I don't know anything."

"We need you." With that, the ᐱᓄᑭᓯᐢ drifted into his mind and remembered different deeds and accomplishments. In his mind he saw all of the great things that Cree leaders had done in the past. All of their great speeches, all of their great triumphs, the swings of their war hammers in battle. All of them made his thoughts brittle and his bones dry, to the point where his being collapsed into these moments. He relived those moments, he became those moments, and he fell into a trance–like state.

"I need some of this bannock." He paused. "I can't live without this bannock."

The old man thought that this was a bit much, but said, "tâpwê, wîhkisin ôma."[147]

---

146   "I am just a younger person."
147   "Yes, it tastes good."

AFTER ᐱᓄᑭᓯᐤ BECOMES A MAN: PART TWO

ᐱᓄᑭᓯᐤ had really begun to change. At first, he seemed like a boy who was wide-eyed about the world, and all of the old people would gather around him, and try to pass on stories and knowledge to him. What they really seemed to like was the way in which he seemed to be able to pick up Cree so fast. Some of the others had been on the reserves all of their lives, and they didn't seem to know half of the words that he knew. He also had a gift for storytelling, and not just in its own right, but in the kind of storytelling where you would get things together, kind of like a puzzle. He was a puzzle storyteller maker.

The world changed one day. And, the events involved Cash and ᐱᓄᑭᓯᐤ. Cash had always been great amongst the old people. When he was younger, they would always give him candies at the rodeo, at a time when rodeos were bigger than pow wows. This was a weird period when Indian people were wearing cowboy hats and they had short hair. There weren't a lot of neechie cats who had long hair at that time. They also wanted to show those môniyâw punks that they were brave. Now that the old time horse raids were over, the best way for them to show that they were brave was to face a bull square in the arena.

Cash always seemed to take advantage of the kindness of old people. His grandmothers and grandfathers had been close to all of the old people. They knew their language. They knew their stories. And they knew their songs. There was a way that the old people talked. Cash got restless standing with them, and the older he got, the more he wanted to run instead of just standing; he wanted to run to pimpâhtâ, maybe even pimihââ. The old people had given him a place to stand but he wanted run.

The difference with ∧ᗡPᓀᒋ was that he came from a place of non-being, to a place of standing with the old people. It was that standing with them that seemed to make the connection with the old people even stronger. The old people liked that because they felt that he was standing with them, listening.

One time old Pâcinîs was wanting to go to town. He had just gotten his old age pension cheque: "tâpwê miywâsin ôma. kisêyiniwi–sôniyâwasinahikan."[148]

"Kitâpwân," itwêw the Senator.

"âya, ê–isi–nôhtê–pimâcihoyân ôtênâhk."[149]

"Môy, nikaskêyihtân ta–pamihcikêstamitân. nimihtâtên ôma. piko ka–atoskêyân âtawêwikamikohk. mihcêtawak pîwâpisk–astotimiwak ê–wî=pê–âtawêyân. misi–tourist–kinwiya–otâpânâsk."[150]

"Hâw mâka. Namôya nânitâw."[151]

They talked for a bit longer about life. They talked about what was happening off the reserve, and about what was happening happening in the country. In the not so long time ago past, the not so kayâs time ago, Pâcinîs had been involved in the League of Indians. Then life got hard for them when the clamp down by the Indian agents happened, and then everything changed for the worse. The war changed everything, and all of the ones who had persisted just kind of stopped what they had been doing. Once they had packed their stuff in for the war, they had put aside their ideas, put aside all of the movements, but they bundled them up for another time. It was like they put the kindling, the embers of that fire out for another time

---

148   This is truly good. The pension cheque."

149   And, I would like to town.

150   "I cannot drive for you. I regret this. I have to work in the store. There will be many Germans who will be coming to shop. They will come in the big tourist vehicle."

151   "Okay, then."

when the fire would come back. On the reserve, there were old people who put the fire deep within them and waited for the right time for someone to take that fire into the future.

Cash took a lot for granted. Cash was around all of those old stories and those old timers. He knew these stories and words, maybe not quite as well as the Senator, but he really did know the stories, and had he wanted to. He could have been one of the old men that they called upon to speak at gatherings and events. But Cash always had one eye to the future, looking to where his heart was.

It was one day when they were all going to town. Cash and ᐱᓄᑭᓯᐢ had been in the back of the truck with a couple of other young people. The old people used to try to coax them into the back of the truck by appealing to the young people but also by telling them that they were being traditional by sitting in the back of the truck. By doing so, they were like old time Indians riding horses, the wind in their hair, tousled, twisting in the air like moving baroque sculptures.

That day Cash and ᐱᓄᑭᓯᐢ sat up in the back. They were both wearing jeans and white T-shirts which seemed to be a rez uniform of sorts. Cash was standing up for a bit leaning against the cab of the truck, facing away from the direction of movement so that loose flies would not hit his face.

"So, hotshot," Cash paused and opened up his pack of Marlboro's and lit one up. "You think you are a real Indian now?"

"ê–nêhiyawêyân. nikiyokawâwak kêhtê–ayak. Kiya mâka? kiyotê,"[152] he paused.

"Tânisi ê–itêyihtaman ?"[153]

"Nimosôm," he said with sarcasm and he looked

---

152   "I speak Cree. I visit Elders. What about you?"
153   What do you think?

at him straight in the eye. Cash had always found it funny that môniyâw social workers and môniyâw interpreters, soothsayers of First Nations culture, had often proclaimed that neechies did not look at people in the eye.

Cash, in keeping with Cree custom, had to take his challenge, or he would be considered to be weak.

"Kîspin kinêhiyawân, môy ocihtaw ê– nêhiyâwiyin."[154] He paused, after making sure to take a tug on his cigarette, and then he smoked it to the bone before butting it on in the metal frame of the truck. Cash kept looking at him doing his best neechie James Dean, "kiya nêhiyawâhtik piko."[155]

---

154   "If you speak Cree, it is not because you are Cree."
155   "You are nothing but a Wooden–Indian."

AFTER ᐱᓄᕆᓯᑊ BECOMES A MAN: PART THREE

Cash was on another business trip, but he made
sure that the chicken and gravy kept being dished out.
Little kids dreamt rivers of Cash's Fried Chicken gravy. He
had been trying to convince Nadine to set up a bakery to
supply him a steady source of bannock. He thought that
would really push the chicken out into the white market,
but ol' Wally at the Department of Indian Affairs thought
the opposite. He said that the average whitey wouldn't
eat bannock – he said it had a weird sound to it. Cash had
appealed to him on the grounds that bannock would really
take off because bannock was from Europe, especially from
Scotland, so it should appeal to the average white person.
In the Indian Affairs board room, the debate went back
and forth like a quick pink pong game. Wally retorted that,
"Sure maybe kayâs ago it was from Scotland, but a lot has
changed since then." He slapped Cash hard on the back,
there were a couple of scotch on the rocks, and he said,
"Get your ass on that plane and hustle that chicken." Cash
was flying to California to try to set up a meeting with Cher.
They were going to try to get her to endorse Cash's Fried
Chicken.

While he was gone, the people were really talking
on the reserve. The old people were really talking about
how Cash never came to visit them anymore. They were
saddened by this, and they wondered what they could
do to try to bring him back to the fold. One old man
commented that Cash was like those buffalo bulls that
would hang out along the side of the herd, and not really
stand with the herd. Another old guy said, "What the heck
are you talking about, the buffalo are all gone."

Another person said, "In the old days our people

shared." The person was talking indirectly at first, how Cash was not sharing as much as he should. While Cash's Fried Chicken had not really broken into the môniyâw market, that was okay. The chicken, and the demand for it, was spreading across the prairies, and everyone seemed to want a piece of it.

One person got up and pulled his braids slowly in a dignified manner, and leaned back a bit, and said, "The chicken is our new buffalo!" With that, a series of "ahâw miywâsin ôma" were heard throughout the band hall. Many people got on their feet and cheered. Someone said, "That Cash is stealing from the people. We never stole from each other. We just shared."

Another man got up and said, "Cha. Quit lying. We used to steal horses from the Blackfoot all of the time." The people went back and forth with debating points about what was happening on the reserve. Finally, someone asked the Senator what he felt. At first he really didn't want to talk, but they really wanted to hear his advice. People always wanted to hear from the Senator, and they always welcomed his council. Someone reminded him that his name was actually the Senator. They reminded him that his name actually was one which demanded that he help his people. That his job was to give people advice, and that he was like a Senator to the people of the Roman Republic. He gathered his strength, gathered his voice, and gathered his sound.

"Neechies, countrymen, lend me your bannock." He paused. "Just jokes." Everyone laughed. Then, as Crees often do after telling a joke, often get tâpwê[156] solemn. He cleared his throat, and then began to do what Crees do best – orate.

"Mistahi ê–pîkiskwêtamohk. Mistahi

---

156   truly, very

niwîsakitêhtên, êkwa mistahi ê–pîkwêyihtamân ôma,
êkwa ê–itêyihtaman."[157] êwako ôma ê–mâmitonêyihtamân.

A younger person got up and spoke, "We are all
turning on each other because of Cash and chicken. Indian
Affairs is using their economic development money to
make us fight each other!"
The room became very quiet, and after the initial blast
of his words, the people started to nod, noting their
fundamental agreement with his words. And soon
there was a slow rumbling of voices, and eventually the
rumbling found form. They all wanted Cash out.

---

157   "There is a great deal of talking. I have a heavy heart,
and I am very worried. This is what I think."

FIRST SPEECH AS CHIEF

ᐱᓄᑭᓂᕁ had the crowd excited. The reserve had not seen so much excitement since Dr. Charging Horse had been to the reserve and given his great speech. It was interesting to think of all of the things that happened since he had left.

ᐱᓄᑭᓂᕁ slowly moved toward the front of the room. The whole crowd gravitated towards him like water moving along the bend of the hill. He pranced up to the stage. His flared cords, his wide lapels, and purple shirt. He had been reading one day in the pawn shop and he had grabbed a book on the history of the Roman Emperors.

After reading this book he was alarmed by the power that these old môniyâws had but at the same time he was intrigued by it. He was intrigued by the way in which they would move crowds, and by the way in which they would move around in the chariots. It was also a bit lost on him that only the emperor could wear purple. ᐱᓄᑭᓂᕁ had an old chuck wagon built as a Roman emperor chariot. Some people thought this was a bit crazy, but others thought that it was good to have a chief like him who was booked up in the head liked him. People admired his daring and they were waiting to follow him into the fray. He approached the podium and began to speak:

"My people, for too long our people have been in the kitchen of colonialism, and have been slowly rising. I say awas[158] to the Indian Act!" People cheered. "I say awas to the Indian agent." More people got up and cheered. "I say we rise up and quit being little Red awâsisak of the queen and start being awas–ers." One lady fainted as soon as he uttered these words.

"It is time we take control of our destiny. It is time that we quit dancing for Indian Affairs and just act like Indians and get our affairs in order." People were ecstatic. There had not been this much excitement since the days

---

158   "Go away!"

of jousting in the war years. "Kayâs aspin paskwâw-mostoswak kā–mîhcêticik."[159] One old lady wiped tears from her eyes. And to reach out to the younger people he shifted to English. "Young people, you make my heart soar like an eagle. You are like wind which helps me fly higher." He paused to focus his thoughts and words. "Like I said in Cree, we no longer have buffalo." He could see the way the young people looked at him while he spoke. Mâh–mahkicâpipayicik,[160] and he continued, "Now, my young people, you make us all so proud. The buffalo are not very numerous but, as you know, our chain of Chief's Fried Chicken has spread across this country. Today, we can say that chicken is new our buffalo."

---

159   "It has been a long time since the buffalo were many."
160   their eyes became very big

BANNOCK RISING

The time had come when ᐱᓄᑭᓯᐟ had become the Chief, and he was now the sole boss and driving force behind Chief's Fried Chicken. It was no longer known as Cash's Fried Chicken. He had given many people on the reserve jobs. He had even introduced the wîhtikow bucket. That was the bucket that had no limit – you could eat as much as you wanted. You just had to come to one of the outlets and bring the bucket and it would be filled with chicken.

ᐱᓄᑭᓯᐟ had used the money from the chicken to pave roads, to get old people walkers, and to buy the kids a bus for sports events. There would be few people at this time who would have had anything negative to say to him or about him. Those that did were quietly keeping their opinions to themselves – people like the Senator. He knew that the Chief was on the rise and he did not want to get in the way of that. He knew that people would not be open to what he had to say. Nor would they think that the Senator was being fair.

The first location of Chief's Fried Chicken had become a bit of tourist destination. There were shiny yellow canopies around the building. The yellow canopies caught and mirrored the glistening of the sun. In fact, the light of the sun made it look like there were several little suns on it. It was probably due to this light that so many people were drawn to it. Also, the success of Chief's Fried Chicken bought the people a measure of pride knowing that there was an idea from their reserve that had reached out from the small corners of the reserve and had made an impact throughout a wider world. Gone were the days of the pass system where people were controlled in terms of their travel. Now the Department of Indian Affairs actually encouraged them to go out in the world. They even gave grants of money to help people make more money.

The thing is that when the chicken store really

caught on it became a centring point, and indeed in time, it became a centre. People used it as a marker to get from one place to the next. For instance, if they were going to old Earl's place, they would say, "It is 2 miles west from the chicken–kamik." In fact, it became so central that people just started to call it the kamik. and they called the people who would frequent it the most as gammies. It got to the point that at times, band meetings were even held there, and people with very full faces and greasy lips, would smile, as Chief ᐱᓄᑭᓂ conducted business. There were, of course, some who questioned this. They wondered if it was ethical for the Chief to conduct community business at the "kamik," but others just hushed them up, and made a hand movement for the people to be quiet so that they could savour their chicken in peace. People like the Senator were amazed at what a powerful force the chicken was.

   With all of the changes, the Third Hand Pawn Shop kind of got left behind. This hit the Senator particularly hard. Not just in the pocket book but also just in terms of his spirits. The Senator's day old coffee in his little café could not compete with recently deep fried chicken. The mantra of the chicken store was "It is a good day to fry." For some reason the smell of deep fried chicken could be completely understood. "Why did the neechies go crazy for it?" That is something that the Senator could not completely understand. He could understand the ways in which people seemingly had given up the old ways in order to fit into the new way of life. The people no longer went into the bush as much as they used to. In fact, some of the old ways had been changed, but some of the old ways had also remained the same. For instance, young boys no longer hunted a moose and had a feast when they were roughly 13 like they used to. They never had the right of passage and were doomed to be boys forever. What happened to the Senator and Jingles at the zoo pretty much ended things – people didn't seem to want to take the old ways seriously anymore. They seemed to be happy to do things in a new way. They seemed all too easy to change. They seemed so willing to change the way that their ancestors had done things. They seemed so willing to be "modern Indians."

The Germans stopped coming to the Third Hand Pawn Shop and this was hard on the sôniyâw bottom line for the Senator. But he still had the Rabbit Root business, and to be honest that was really what was keeping him in business. The Germans were quick to change the focus of their attention. The Germans were quick to get pictures at the new chicken palace. There was a big chicken outside of the store. They claimed that it was the biggest chicken in the world. One old Cree from the area saw the chicken and thought it was sacred, because it was white, and he asked his grandson to pull over so that he could sing an honour song. The honour song that he had in mind was actually a Cash Williams classic. He thought it was a sacred albino chicken. He walked up to the albino statue and pulled down his cowboy hat, and put his hand on his heart, and closed his eyes, but just before he was about to sing, his grandson tapped him on the shoulder and told him that it wasn't an albino chicken, but just a regular chicken, and many of the chickens, though not all, were white. The old man reportedly replied with "kah." and lightly shook his head and walked away.

Another group of people who were called tîhtipowiyiniwak, the rolling people, or called "Holy Rollers" in English. They were led by a half Hutterite, half Cree man whose name was Zebediah. He was quite adamantly against the large chicken statue which was an idol, an idol that was leading people astray. He even went as far as to call the chief a Baalist and had openly called for the burning of the idol. Some people asked the chief why he just didn't press charges against him for saying these things. This was the most obvious course of action. ᐱᐳᑭᓓᓫ took the time to listen to them, he felt that he had to listen to them. This was a tricky one, because while Zebediah was half Hutterite, he still had strong ties to his other community. He was hard working, just like both of his peoples, and he had focus. It was this sort of focus that could cause a great deal of trouble for him. It was this sort of focus that could upset the balance of things for the chief. Without the Hutterite chicken, ᐱᔪᐱᓂᕝ would be in a very difficult position indeed. The Hutterite chicken had been the backbone of his growth, and indeed had been the backbone of his success. There would be no "Bannock rising" without it. Zebediah being the half breed cultural interloper was the bridge between the people and he was a bridge that was needed. ᐱᔪᐱᓂᕝ could not swim across the water of the cultures. He needed his bridge. So he couldn't really challenge him directly. He had to challenge him indirectly. He called a meeting.

BANNOCK RISING: PART TWO

Papoose Face stood by the chief, wearing his leather coat. Beside him Bannock Slap also stood – not really saying anything. He always wore sunglasses to the point where some people even wondered if he had eyes. There were rumours that he was the product of some awesome and crazy Indian Affairs experiment which was to give him super abilities – in fact they said that he had super seeing. But other people didn't say anything they just accepted his silence.

"The Hutterites are here." Cash nodded to Papoose Face in a matter of fact sort of way. Like he was Walter Cronkite reading the news. Papoose Face was his right hand man. Once Cash had been muscled out both Papoose Face and Bannock Slap took over. The trick of things was to not push too hard against the old people. There were a few of the older ones like the Senator who slowly were being pushed out the action and out of the loop. It was called the classical pull and hug move. He had done this so many times, bringing people close to him and then cutting them out that it become so common that no one even noticed it anymore. It was often coming when he would give someone the wîhtikow bucket pass. That in and of itself did not mean everything but at first when someone first had the wîhtikow bucket, they were giggly and happy. Usually people did not expect what would happen next. All of the things happened so fast, each in succession, that they never really saw it coming, even though all of the signs were there. It was the brutal efficiency of the way that he did it, the way ᐱᓄᐱᓂᕉ pushed people away was almost poetic. It was a combination of gentleness and brutality which gave him so much power.

Another thing that gave him so much power was that while he was pushing people on the outside he was also still sponsoring the weekly night of stories. This got all of the old people on the reserve together, and it also got the young people. Because of the extra Cree classes that he was also supporting people seemed to be more tolerant of what he was doing to shut people down.

The tricky thing about the Hutterites was that he could never offer to give them the wîhtikow bucket so that he could get on with the process of putting them on the outside. In a way, you could say that they were seemingly invincible.

They had the place determined where they were to meet. It was technically outside of the reserve limits. The Hutterites actually pulled up in a buggy and the Chief pulled up in his Black Lincoln. The buggy and the Lincoln moved closer and close together until they rested side by side. The Hutterite horse was lightly neighing.

The Chief rolled down his window, and the curtain of the buggy slowly moved to the side.

The Chief spoke, "You know that we need the chicken." He paused, "We need your chicken."

Zebediah kept looking forward without flinching. He just kept looking forward, waiting for more words from ᐱᔪᐱᓯᔅ. ᐱᔪᐱᓯᔅ, with his window open, cleared his throat, and continued, "Look Zebby, we know that with all of the parking lot hustling, at bingos, outside of stores, that you can never sell the amount of chicken that you can sell with me."

Zebediah kept staring forward almost in a trance like state. It was kind of spooky. But ᐱᔪᐱᓯᔅ kept talking for a bit, and then Zebediah finally interrupted him and said, "Ja, it is goot. It is miywâsin," he said with a Hutterite accent. "The chicken sales. It is sure bet," he paused for a bit though and said, "You know some of the Elders say that it is changing us. They say that it is making the young people lazy."

ᐱᔪᐱᓯᔅ looked at him nervously and asked him in a hunkered down and hushed tone, "do you mean Elders from the reserve?"

"No. No," said Zebby. He said it in a dismissive

tone. "That part of the engine is more your business than mine." This time Zebediah actually got somewhat emphatic and started to wave his hands around. "No, you fool. I mean the Elders of the colony. They say by selling all of our chicken to you, that it is making our young people weak. It is as though they no longer know how to sell and hustle anymore. We get the big cheque from you, and then that is that. It is as though they don't don't know how to sell do anything. They have forgotten to dig deep into themselves to try and sell something."

ᐱᐅᐱᓈᐟ, always the orator, and always the one who would try to find a way to spin things to his favour, said, "Zebby, cihpîsis. Don't get mad. Moy gootwâsin ôma." He smiled, lit a smoke, and gave it a tug. "Look, your people, or at least your mom's people, are some of the hardest working people I know. You guys keep working and working and work together. Mâmawi–atoskâtamahk tâpiskoc kayâs ago nêhiyawak." Just like the Crees of old."

Zebediah started to move his head in agreement but he continued to look straight ahead. "Why thank you ᐱᐅᐱᓈᐟ. It means a lot to hear you say that."

ᐱᐅᐱᓈᐟ then went on to say how he envisioned getting some of the Hutterite lads truck driving training so that they could drive the big trucks to deliver Chief Fried Chicken. They were in the process of setting up shop in the United Sates. People there as well as in Germany were so hungry for Indian culture that they seemed to crave whatever ᐱᐅᐱᓈᐟ was hustling. He was hustling a Native American experience so he hired flute players to play live, especially on days like Valentines Day and cheque day, to try to create the right ambience. This had seemingly had found the mark. ᐱᐅᐱᓈᐟ had been piloting two stores in The Bay area. These had done very well. The locals loved his chicken, and having a Native American experience, but they also were inspired by the fact that the chicken was considered to be organic and free of chemicals. The hippie market was huge in The Bay area. They just couldn't seemingly get enough of it.

In what perhaps was his most interesting move yet, he thought of another market. He had been the master of getting the locals to like his stuff, and had a good stretch of stores across Saskatchewan, Alberta and southern Manitoba, but perhaps his greatest feat yet was his penetrating the high end market in the financial district in New York City. Instead of using Hutterite chickens here, he used pihêwak, prairie chickens, right from the bush. On the mugs, it said that the meat had been compassionately hunted by real Cree Indians of Saskatchewan. The patron not only received an embossed leather book in Cree syllabics which was called "The Ballad of ᐱᔪᐱᓯᐢ," but they also received an 8–track recording of it. ᐱᔪᐱᓯᐢ had hired some of the local round dance singers to sing a ballad for him. Not only did the book have that ballad on 8–track, but it also had glossy pictures of the men and women who had been hired to hunt the chicken. These hunters had become minor stars and celebrities and this fame had further dampened any criticism. These hunters were invited to come to dance at Studio 54. Rumour had it that one of them had even been flown to New York for a Village People concert. He stood in for the Indian who had developed a throat infection. It was hard for anyone to take down the chief when he was making some of them rock stars. There were still a few people like the Senator who stood in his way but these voices were slowly getting muted over time. The Senator thought that maybe he might be exempt from the wîhtikow bucket take down because he was the one who had put the last Indian element on ᐱᔪᐱᓯᐢ when he was still in wooden form. He also had thought that perhaps because he had been like an uncle to ᐱᔪᐱᓯᐢ that ᐱᔪᐱᓯᐢ might let him off.

CHIGGEN: THE NEW BUFFALO

The rapid rise of ᐱᑭᕐᑐᐦ's power was quite startling to the people. They could not believe how quickly the bannock of his personality had risen. Things had changed a lot in recent times. The Chief had broken the game wide open. He threatened the established order of Indian Affairs and the established system of the Indian Act.

Cash had only taken things so far. His family had worked hard to get along with the various string of Indian agents who had worked on the Broken Elbow reserve. Because of that Cash's family was never poor and they had always had enough to eat. They had gone along with the system and had tried to get benefits form the system. They had had one thing going for them. They were fair-skinned Indians and that had been a sort of passport into the world of the môniyâw. They played the hard line Treaty position at times but then they played the happy-go-lucky fort Indian line when that suited their interests. They seemed to be always playing things on both sides. They had played this well over the years. But the ends of the game that they had been playing just seemed to get tighter. It got so tight that the string that had been holding everything together just sort of snapped.

The Chief's Fried Chicken empire moved from being a localized phenomenon to becoming more of a regional phenomenon and this made the boys at Indian Affairs very pleased and very happy. The Wahwâ-man had even gotten a promotion out of the whole thing somehow and in the hustle and bustle of it all his study on rez dogs was put to the other side.

Then one day, ᐱᑭᕐᑐᐦ just walked right into the office of Indian Affairs – the district office of Barney and said, "We don't need your money, or your goddamn grants." He ripped up the agreement that he had with the Department, and threw it on the ground. This made him wildly popular with the people especially with the older people who had lived so much under the rule of the Indian Act. Cash, they said, had been a good Chief but he was too much of the same old, same old. He could get money from the Department but ultimately he was still under the control of Indian Affairs. Now, Cash was pushing Chief's Fried Chicken, and they were pushing it hard and fast. People were proclaiming 'Chicken is our new buffalo." People put the saying on bumper stickers. They even put it on T-shirts. The neechies needed a rock star with hustle, and the hustle is what seemed to spark it.

With the expansion of Chief's Fried Chicken, ᐱᑯᐸᓂ had had a sit down with some of the Hutterite family heads and secure a good solid chicken supply for years to come – he even helped them expand some of their operations. He was hiring truck drivers. He was hiring people to make the bannock that would go along with meals: all of the bannock making was done under the guidance of Nadine's ohkoma, who prepared kits with the help of people that they trusted and then these kits were sent out to all of the branches. Then the cooks would just put them in the oven and fire them up. The fresh bannock was then included in the extended family meals. Everyone seemed to love this bannock and one could say that the bannock had played a key role in the expansion of the chicken.

Nadine's ohkoma was willing to help because she saw it as trying to help her granddaughter to travel. It helped her fly out to Europe where she toured the book and literature festival circuit. She had a new book out that had been received with great critical success, but moneywise – that was something that Nadine would have to wait for. She was hoping that she would be able to make more money down the line so that her ohkoma would not have to work so hard making bannock.

ᐱᑯᐸᓂ had attracted people around him, not only because of his ideology, but also because of the simple fact that he had money. He was flush with money. The kind of money that neechies just weren't use to. The kind of money that could get things going, the kind of money that could get the job done.

There were two men in particular that gravitated toward ᐱᓄᐱᓂᑊ. One was Papoose Face and the other was Bannock Slap. Papoose Face was from a nearby reserve. He had chubby cheeks and had a high pitched voice and was quite dark. He did not say much. Papoose Face was not really tall, but tall enough. The thing that made him stand out was the fact that he had very broad shoulders and a very hefty build. Bannock Slap had been in the army, and was tall – he was about 6' 2". He had a good build on him. He was cocky and he often chewed gum. He liked to taunt and tease people. He was noted for the bannock slap that he could deliver. Both of these men wore black suits and both always had thin, black ties and black sunglasses. They both had neechie mullets and they would say, "All business in the front and all fun in the back." People started to refer to them as the neechie mafia.

Wherever ᐱᓄᐱᓂᑊ was, Papoose Face and Bannock Slap were there too. They were his left hand and his right hand men. If you wanted to talk to ᐱᓄᐱᓂᑊ, you had to get through these two. Since Papoose Face did not say much, people usually had to go through Bannock Slap. If Bannock Slap didn't like what you said, or if he thought you had been disrespectful to his boss, then he would bannock slap you. He was from the Broken Elbow reserve and was Napoleon's nephew.

JINGLES GOES TO THE BUSH
AND BECOMES A HUNTER

Cash's, son, Jingles, was charismatic and good looking, but retreated to the bush once his father lost power. He became content in the bush, but he was genuinely saddened by his father's misfortune.

The neechie hustle had made him tired. He was tired of his father talking about tradition and then on the other hand filling his pockets with sôniyâw.[161] It caused him to retreat into himself more and more and he consistently turned down various opportunities that his father presented to him.

Kihci Lars was taller than many on the reserve. Kihci Lars was afforded a great deal of respect. He was 6'4", and had a beard that was mostly brown, but as it grew out often had red and blonde in it. He was ½ Cree and ½ Swedish. He would wander the forest wearing his buffalo robe, and sometimes he would wander the roads of the reserve. He would pause in his wanderings, hold his staff, and look out into the horizon. The nêhiyawak in the area felt comfortable with him. He spoke Cree but also kept aloof of the reserve to some extent. He had often taken young men into the bush to take them on their first moose hunt. He also had often officiated over the first moose feast. But not so many young men observed the moose hunt now. It was rumoured that Kihci Lars sometimes sacrificed moose to honour Odin.

The Senator would sometimes hire Lars to hang out at the Third Hand Pawn Shop. Some of the Germans were fascinated by him, but others would point at him, and would say, "Nein, er ist nicht ein wirklich indianier."[162] Other times German families would bring their children to see Lars and his great feats of strength. They would say,

---

161   money
162   "No, he is not a real Indian."

"Ihn sehen, kinder. Ein Indianer kennt keinen Schmerz."[163] Kihci Lars had even created a wooden teepee that Mattias Sjöberg from Ikea reportedly had offered to buy from him.

The cabin of Kihci Lars was located in the bush north of the reserve. It was part of the reserve that edged the rivers. It was to this cabin, and to the sanctuary of the bush, that Cash retreated to in order to find peace and balance.

Jingles remembered the conversation he had with Lars when he first went to the bush north of the reserve.

Lars approach him with a warm smile, stood outside of his cabin, leaned into his staff and said, "tawâw."[164]

Jingles answered him, "kinanâskomitin."[165] He paused for a bit. "I want to get away from the reserve. There is really not much for me there."

Kihci Lars answered and said, "The bush is where you can still be an old Cree. Aya, how do you feel about your dad not being Chief anymore?"

Jingles lifted his eyebrows, shrugged his shoulders, and sighed. "Well, chiefs come and go. People seem to want the chicken more than anything. It is good for people. People are getting jobs, but ..."

Lars smiled and put his hands through his beard, "Yes, kitâpwân.[166] People seem to have lost focus."

"My dad did lots of good things, but he forgot lots of practical things. Like flooded reserve roads, and the needs of our rez dogs and so on. He just got so focused on the chicken," Jingles said with resignation.

There was a rumour that there was gold in the bush around, but no one really pursued it because it was purported that the Senator had proof that the Broken Elbow reserve had a claim over the bush stashed in one

---

163   "An Indian knows no pain."

164   "Welcome."

165   "I thank you."

166   "You speak the truth."

of his old books. The rumour had been enough to prevent various companies from wanting to lay claim to the area. They were content to try to wait until the day came when perhaps the Senator would pass on and his knowledge of this old claim would pass along with him. Some of the big companies, they said, were waiting until this happened and they could then move in. They thought that if they pushed the issue now, it might cause the Senator to spread his knowledge. It was reported by some that the president of one of these companies passed a silver briefcase to ᐧᒪᑯᐧᓐ to keep it quiet. They said it was this money that allowed Chief's Fried Chicken to expand into the United States.

But waiting for someone to die could be a very long waiting game. A game that could get old, while waiting bodies became waiting bodies riddled with arthritis. It was a waiting game that very few were prepared to try to beat the Senator at. It was the existence of these alleged papers, and the alleged existence of a map that some say had prompted the Department of Indian Affairs to give the Senator a grant. This grant allowed him to open his pawn shop. The Senator never said either way whether he did have the map and the other papers but had on a few occasions used the possible existence of these things to get leverage in various situations.

The existence and power of these "possible" documents had accumulated in the area so much that it had become a bit of a legend amongst both the neechie and môniyâw[167] folk. That was one thing that could not be denied – there was no shortage of these legends. The earth of the territory was so full of stories and storied song that one could say that Kihci Lars had become part of this storied landscape.

It was the place in the bush where Jingles had retreated to once his father had lost the election to ᐧᒪᑯᐧᓐ. It was where Jingles thought he would try to find

167   white person

himself again. It was in the deep bush, under the guidance of Lars, that Jingles had hoped to find his centre again. Away from the distractions of the reserve, away from the distractions of the fried chicken and away from the love of money and power. Jingles emptied his mind, which had been full of all of these distractions, and pursued the life of the bush. He became a very good hunter. The people spoke with admiration about how he had learned to make his own bow and arrow fashioned of chokecherry wood. They said that he was becoming skilled at hunting and that he loved the life so much, and was so happy to be away from the spotlight that his father had created, that there would probably be nothing that could ever pull him out of the bush. The Germans who had come to the Senator's shop so often in the past, came sometimes in small guided tours to meet this legendary hunter.

ᐱᗜᑭᓀᑊ'S SPEECH TO EXPAND THE CHICKEN EMPIRE

It was during his time in the bush, when ᐱᗜᑭᓀᑊ really began to expand the chicken empire. More and more chains were being created all over. There was even talk of a chain being created in Europe – in Germany. ᐱᗜᑭᓀᑊ was really pushing hard to develop the chain. Ever since ᐱᗜᑭᓀᑊ had taken human form, he seemed to be a neechie emperor, a man driven by great ambition. This ambition was not only to prove that he was a great leader but also that he was from a great people – namely the Crees.

The word was that he was expanding to upscale markets, not only in Europe but also to large cities in the United States starting in the Northeast portion of the United States – especially in New York City with all of the splendour of the Manhattan skyline.

The people of the reserve were having their pictures taken by some very flashy cameramen. The rumours abounded that these men were doing some special shoots for the Western Producer. Everyone was excited by the attention that the cameras were giving them.

The people were talking about the excitement that was being generated by the song that ᐱᗜᑭᓀᑊ had on the hit parade. It was called "Neechie Hustle," an instant disco classic. Not only was he a leader, but he was also a DJ. Rolling Stone magazine had ᐱᗜᑭᓀᑊ on the cover. He had braids, and looked terribly handsome. He got so much fan mail that he had to hire two summer students to answer it.

ᐱᗜᑭᓀᑊ was hatching a scheme to expand Chief's Fried Chicken. He hinted at the expansion in the Rolling Stone article, but knew that he couldn't let the lynx out of the bag just yet. He hustled the hustle but needed time to fill it in and shape it. That is why he was going to the bush—to get away for a few days. He didn't have that luxury but he was going to make the time.

He told Bannock Slap and Papoose Face that he was going to take a few days off. He told Chiboy, his most trusted assistant, to settle in and saddle in, and that he would have to hold down the fort for a bit. Then he got ready to go to the bush. ᐧᓄᑭᓀᕽ had become so flashy that even his horse had beadwork. He had commissioned the finest beaders north of the Rio Grande River. The cut glass beads caught the light from the sun, and cast them in patterns of light and shadow on the shiny surface of the horse's hair. The horse was tied up in front of the band office. There were several little picnic tables with umbrellas whose poles stood up, and could be unfolded to provide cover on rainy prairie days. It was at those picnic tables, and indeed sometimes under the umbrellas, that ᐧᓄᑭᓀᕽ took a page from the playbook of John Dief the Chief. He tried to spend time with the people. He tried to keep the channels open with the people. He took the idea of the Indian agent and tried to turn it upside down. He wanted to be the anti–Indian agent.

On these sunny, early spring days, he had several people gathered around him. They had filled the chairs of the picnic tables. The main deep fryer cat was there handing out chicken to everyone who was sitting at the tables. Two of the people had copies of the Rolling Stone for him to sign. There were a few people who were also there, sitting in cars. He knew that the people had been really impacted by Dr. Charging Horse. The acceptance of Dr. Charging Horse was all the more exceptional, not only because his first name was Lester, but also because he was a Blackfoot whose ancestors had been rivals of the Cree ancestors. Because he had been able to cross this boundary so fluidly, it brought home to ᐧᓄᑭᓀᕽ that he could cross the boundaries between being a wooden Indian, becoming an Indian, and then becoming the Chief. He also hoped that by bridging the boundary of the known reserve into the territory of the bush, often called no man's land, that he would be crossing the borders of the unexpected yet again. It was only by crossing these borders that the Cree people could hope to find their rightful place in history.

As the people had gathered around him, they were genuinely excited by his leadership, and wanted to spend time with him. The people gathered around the picnic tables were like a living, breathing collective organic newspaper.

"Chief," said one of the locals, "what was it like being a nêhiyawâhtik?"[168] Someone else said, "Sssh. You should not ask him about that."

ᐱᓄᖃᖓᕆ smiled and looked around. He could see that despite the fact that the people were genuinely interested, they were afraid to ask. They had held back out of fear or a certain respect for the Chief—it was not known which. That was the thing about ᐱᓄᖃᖓᕆ. The people followed him not because they were scared of him but because they genuinely respected him. In the older times, people followed the Indian agent not out of respect but because they were scared. Of course the Indian agent would throw the people little trinkets for following him. That is how ᐱᓄᖃᖓᕆ was different. He did not give people trinkets – he gave them grand and lavish prizes, or gifts, whichever way one wanted to say it.

"My people, fellow band members," ᐱᓄᖃᖓᕆ itêw. He saw flashes in his mind of those times when he felt claustrophobic in his wooden form, but over the time he had learned to still his mind. "I know that you are all very curious about my time as a wooden Indian." Some people looked away when he said this because they did not want to seem too eager to look. Even though they wanted to know, they did not want to be seen to be too eager. "The time when I was a Wooden–Indian was like when a butterfly is waiting to be born. The world outside is muffled to some extent. The outside world is a blanket of unfinished whispers. The sound is scattered and unformed." He

---

168   wooden Indian

paused, and put on his glasses for dramatic effect. "Then there was a brilliant flash of light which radiated not only from my mind, but also as I have been told, radiated in all of the land around." Everyone looked at him now, their eyes wide – even those who had previously averted their gaze. They wanted to know very much what he had to say. "Then I came into my body. I came into my flesh and I felt the warmth and saw fully formed images for the first time." With that everyone said, "ahâw."

A few speakers got up and spoke, "Okimâw, mêtoni kinanâskomitinân, Mêtoni ê–kî–wîcihiyahk. Piyisk niya êkwa niwâhkomâkanak ê–sôniyâhkêcik."[169]

Another one got up and spoke, and thanked the Chief for helping him find work, for creating business opportunities on the reserve, and through the enterprise of the Band. "I will never have to work for Indian Affairs ever again." With each part of the story, ᐱᓯᒼᐤ would make the classical Cree sound of "mmmh." Which acknowledged that he had heard their words.

ᐱᓯᒼᐤ told them that they were expanding Chief's Fried Chicken to New York City, and that they were going to sell chicken at upscale restaurants. But it was not going to be the chicken that they had bought from the Hutterites. No, it was going to be wild prairie chickens hunted by Cree Indian hunters. He showed them a mock up of the embossed book cover and flipped through the pages. Everyone was excited about it. He asked who supported him and they all yelled back in unison "niya." It was the populism that fuelled him but then he had them express their views in case anyone ever asked about the legality of what he was doing. He had been advised by his assistant, Chiboy, that legally it was like having a band meeting.

ᐱᓯᒼᐤ told them that he was going on a journey, that he was going to the north side of the reserve. He was going to go into the bush country.

169   "Chief, we truly thank you. Truly, you have helped us. Finally our relatives are making money."

"You are going to see that crazy Kihci Lars," one said.

"I am going to visit Kihci Lars, but I want to visit Jingles too."

"Tânêhki ê–nôhtê–kiyokawat okosisa Cash?"[170] the one said.

"Mahti pâkitinihk,"[171] another said.

"My people," he said, "I know that some may wonder why I will visit him. Why would I visit the son of my former rival?"

With that some people said, "Tâpwê. Why do you want to?"

"Yes, he is the son of Cash, my rival, but he does have strong skills of his own." He paused briefly, "Remember I am only your chief as long as you want me to be. I want everyone on the reserve to be as strong as possible as a group. I want our reserve to be something that we can all be proud of." While he was talking, Bannock Slap and Papoose Face stood by him with their arms crossed. They had their long hair tied tight in braids, and their sun–glasses covered their eyes and emotions.

"I want Jingles on board. I want to take him with me to New York. I want him to be the poster boy for our launch over there. The bottom line is that Lars looks too môniyâw. The people want a real neechie to buy chicken from. A môniyâw looking fella won't be able to sell the chicken."

One of Cash's friends from childhood said, "That is bullshit, and you know it. Colonel Sanders is a môniyâw, and he sells chicken!"

That was the first time since Cash left that someone had openly challenged ᐱᓓᐯᐅᐨ. After he said that, a complete and utter silence spread across the gathered group. Cash's friend pushed his way to the front and said, "Yeah, that is right, 'Chief'." He said Chief with sarcasm. "You are some piece of work. You are a wooden Indian and

---

170   "Why do you want to visit the son of Cash?"

171   "Please let it go with him."

you should not even have status – let alone Treaty rights."
Two other people in the growing crowd shouted out their
agreement but other people in the crowd also voiced their
support for ∧ᗺᑭᓓᓂᐣ. A couple of little fights broke out.
Some of the pushing led up to ∧ᗺᑭᓓᓂᐣ and with that
Bannock Slap did what he did best, he bannock slapped
one person, who got too close, and Papoose Face put
someone else in a headlock.

"My people," ∧ᗺᑭᓓᓂᐣ said, "let us not fight each
other but let us fight the limitations and the shackles of
the Indian Act." Some people applauded but many seemed
unsettled. They were unsettled by the minor display of
violence by ∧ᗺᑭᓓᓂᐣ's associates. After the meeting,
people slowly went their own ways and there was some
general talk about his plan and how Jingles was going
to be the poster boy for the new launch of the upscale
chicken. Many of the people spoke about how they thought
that this was a good idea, but some people just walked
away without really saying anything. Whatever the case,
∧ᗺᑭᓓᓂᐣ knew that he had to head to the bush. He needed
Jingles to be his poster boy for the expansion of the chicken
empire.

GETTING JINGLES ON BOARD

ᐱᓲᐯᓯᐟ rode his horse towards the stretch of the reserve. At first his ride was smooth, the horse moved at a steady pace. As he trotted on he stopped at a few people's houses for tea. They would invite him with great solemnity and with great ceremony. He drank Red Rose tea and was very happy with the support that he had from his people. As he travelled northward in the reserve, he was welcomed in homes, and asked to spend time with kids to tell them stories, and speak Old Cree.

As he continued on his horse, he felt the weariness of his horse and paused at the end of the reserve. He leaned down heavy, arching his back, with his head down. One of the Germans named Helmut who was a frequent shopper at the Third Hand Pawn Shop, took a few photos of this position and made some posters of it, and sold them at his Butcher shop in Dusseldörf. Another Deutscher saw this poster, and started to sell stylized images of it, and before you knew it, he was all over the place – the ᐱᓲᐯᓯᐟ, that is. Then before you knew it, it became an iconic image and some described as the "end of the trail." Then as the image spread throughout the world, every second Indian claimed that the Indian in the picture was their mosôm at the end of this or that battle.

One would think that a leader such as ᐱᓲᐯᓯᐟ would welcome such a thing and perhaps that they would indeed embrace it themselves. It was true that at this critical phase in the story ᐱᓲᐯᓯᐟ had not been consumed by his own ego. Even at this stage he was grateful to be in human form. He still had those claustrophobic flashbacks of being a wooden Indian, trapped in the wooden form. But as long as he had access to the four primordial neechie elements: KFC gravy, tears of a midnight bingo caller, chokecherry wine cured under a full moon, and bannock from the original recipe, he could maintain his human form.

As he entered the bush he could hear the flutter of various animals. He could see where the light of the sun broke the canopy of the trees and lit up the floor of the bush. He rode the morning into the afternoon and the evening until he finally reached the place close to where Jingles was camped.

He could see the flame of his fire licking the space of air around. He could see Jingles poking in the fire. He could see what he thought appeared to be a pot of tea brewing over the fire.

Jingles was really never much for pow wow dancing. In that way he was like Buddy Bradley. He did not want to be defined by the narrow stretch of small slender boxes which made people feel comfortable. He often got bored at pow wows and would cruise around and check out the various vendors. There was nothing like checking out vendors first hand at a Pow wow. It was like having a living Sears Wish Book right in front of you. And to top it off you have some healthy French Fries bathed and soaked in crazy gravy. Years later, Starbuck Indians would be appalled by such culinary choices. But, in fairness, the game back then was different. People were just happy to eat something besides moose meat.

Jingles did not want to be a pow wow dancer as his mosôm had wanted him to be. He had always imagined that maybe some day he could be a dancer on the TV show Solid Gold. He dreamed of being one of the solid gold dancers. Jingles found some of the self–congratulatory machismo swagger of the older Crees to be somewhat tiresome. He was interested in a bigger world.

By the light of the fire, he sketched his ideas. He had often imagined that he could open a disco in the middle of the bush. He had approached his dad Cash, but his dad laughed off the idea. His dream was to get everyone from the pow wow trail under the brilliant disco ball. He had also sketched platform moccasins that would have little minnows from the Saskatchewan River swimming in them. People could see them through the open glass. He even imagined some day that he would go to some grand disco and ride in on a horse with flashing lights on the sides of the horse.

As ᐱᓄᐳᓂᐤ slowly approached Jingles, he could hear Jingles humming a song. ᐱᓄᐳᓂᐤ recognized a distant disco beat in it. The song was ᐱᓄᐳᓂᐤ's song "Neechie Hustle" and he could see Jingles do a bit of dance. Some fancy footwork to be sure. It was not like anything that he had seen before. The dance moves looked like he as making bannock or something. It was intense footwork.

ᐱᓄᐳᓂᐤ approached and called out. While they were at the bush it may have seemed a bit strange perhaps for him to knock on some door that perhaps did not exist. Instead the bush call out was perhaps the best way to get someone's attention.

"Tânisi," ᐱᓄᐳᓂᐤ said. At first, it was as if he did not hear him because he was so into his song. But the horse of ᐱᓄᐳᓂᐤ neighed and moved his head and his body to greet the presence of Jingles. Jingles slowly stopped what he was doing and smiled a bit. He had to squint because he had lost his Indian Affairs glasses somewhere in the bush and would have to go to the city to get another pair of glasses.

"Tânisi nisîmis,"[172] itêw .

"Tânisi okimâhkan,"[173] replied Jingles.

Jingles paused for a moment but he did not feel a need to talk about the ousting of his father and the way that his father had lost the election. Rather he was happy to just sit by the fire, sketching and imagining what disco could be.

"Well, my friend, the chicken sales are doing very well."

"Yeah, Kihci Lars told me that the sales are really

---

172   "Hello younger sibling."

173   "Thank you Chief."

expanding."

"You know my boy," ᐱᔪᐯᑊ said, "They have been very good indeed."

"That is good," he paused. "Are you still getting the chicken from the Hutterites?"

"Yes we are my boy."

"You know, Chief," he said, "I have to confess that I really like it here in the bush. I like it away from everything."

"Mitoni miywâsin ôma my boy."[174]

"But I have been thinking that it may be time to leave the bush now." Jingles was sketching again.

One could undoubtedly ask why ᐱᔪᐯᑊ himself did not become the poster fella for the chicken. The reason was quite straight forward. He could not take the time off to go to New York.

The light of the fire continued to move around, continued to shimmer in the bright spaces around them.

ᐱᔪᐯᑊ began to ask Jingles more questions. This time about dancing. "Kitakahkêyihtên cî ê–pwâtisimoyin?"[175]

Jingles shook his head slightly and said, "môy mistahi. Mihcêtawak takahkêyihtamok ôma, aya môy niya. Aya, nitakahkêyihtên ê–nito–wâpahtamân êkota, apisîs, aya môy kinwês."[176]

ᐱᔪᐯᑊ smiled and said, "I heard though that you like to dance, I heard from a lot of the old people that you really like to dance."

"Yes, that is true and that is one of the things that I miss the most in the bush. Sure, Kihci Lars likes to get drunk sometimes on le pôkêt and pull out his fiddle and dance around but that still is not really the kind of dancing that I want to do. It is not really the kind of dancing that

174   "That is truly good my boy."

175   "Do you like to pow wow dance?"

176   "Not much. They are many who like it, but not me. But I like to watch it a little, but not for long."

interests me," Jingles said.

ᐱᓄᑭᓯᐧ looked at him with great interest. "Well, you are hunting a lot. I heard that you are getting quite good at it."

"Yes, I am. I like going out in the heavy bush," Jingles said.

ᐱᓄᑭᓯᐧ knew that he had an opening that he could move into. "What would you say if I tell you I have an idea of how you could do both."

"Hmm..." Jingles paused for a moment, and then grabbed his sketch book. He started move his pencil around the surface of the sketchbook. ᐱᓄᑭᓯᐧ moved a bit closer to Jingles and asked if he could take a look.

"Sure," said Jingles.

ᐱᓄᑭᓯᐧ looked at the sketches, "Seems like you really have some great ideas for disco."

Jingles put down his sketching pencil and shared his joy of disco, "Yes, I really like your song called the Neechie Hustle."

"I heard it playing as I was coming close."

"My dream would be to dance in a real discotheque and to ride in on a horse with disco lights on the side. Dismount and then show off my platform moccasins."

ᐱᓄᑭᓯᐧ replied, "Let's do it."

"What do you mean?"

The pitch of ᐱᓄᑭᓯᐧ's voice went up, and his excitement and eyes seemed to draw Jingles in, "I want to pay you for designs and have you help launch a new upscale form of Chief's Fried Chicken in New York City."

"Wahwâ," Jingles almost sang this.

The Chief could hardly contain his excitement, "And the launch will be at Studio 54."

Jingles answered, "I am in!"

NEECHIE HUSTLE

The Cree hunter, Jingles, had been asked to go to New York with the Chief. They had planned to have the big launch of the upscale form of Chief's Fried Chicken. It was going to be made with wild prairie chickens and sold with corresponding embossed books which celebrated the life and lifestyles of the authentic Cree hunters. People like Jingles loved this pitch and believed that they were going to take New York by storm. They had been penned up for so long, and now all of their energy was about to explode onto the world scene. The time of the Indian Act was over, it was time for Indians to start acting out their neechery. It was time for neechie hustle.

They had met happily in front of the Chief's house. ᐱᐅᐯᓯᐣ had agreed to drive Jingles to the airport. He was going to borrow the school bus. They hoped against hope that the bus could make it to the airport despite the many miles that had already been put on the engine. The Chief had temporarily extended his lines of cash and credit for the expansion and launch so the bus would have to do. The chief had promised the school a new one, once the deal in New York was sealed.

They got to the airport and were about to take off on the plane, and Jingles said that he was going to get militant and tell the people at the border that they were agents working for the man. He had his obligatory red bandana on, his obligatory militant regalia. He also had his choker with the seemingly obligatory turquoise elements. He had bought it once when he was in New Mexico during a conference. He was one of those Indians that was always going to a conference. The other neechies around him always teased him about being all "conferenced up." Some neechies were booked up, some were smudged up, but this neechie was "conferenced up." Every neechie worth the grease in the bannock of their being had a bit of the neechie hustle.

The original neechie hustle started with the Wahwâ–man himself. They say that his hustle was so grand that no one could stop him, that he was an invisible tidal wave of funk. The old ones even said that he had invented disco when he put the little blinds on the ducks – but that is another story for the winter months.

As Jingles approached the limo that ᐱᓄᐯᓲᕆᐣ had hired for him, he got increasingly nervous. On one hand, he was filled with a great deal of self–doubt. On the other hand, he was grateful that he was away from the ugly racism of Saskatchewan. He remembered when he would go to town and the way people would look at him when he would enter a café. All of the heads of the people would turn to him, like the heads of sunflower plants as the daylight entered the long and full prairie fields. Now he wondered what it would be like when he entered this disco place, this famous nightclub. He used to laugh about how people would talk, well the older folk anyway, about the bands that play at the bars. They would call them orchestras. The word "orchestra" made their musical enterprise sound so magical and mystical. That is exactly the kind of place that Studio 54 sounded like. And it was exactly what ᐱᓄᐯᓲᕆᐣ was. He was a magic man, like the Wahwâ–man, and indeed he made people feel magical. That was just the kind of guy that ᐱᓄᐯᓲᕆᐣ was. He could walk into a room and change everything. That is why so many people like Jingles gravitated towards him – he was kicking the man in the pants, and the younger people of the reserve, propelled by the stories of the Older People, were realizing that not only was "the man" they were fighting not just in the world, but the man had tented inside of their minds and their souls and indeed in their hearts.

The limo driver had been told by the people at Studio 54 where to take Jingles. The limo driver was seemingly bored and intrigued at the same time by Jingles in his get up with his big headdress. The limo driver told Jingles that he was actually part Cherokee, that one of his grandmothers had been a Cherokee princess. Jingles laughed and said that one of his grandmothers had been a redneck princess. The limo driver did not know what to say and he tried to fall back by feigning boredom, but he could not seem to get back into the rhythm of the words and the flow.

"Here you go, Jingles," he said in a way which suggested that he could not believe that an Indian from the middle of nowhere, from a state, nay a province which the limo driver could not even pronounce, was getting into this club. There were lines of beautiful women who were remarkable in their beauty and in the way that they were dressed. Jingles had to shake his head again. He could not believe that he was in this huge city. When he was younger he remembered that they could not leave the reserve without a permit. Now he was free to roam the earth and he was roaming this crazy city that seemed to be on fire. He tried to find some memory, some element, which could perhaps give him some measure of comfort. He searched his mind as though it were a grand library of index cards. He searched to find some comforting words of the Senator. He remembered the feeling of fire, just like the fire that he felt from this city. He tried to make sense of this feeling of fire that he was feeling as he got closer and closer to the arena of Studio 54.

As the big bouncer with steely blue eyes ushered him through a side door, he could not help but think to himself, "Boy, you are in the big tent now. You are not in a berry picking tent in Canada."

Jingles, in the midst of all of the bright lights of

New York and the hustle and bustle of the city, paused and thought about the words and what they meant to him. For some reason the words resonated more with him in Cree than they did in English. He did not want to be a takay. He also thought about the fire that he was facing. In fact, he felt the fire deep inside of his soul and deep inside of his belly.

He was ushered into a side room which had all of kinds of blue light in it. There were handlers waiting for him. They were getting him ready for his grand entry into the floor of the dance club. Some of the people called it the killing floor. People were buzzing around, buzzing around the room and giggling. "Oh my God!" one of them said. "That is a real Native American hunter." Another said, "I know. He is so sexy. I want to be with him." They all screamed and giggled his name. He got ready as he was about to make his entrance.

The place was full of lots of really cool and famous people. Elton John was there with his famous glasses. The word was that a lot of neechie cats were leaning heavy on the Department of Indian Affairs to provide them with fancy cat eyes like that but the word around Nanabush's campfire was that the Department of Indian Affairs was not budging in any way. Diana Ross was there, dancing and swaying to rhythm. Andy Warhol was there, of course, planning a new series on famous rock star Indians, and as soon as he saw Jingles come in, and as soon as he heard the people go wild, he knew that he was onto something. He knew that the force behind the rise of ᐱᓄᑭᓈᑊ was something that he wanted to be part of. Warhol always had a sense of what was going on. You could say that he was a cultural barometer of sorts. Warhol knew this cat was going to fly higher than a rocket ship. This cat was going to fly higher than the stars.

The crowd went crazy, the hips and lips on the

dance floor moved in a crazy frenzy, just like a round dance back home in Saskatchewan. There was a hell of a flicker show, Jingles thought. The announcer proclaimed and testified into the mic: "Everyone. All of you crazy cats out there. We have a treat for you rainbow children tonight. We got ourselves one crazy Native American right off the reservation! He is here tonight to help launch the famous Chief's Spirit Chicken, a new line of wild chicken hunted by authentic Cree hunters. And the launch of this product is happening right here, right now!" Everyone danced and clapped as a pow wow remix of "Neechie Hustle" filled the club.

Now this is where the story starts to get funky. The tables of the freshly cooked wild chicken were in the back with Nadine's mom's bannock which had been flown in by a special jet. Jingles thought that this flicker show was more magnificent than the light show of the northern lights of long, summer, prairie nights. It was also sure to put to shame the fireworks shows of the Sports Days of the reserve. As Jingles came out on a horse, the crowd went even more wild. Diana Ross swung her hips harder, the crowd moved their lips harder, and the hands of people clapped even harder and made a form of indoor thunder.

The scene was magnificent. Jingles came out on an old mustang that ᐱᔪᐯᓯᕻ had flown in from the Blood reservation. The horse was black and white in body with magnificent black spots throughout. The black and white colouring looked magnificent in the disco lights. In fact, it almost looked translucent. There were blue lights that had been attached to the horse with Jingles's name in syllabics on one side, and pahkwêsikan on the other side. One fella who had flown in from Los Angeles was heard to say, "This is just out of sight!" Jingles also had a fantastic headdress on, speckled with brilliant lights, and it moved like a beautiful electric storm as he swaggered, while the people layered up their consciousness. At the bar they were drinking "The Cosmic Cree" which was vodka mixed with Saskatoon berries and a rare plant found in the hilly areas of Alsace–Lorraine. The crowd moved and parted as Jingles entered the floor like a triumphant conquering Roman general. His horse kept perfect time – the beautiful horse named "Osâm–mistahi" would take two steps forward and then one step back. Beautiful models of all shades of the pîsimwêyâpiy?[177] would yell out to Jingles, "can I touch your horse?" Jingles nodded and thought to himself, if only those smug rednecks, those funky reznecks, and, of course, all of those funky whitenecks, the cool môniyâwak, could see him now.

Jingles kept moving and dancing. He was wearing his platform moccasins with little minnows from the Saskatchewan river swimming in them. He had an electric breast plate that kept flashing Cree words in syllabics like "freedom," "wahwâ" and other cool words. Jingles became convinced that disco was a powerful tool of political liberation. Marlon Brando had flown in for the launch of Chief's Spirit Chicken. Brando raised his drink and nodded with approval as Jingles passed by. Brando was taking a well–deserved break from the filming of Apocalypse Now. Andy Warhol was heard to say, as recounted later around Nanabush's campfire, that the kihci art napêw himself pointed to Jingles and said, "That man is a walkin', talkin' loaded gun. He just needs to be pointed in the right direction."

---

177   rainbow

THE HUSTLE CONTINUES

After that night, people could not stop talking about Jingles. Things got crazy and they got crazy fast. The "Neechie Hustle" became a big hit on the circuit, and was one of the hottest tracks of the summer of 1976. Jingles also invented a new dance that went along with it. Jingles even had his mugshot for and afternoon in a big TV in Times Square. Andy Warhol even did a series based on Jingles, which sold out even before he was finished. These paintings were the hottest things that summer. Marlon Brando used his influence to get an exhibition of the "The Native American and Disco" which was a huge success. Marlon Brando even had Jingles do a walk on for *Apocalypse Now*, he was the guy that killed the bull.

It was a spectacular time. Everything changed quickly and it was all amazing. Things got a little crazy, there was a lot of kneading bannock, and a lot of grease, and the lights of the shiny disco balls just seemed to make everything shinier.

PASKWÂW–ISKWÊW STOPS MAKING BANNOCK

Things got crazy after the Studio 54 launch. Jingles had served moose meat at Studio 54 from a moose that he had killed. He wanted to make up for the fact that he had previously not done the feast right, all those years back in the 1960s after he and the Senator had gone to the Zoo. People loved the moose meat but ᐱᓯᒼᐤ was not that thrilled by this, because he said their job was to sell chicken not give away moose meat. "You have to make sôniyâw Jingles. The trip isn't paying for itself." After the successful launch in New York City, everything seemed to pick up at an even faster pace. The bannock slaps from Bannock Slap got greasier, and the lard in Papoose Face's cheek, seemed to jiggle more when he would talk.

Then ᐱᓯᒼᐤ went to go Nadine's ohkoma to get the next batch of the special pellets that she prepared to animate the bannock dough. She had greeted him with an icy silence.

"What's wrong?"

She didn't say anything it all. She just ignored him and made tea for everyone including Papoose Face and Bannock Slap. They sat and drank it.

"I am not making the bannock anymore," she said.

The boys were used to intimidating people to get their way but they knew that this way would not work with the kohkom. Those ways of neechie hustle could not be applied to the kohkoms. Everyone knew that kohkoms were the ones who had all of the power. And, in ᐱᓯᒼᐤ's case, she had the power to make him lose his human form and revert back to being a wooden Indian. They left realizing that they were in a bit of a pickle

– what would they do now that they didn't have this bannock anymore? They would have to just sell everyday bannock but people would notice the difference – at least the Indians would. Maybe it wouldn't matter that much, they thought. The real problem was that if ᐱᖁᑭᓂᖠ didn't have the bannock dough from the original bannock recipe then he would turn back to being a wooden Indian.

PASKWÂW–ISKWÊW STOPS MAKING BANNOCK: PART TWO

That night ∧ᓄᑭᓂᐦ fell into a deep sleep. In that deep sleep, he dreamed of the expansion of Chief's Fried Chicken. He also saw himself slowly turning back into a wooden Indian again. He felt his body become heavy and hard to move again. He had been drifting above the earth but now his body became heavy and he fell towards the centre of the heavy earth, to the centre of where he was. This new heaviness was now his skin and his body.

He was in an open area, like in a western. Dust seemed to gather and rise from the wagon roads, and seemed to pull him in. The force of heaviness that he felt in his wooden body seemed to pull him into the road and dust. There was an openness on the road and an openness in the sky which seemed to pull him to this place. Everything he was, everything he had been, was right then and there. He heard a mystical booming voice say, "Think of the sound of one hand making bannock."

The streets were empty until he saw a shadow push and pull the light by entry to the saloon of the town. Then that shadow grew more and more into the light. Eventually he could make out the form of a wooden Indian. The form moved out to the road to square off against him. He could see the other wooden Indian had guns by his waist and that he had a cowboy hat, spurs, a black vest and black pants, and a white cotton shirt that seemed to catch the light of the sun in a certain way.

"My name is Kaw–Liga, and I am here to challenge you," he paused for dramatic effect. "There is only room in this town for one wooden Indian."

"Well," said ∧ᓄᑭᓂᐦ, "I guess that is me."

"No, nîci–nêhiyawâhtik êwako niya poko."[178]

---

178   "No, my fellow wooden–Indian, there can only be me."

The sun seemed to draw the light up to a higher point in the sky and to cast longer shadows on their figures.

A crow who sat on a nearby pole let out a sound and they both drew their weapons. ᐱᓄᐲᣵᣞ was fast, but not as fast as Kaw–Liga, and he could feel the hard stiff metal bullet sink in his wooden body. He felt his body get lighter again, and the earth below him opened up and welcomed him into a great place of warm light.

Then he woke up. It had been three days since he had put all four of the Indian elements on his body. He noticed that his joints were stiffening up and that his one index finger was turning to wood. If the kohkom would not make the bannock than he had really one choice. Storied verse had told of the original bannock recipe being in a treasure chest, shipwrecked somewhere in the north. Somewhere along the Hudson Bay. He had heard the Senator talk about it, and he was keen to send Papoose Face and Bannock Slap to get it. Time was not on his side – the sooner they could get it, the better.

As ᐱᓄᐲᣵᣞ expanded his chicken empire, Paskwâw–Iskwêw eventually got tired of making the bannock for Chief's Fried Chicken. She had told the Senator that she never believed in what ᐱᓄᐲᣵᣞ was doing. At first, she believed in ᐱᓄᐲᣵᣞ in the same way that she had lost faith in what he was doing. Initially, she had believed in both of them, but then as time went on, she really started to doubt them, and to doubt what they were doing. Sure, they brought jobs, but at what price?

Looking back now, that is something all of the hustlers understood. The kohkoms were beyond the hustle. They were the force that gave us form after the troubles of 1885. They were the ones that pulled together the pieces, and held our communities together. Without the kohkoms we would have been finished a long time ago: our languages would have fallen to the wind, and scattered like the leaves of fall.

Paskwâw–Iskwêw was firm in her conviction not to provide the bannock despite all that ᐊᓄᐯᓀᕁ had done. Despite all of his efforts, he could not break her resolve. He had the band stop delivering her water. He also had the garbage man stop picking up her garbage. He also tried to cut off her social assistance payment cheques but he was limited in what he could do because, despite his rise to power, she was still very respected by the people, and was a full–fledged member of the kohkom network. No matter how high a chief would rise, he could never completely go against the kohkom network. They had a great deal of power and influence. There was really no undoing it.

She was always busy: helping the kids of the reserve, helping the wounded rez dogz get nursed back to health. She was a strong woman, she had medicines and always stood independent from the Church and the Indian agent. Sometimes in the middle of the night she would get her horse and travel through the night. She would go from relative to relative and visit. She was always a great storyteller.

Without her bannock, ᐊᓄᐯᓀᕁ was in danger of losing his human form. He was no longer able to get the bannock of Paskwâw–Iskwêw, and he could feel that his body was beginning to change. He could not see it in his face directly, but he could feel the wood again. The last thing that the Chief wanted to do was to take the form of a wooden Indian again. As a wooden Indian he could see everything but he couldn't talk: it had pissed him off that all he could was witness the world around him and not be able to do anything about it.

The Chief could feel the effects of not having the bannock. He felt his blood as though it was hardening. He could feel his limbs getting less limber with time. He found it more difficult to do his daily exercises. He used to do a lot of stretching first thing in the morning. He would do this while he was drinking his morning coffee. He would set the exercising mat beside him and would get into the rhythm. He would do this with the sound of birds, and he would feel the sway of the trees, and the way the wind would catch pieces of the lonely, errant, struggling wind.

As the days passed he became more and more stiff in his mind. He would increasingly have visceral flashbacks of when he had been in the museum. He remembered the way that the Germans would stop and look at him. He would remember the way that they would speak in a hushed tone. He did not understand their words in a word by word manner, but rather he understood the tone and nature of their words. He understood the emotions and feelings of his words and in this way his understanding was more complete.

He had tried everything to get Paskwâw–Iskwêw's grandmother to make bannock so that he could keep his human form. He was very afraid to take that form again. He was scared to revert back. He was scared to move back into the land of the shadows, back in the shadow of the bannock, the land of the bannock shadows. That was a place without full shape, a place without full colour.

GETTING THE ORIGINAL RECIPE

Now that Paskwâw–Iskwêw refused to make the bannock from the original recipe, ᐱᔪᐱᓯᐢ was desperate to get more the bannock in order to keep his human form. The first step was to get the old book from the Senator's Third Hand Pawn Shop. In that book, he knew there was a map which could help him. It had a map which had the location of a shipwreck from the Hudson Bay Company which had the original bannock recipe. It was this recipe that could help him make bannock to keep his human form.

At first without the elixir of the four neechie elements: KFC gravy, chokecherry wine cured under a full moon, tears from a midnight bingo caller, and bannock from the original recipe, his body was becoming wood a little bit at a time. There were little patches of wood which were emerging on his body. They were barely noticeable and ᐱᔪᐱᓯᐢ would cover them up. He covered a couple of them up with bandages. He had a little bit of bannock in the fridge which he could use to keep his human form. But, he would have to use it sparingly. He would have to try to make it last as long as he possibly could. He also had a couple of pieces in the freezer which he could pull out and thaw. Not only was he worried that a wooden appearance would throw people off, but he also worried that he would not be as limber, and would not be able to move around as much.

The book that had the secret map was called The Ancient Book of Cha. The book was full of Cree wisdom, and had many interesting phrases and expressions. The map was on the last page, but in order to be seen, it had to be held up to the light of a campfire. ᐱᔪᐱᓯᐢ had learned that Paskwâw–Iskwêw had drawn the map in the book as a precaution in case anything ever happened to her. She knew it would be safe and she trusted the Senator.

One night when the Senator was out at Bingo, Papoose Face broke into the Third Hand Pawn Shop and ripped the page out of the book. He carefully cut it using a razor, and made haste with it. ∧ᴖᑭᓂᒉ had bet that the Senator would not miss it because the Senator seemed to have forgotten about it. Then, once Papoose Face had it securely in his possession, he went to see ∧ᴖᑭᓂᒉ and gave it to him.

∧ᴖᑭᓂᒉ put the page from the Ancient Book of Cha up against the needed campfire. He found the location of where the scroll of the original recipe was—it was a bit north of present day Churchill, Manitoba. He summoned Papoose Face and Bannock Slap, "Boysak, the location of the shipwreck was just north of the town of Churchill Manitoba."

"Ok boss," said Bannock Slap. "We will go get it." The boys made a plan to go Churchill by train. They would then take an ATV to the particular spot. They gathered their stuff as quietly as they could so as to not draw too much attention to themselves.

Papoose Face and Bannock Slap got in their car and drove in to the city to take the train to location. They had packed clothes, snacks, and brought some chicken with them to keep them going for a bit. They used their Treaty cards to get discounts, and they sat on the train with their black sunglasses on. They had their arms folded and sat across from two Wonder Bread Eaters who shifted nervously in their seats, after a couple of attempts of small talk had failed.

The train ride was long, and the two would take turns sleeping in the sleeping cabin. At times, Bannock Slap would read his newspaper and would order coffee from the meal cart. The coffee helped them stay awake and gave them focus. As they were moving, Bannock Slap opened his eyes, and rubbed them slowly. A few minutes passed and he could hear the clank of the metal of the train upon the rail. Then there was the sound of the motion of the train, like an ongoing passing humming wind, which filled the space of the cabin. He shuffled his body about, and looked out and imagined what the recipe would look like.

The boys got off the train and went to the point where they were to get the ATV. They got it and eventually got to the outcrop of stone by the shore where the ship was hidden. They put their supplies on the vehicle, and loaded it up and made their way there. They stopped after awhile at a designated point where they had confirmed the pick up of the extra supplies through the use of their satellite phone. After they made contact with the suppliers, they worked their way to the point on the map along the shore close to the ship. On the way there, Bannock Slap turned and said to Papoose Face who was behind him, "Do you think that we will see a polar bear?" He feigned a laugh, but Papoose Face as usual, did not say anything. His jowls just moved about a bit from the wind.

They finally made their way to the place near the shore. They knew they were close by because of the rising ridge. They carefully parked the ATV and opened up the one box. There was a wet suit, and fins for both of them. They had to put these on, and then go into the water. Then they had to swim under water a bit, and they would resurface on the other side, inside of a concealed cave. Then they would go and retrieve it.

They got their gear on and then they went underwater to the special point. They swam underwater and then re–emerged in the concealed cave above the water. There within the concealed cave was the shipwrecked Hudson Bay Company ship which had the bannock recipe scroll. With the passage of time, no one is sure how the ship ended up there. Some say that magic was involved, and there were many over the years who came to look for it.

As they approached the ship, they made their way to one of the chests. It was there in a hidden compartment, where they found the scroll of the original recipe. Through this recipe, it could be envisioned that ᐱᑯᐸᑦᓯᑦ would find his way back to his complete humanity and form. With that Bannock Slap carefully opened the water, proof metal case, and put the recipe in it. With that, they headed home.

242

THE BUFFALO UNICORN

The Senator loved to drive, as he was always driving, ê–pâh–pamihcikêt. And as he was driving he was often hungry, ê–nâh–nôhtêkatêt when he was hungry he would often stop at a diner somewhere on the road. There was an 8–track player on the bottom of the floor of his car. He could see a CCR 8–track on the floor by the player. He pulled the reins of his metal Red River Cart again, thinking that he could feel the pull of imaginary metallic horses. He was deep in thought, listening to John Fogerty singing the buffalo home. He thought of Nadine and tried to tuck in his belly. It hurt a bit but he knew next time he saw her he would do neechie plastic surgery and duct tape the rolls that he had.

As he kept driving, the sky began its turn from day and the heavy orange of dusk flushed the landscape. The daylight was stubborn and persistent, and clung to objects as its source, the sun, passed over so slowly into the horizon line. As the daylight retreated from the skin of the earth, the Senator rubbed his eyes a bit to make sure that he was seeing everything clearly.

He swore that he heard John Fogerty's voice slow down a bit but then he shook his head, hoping that this would knock him back into the world and back into his body. Then, as he was looking at the road, he swore that he saw a purple deer walk across the road. Then once again he shook his head, hoping that would knock him back to his senses. Everything seemed to be back to normal, or at least as close to normal as things can get for the Senator.

But things seemed to get weird again. John Fogerty's voice seemed to get very slow, and his words became drawn out, and the speed of his truck seemed to slow down. And the sky seemed full of heavy bannock grease clouds which seemed to drip onto the land. From the 8–track player, various psychedelic forms and colours seemed to rotate out. It was like all of the sound was becoming solid form. At first the Senator thought it was funny. Funny in the same kind of way when someone farts and you burst out laughing. But then the truck seemed to levitate a bit, and move off the pavement, and then while in mid–air, it started to rotate around. The trees became multi–coloured lollipops. The truck moved up to the sun, and then with that came a great flash of light.

The Senator felt like he had been bannock slapped and he slowly opened his eyes. He could see the fantastic colours around him, and it was like those colours were inside of him twirling around and he felt like the local Salvation Army store with so many amazing colours. He felt magical. He felt giggly. One of the things that he noticed right away was that he no longer felt a pain in his hip. It felt limber and elastic. He also felt twirling purple threads of light that came radiating out of him, and it seemed like there were more that were coming out of his hip. He felt like he had long light purple and radiant yellow threads that became rich, thick braids that radiated out. He grabbed the open air around him, and he unconsciously grabbed for bear grease to rub through his hair. Instead of bear grease, he reached out and found something else, he reached out and found something even more magical than masko–pimiy. He grabbed some strange elixir that he bunched in his hand and ran through his hair. He felt the magical pull of it through his hair. He felt young again, like the time when he and Cash had gone to Europe to sing pow wow. He felt his body lift off the ground and he started to fly. It was like little magical hands were lifting him up. He could see the stretch of the prairie and a patch of forest in front of his line of sight. He felt like he was a bush pilot again and was floating through the sky. The sky was bursting with magical reds and oranges. The sun was a sparkling brilliant light that cast over the landscape. Bursts of green, washed out tans, and faded blues filled out the various forms below. The clusters of rocks seemed to vibrate. The vibrant orange grass swayed in the wind, clawing and feeling into the sky.

Then he felt the gentle glide of air beneath him.
He felt little currents, like little river currents, underneath
himself and was propelled upwards. He felt a gentle nudge
and he noticed beneath him was the pink buffalo unicorn.
It was so majestic. She shook her head, and caused the
air to dance. The unicorn shook her mane and it caused
another vibration, and the Senator felt it as an electric
pulse that seemed so powerful. He then felt the unicorn
move below him. The flight of the unicorn was truly
majestic, and it was in this majestic flight that he had never
felt so alive. He felt the power of the bannock force flow
through him, and move throughout him.

The things that he saw that day transformed
not only him, but transformed his soul as well. He saw
magnificent rivers of gravy; he saw herds of unicorn
buffalo roaming the fields in their wondrous pageantry.
This pageantry was like a speckled angel and the Senator
just seemed to get lost in it. He could feel the unicorn
beneath him, and he could feel its movement. It was a
strange sensation. It was like time really did not matter to
him anymore. It was like time was just a stretched out hide,
a frayed possibility that had somehow lost its form and
had somehow lost its place. It was frayed around the edges
and was difficult to control, it was difficult to tie it up and
measure it. It was difficult to try to control it. It had to flow
– just like the flowing movement in the sky.

It had been a long time since the Senator had felt
so free. He felt an unbridled freedom. And in many ways
he felt like a buffalo that was breaking out of a fence,
and he was pounding the open prairie again, free, feeling
the blades of grass, but now he could feel the blades and
little stretches of the wind, as they wrapped around him.
It made him smile, because it reminded him of when he
and the rest of the gang had got into the SS 3000 teepee,
and they had those brief minutes of flight. It was in those
moments of flight when they believed that they could do

anything. At that moment, at that time, they truly believed that they could do anything. They even believed that they could make it to the stars. It was not every day that Indians tried to make it to the stars, but the Senator and the others were not everyday Indians.

The unicorn looked back at him and seemed to smile at him. The magical horn of the unicorn pushed ahead, and created a space for movement. It was that place of movement which was filled with magical colours and magical feelings. It was these magical thoughts and these magical feelings that seemed to make him forget things. He thought of Nadine, and how nothing seemed to work out with her no matter how hard he tried. And he felt a pulse from the unicorn's body, and the unicorn shot all of this negativity from its horn. And after that, he felt light, and, indeed, stronger. Then he thought about how the Treaties were not being honoured, and how Trudeau seemed to be really against the Indians and it was unclear how things were really going to turn out. The Senator thought all of those negative things, and felt the energy of these things pass to the unicorn, and then he felt them shoot out of its horn. Each time the unicorn would look at him, she would almost smile. There was a gleam in the unicorn's almost–smile that reminded him all of that was missing in the world, and helped him shape his world. The world seemed warm and kind, like the reassuring words of a kohkom in the playful days of a summer on the reserve.
They seemed to fly in the sky forever, the unicorn magically propelling herself as well as the Senator high into the sky. In this wondrous land of the sky, the Senator did not need a permit, nor did the Senator have to answer to a Chief, a Chief who may have let power get the best of him. Here, out in the open air, he had no one to answer to, except the magical unicorn, mistatim kâ–otêskanit.[179]

As he flew over the world, he saw it busting with magnificent colours. He saw rivers of gravy, lakes of

---

179   literally, "the horse with one horn"

bannock grease, and as he flew in the air above the earth, he heard the whispers of Indian agents agreeing with Indians and of people from the Department of Indian Affairs agreeing to fund new economic ventures on the reserve. He saw massive bingo games which seemed to fill acres and acres of territory. He also saw strange formations which appeared to be made of bannock and which appeared to be some ancient form of Indian writing. The Senator could not read it but yet he got the sense that it was a powerful and wondrous message which seemed to make the unicorn giggle. Every time the unicorn giggled, the Senator noticed a warm sensation move through his body. In fact, the Senator noticed that every time the Senator thought a negative thought, the unicorn giggled and then the Senator could feel that warm sensation move through him.

Then in the clearing ahead of them, far below on the ground, there was a campfire with people moving about the fire. As they got closer, the Senator could tell that they were conversing. He could not make out if they were neechies or môniyâw folk, or both, as he got closer, it did not seem to become more clear. The reason he could not tell at least on the surface was that their faces were concealed. They were wearing dark capes and hoods. They were pointing to the sky, and as a few seconds went on in the flight, he could see that thy were pointing at him and the unicorn. As he and the unicorn approached, the unicorn got skittish and nervous. But the Senator was intrigued, and wanted to move towards the encampment. He was drawn to the five hooded figures. He could seem them looking up, and pointing to him and the buffalo unicorn. He leaned into the buffalo unicorn and tried to move towards the other direction. But the buffalo unicorn tugged and twisted, and then the unicorn buffalo looked at him, but there were no more smiles or giggles. While he wanted to go to see the five figures, the unicorn looked at him again and smiled and sent a warm giggle through his body. The great feeling of the unicorn buffalo was overwhelming; the great feeling of the unicorn buffalo was powerful. The Senator felt overcome, and muttered, "kah." It distracted the Senator from what he was trying to get. But the rush for what he felt was undeniable. It was 100 times more powerful than when he would drink le pôket with the other old fellas.

The Senator rode the unicorn buffalo and they flew throughout the world. They saw many magical things, came to a big field, with the bright yellow sunflowers arching and moving towards him and the buffalo unicorn. Great waves of happiness passed through the buffalo unicorn and through him. The horn of the paskwâw– unicorn was like an antenna that grabbed the happiness and moved it through him. The unicorn's body filtered the happiness and passed it on to him. The unicorn kept looking back at him and kept giggling. Each time the unicorn buffalo would giggle, she would lift her head slightly. Then she would lower her head down and then it was, tâpiskôc, like the buffalo unicorn with wings would turn to look at him. It was like the unicorn buffalo was smiling. When she was smiling, it was like a flash of light came from the unicorn buffalo's teeth. The flash was a glimmer of light like a little star that seemed to rotate slightly.

As they approached the field, they could see various people crowded around what appeared to be the bingo caller at Carnival Bingo. The man looked so different from how he usually looked when he was calling bingo. As they approached and came closer, the Senator realized that it really was the bingo caller from that place and he could see clearly the lines of his face, and the way his face was making the laughter. At first he thought that there were other people around the bingo caller. After all, there were usually people around a bingo caller. The two things kind of went hand in hand. Bingo caller, people. People and a bingo caller. But there was no one else. Just the bingo caller in the middle of a great field, a great field full of sunflowers. Their yellow filled his heart and his mind. It was like the whole field was a burning sun, bright and brilliant. He felt like he was in the middle of a Van Gogh painting, and that he was like a swirling moving colour. He had never felt so much joy in his life. After all of the years, on the reserve, and after all of the disappointment that was in his heart, after tall of the things he had seen, and felt in his heart, his heart had become so heavy, so heavy that he did not seem to be able to carry it any further into the future. But now, he felt lighter, not only in his heart, but also in his body. He felt the motion upwards and he felt the glide on the wings of the paskwâwi–unicorn as they moved upwards towards the sky. He felt so free, free like a bird, like a bird that had been caged for so long, now finally free. He could not believe how free he actually felt.

The paskwâwi–mostos unicorn kept flying but was seemingly drawn to the bingo caller. At first the Senator did not know what to make of it, because the other time they had seen people the unicorn had moved away from them. He had flown away from the five in hoods, the Senator thought. But now the buffalo–unicorn horse–like being, kept flying closer and closer, and the closer that he came to the bingo caller, the more of the warm energy the Senator felt surge through him. It was so glorious that he felt like his body was earth that was being soaked in deep rain. A deep soothing rain. This time the paskwâw–unicorn was not fearful or angry but rather seemed very excited to see this man, this bingo caller who was on the ground. They kept moving towards him, kept coming closer and closer, and the closer they got the more happy the unicorn buffalo seemed to be. The Senator could feel the incredible rush throughout his body, it was like he was freebasing bannock grease, and that grease was moving through his body, his body was holding all of this joy and the Senator did not know how much longer he could actually hold this powerful feeling. Everything had a limit to what they could hold, and the Senator was worried that his body and soul were about at the limit of what they could hold. He worried that his whole being would burst.

They got closer, and he could see the shimmering smile, the wâsi–pahpiwin of the bingo caller. It was deadly and magical. The Senator was so intoxicated with the warm feeling of the unicorn that he could only focus on the good things. He saw flashes in his mind of Sir John A. MacDonald, and saw him eating bannock. He saw another flash of John A. MacDonald dancing pow wow. He saw another flash of John A. MacDonald professing that "Treaties should be honoured." He saw flashes of Nadine saying, "I do. I do." At first it was a just a haze of sensations, then he realized that she was saying "I do. I do." in a white dress. He heard church music. He truly felt overwhelmed and never felt a pain in his hip.

They got closer and the bingo caller waved to him. The Senator opened his eyes, and heard the wondrous, magical words, "You have a good bingo." But the bingo caller was not talking to him directly but it was rather like he was talking to him through his mind. He could hear the words again, and there was no movement of the bingo caller's mouth. He could see the bingo caller and the bingo caller was waving at him, like little Tattoo from Fantasy Island waving at the planes. The unicorn buffalo looked back at him and then he heard the giggliest giggle of all. The unicorn–buffalo glided down to the ground and then the Senator slowly got off. He got off and then touched the ground. But then just a he was touching the ground, he felt another surge of the unicorn power move through him, and this time it was too much for him to hold in, and he started to shake a great deal. He fell to the ground shaking with pure ecstasy. He fell on the ground twitching and twisting. He kept hearing, "YOU HAVE A GOOD BINGO! YOU HAVE A GOOD BINGO!" But the words were so clear and crisp, just like early morning bacon, crackling on the grill. He closed his eyes, and saw the bingo caller giving him a big cheque, then he saw the unicorn smiling the biggest smile that he thought a unicorn could smile, and then he heard the unicorn giggle so loud that he shook the whole earth. It was such a sound burst that people in neighbouring reserves had their honey trucks over turned.

The Senator kept hearing the mantra, YOU HAVE A GOOD BINGO. YOU HAVE A GOOD BINGO and it was like the words were water and rushed through him like the Saskatchewan River. He felt like he was drawing in the happiness and began to wonder how much longer he could hold it in any longer. Just when he thought that he could not hold it in any longer he felt the most vicious bannock slap that he had ever felt in his life.

POW! WOW! The Senator felt another powerful bannock slap on his face. The image began to sink to that point where he felt the bannock slap. He opened his eyes and the vibrant colours were faded, and everything looked more ordinary. He could feel the pain in his hip again. "awiya!" the Senator. The Senator looked around for the unicorn–buffalo but there was no sign of him. "awiya!" the Senator said again. He could truly feel his hip, and he could feel the pain of it. He then saw what looked like a kohkom floating above him. Her kerchief was pulled over her head, so he could not make out her face. She had a little blue sweater on, and a floral patterned dress. She had the pull up moccasins with floral bead patterns.

No longer did the Senator feel that warm feeling in his body. The feeling of warm bannock. Instead he felt the coldness of all things ordinary. Instead of his body feeling like warm bannock, his body felt like cold porridge.

Perhaps what was more disconcerting to the Senator was not so much the bannock slap but perhaps it was the loss of the great feeling of warmth which he had been experiencing up to that point. It was the greatest feeling that he had ever felt, and now it was gone. The kohkom moved down from her elevated position.

"Where am I?" the Senator said.

"You are in the middle of a big field." The yellow that had been there was no more.

The Senator said, "Where is the buffalo–unicorn?"

The kohkom said, "There never was a buffalo–unicorn."

"What do you mean that there never was a buffalo–unicorn?"

"What I am trying to say, there never was."

"But I saw the unicorn. I felt her. She was magical." The Senator then looked to the side and said, with a big open heart, "I have never," he closed his eyes a bit when he said this, "I have never seen anything so glorious."

The kohkom raised her head and lowered her handkerchief.

"Kohkom Paskwâw-Iskwêw. It is you."

"Yes, Senator," she paused, "You were experiencing the lullaby of colonization." The Senator looked at her with great puzzlement.

"The unicorn–buffalo was an electro–magnetic manifestation of the Indian Act," she continued.

The Senator paused for a moment and realized that instead of being mad, he should perhaps wait to hear what they might have to say. He wanted to hear what they knew of what had happened to him.

"Look Senator, I have been watching you for a long time."

The Senator did not say anything as well for a bit. It was one of those moments like when you sit with an Elder and they do not say anything. And you just sit waiting for them, and you get to the point where you actually just begin to enjoy the silence. They all just started to sit comfortably in that silence.

"I am a Bannarchist." The Senator looked at her with a look of puzzlement. With that, Paskwâw–Iskwêw tapped her cane on the ground. With that, a hologram appeared, and the Senator saw the Battle of Caledon, the passing of the title of Bannarchist from one person to the next. The Bannarchist was the keeper of the original recipe.

She continued, "nitohta [180] Senator. The Department of Indian Affairs got concerned about the rise of the neechies. They got worried about neechie hustle." She paused for a moment, and tapped her cane, and instantly there was a hologram of ᐱᓄᑭᑦ counting money. "They were not worried about ᐱᓄᑭᑦ because he was consumed with money," she paused, and his image disappeared, "but they were worried about you. You kept the old value of sharing with others."

The Senator looked again with astonishment. "Look Senator, we do not have much time. Let me explain this all to you. There was no unicorn buffalo, nor was there ever a unicorn buffalo. It was a trick by the Federal government to lull the natives, and to make them complacent. Everybody knows the love that Indians have for CCR."

"Tâpwê, dat is true. They got beats, like they are always singing their hearts out. Sometimes I think that they would be able to sing back the buffalo."

"Well, that is where the government came in. They knew that so many Indian people like CCR, so they thought what better way to trick Indians, then to put secret messages in the CCR 8-tracks. When you would listen to the secret message in the 8-track, you would be lulled to sleep."

"Holeh smokerinoes," thought the Senator, "that sounds spooky." He paused for a minute and looked around. "By the way, where is my truck?"

"Jingles, brought it back to the Third Hand Pawn Shop."

The Senator paused for a moment and rubbed his eyes in astonishment and arched his head to hear more.

"Yes, the family of Nadine are direct descendants of the Scottish Fur Trader McGregor. His father had fled from the battle of Caldedon and hid the recipe. He hid the recipe

180   listen

while he fled through the forests of the highlands. He kept the receipt until his son joined the HBC company, and then was tragically shipwrecked in the Gulf of the Hudson Bay, where they say that the original Scroll of the bannock rests. Despite having lost the scroll, McGregor kept the recipe in his mind, and told his family of it through the ages, and all down the line."

"Kah," said the Senator.

"We are here to not only get you out of the deep sleep of the CCR 8–track, but also to get you to help us."

"There has been a great disturbance in the bannock force, we feel that something will be bursting through from the other side of the bannock into this realm."

"Cha. First I see buffalo unicorns, then you tell me that there is more?"

"Yes, ᐱᓄᑭᓀᔨ is a manifestation of the bannock force. But he is of the burnt side of the bannock. As a Bannarchist I have to protect the recipe, and I have refused to make any more bannock for him so that he will return back to his wooden form. I believe that ᐱᓄᑭᓀᔨ now has the recipe and you must try to stop him."

THE RECIPE MÔY MIYOPAYIN[181]

After getting the recipe, Bannock Slap dutifully brought the recipe to their boss. ᐸᓄᐸᓂᐢ had become half-wooden. He had resorted to wearing a mask to try to conceal what was happening to him. They didn't know what to say when they saw their boss, but they were happy to give him the recipe.

"You know boss," Bannock Slap said, "people are starting to talk. People are saying that you are using medsin and that medsin use is not right. Everyone keeps going to the Senator to hear what he thinks, but he won't say anything. Seems like he just doesn't have the heart to talk about anything since he found out that Nadine is engaged to that Italian journalist."

ᐸᓄᐸᓂᐢ did not say much. He just grabbed the silver metal case which had the recipe in it and they could see that three of his fingers had turned to wood. They were a bit taken aback by them. But they tried to conceal their astonishment. They both looked at each other but then Papoose Face did a silent motioning of Bannock Slap out of his silence.

"Boss," Bannock said and then paused. "People are starting to talk. People are saying that you are using some kind of witchcraft." He told the boss that some of the more superstitious Indians had stopped going to get the chicken from Chief's Fried Chicken. Those was the more traditional and conservative elements. This did not add up to a majority but it did represent a sizable loss in sales. Even some elements of the "so called" progressive elements stopped going, not because of a fear of Indian voodoo or mojo, but because of even a more pragmatic concern. They had stopped going ever since Nadine's ohkoma had stopped making her special bannock. Many of the whites kept getting declines in sales which got the Hutterites nervous and they started to look for other places to sell

181   The Recipe does not work

their chickens. They were trying to find a secure market.

ᐱᓄᑭᓂᕁ got mad when they said this and he started to smash things around. He called them liars. During the melee, which consisted of throwing stuff around while the other two were trying to shield things, ᐱᓄᑭᓂᕁ's mask fell off. Both of his sidekicks gasped, and Papoose Face, after being called "fool" one too many times, felt the grease of the bannock of his face burn, and as he ran out, the rolls of fat seemed to jiggle bit more than normal.

Bannock Slap stayed and helped his boss put his mask back on. ᐱᓄᑭᓂᕁ motioned for him to go away and leave him.

ᐱᓄᑭᓂᕁ grabbed the old parchment which his sidekicks had retrieved from Hudson Bay. He took it down to the big spacious kitchen. It was an underground kitchen bunker where Chief's Fried Chicken did a lot of special and extra culinary developments and experiments. He did not summon any of his culinary minions. He had to make the dough himself because he could not really trust anyone else to see him in his weakened and changed state.

He followed the script of the old recipe which was written in an old style of writing Cree which at times was hard to understand, but he worked his way through the writing of the scroll and he prepared the bannock. He then sang the song of the wooden Indian, and put the four Indian elements of his body: the tears of a midnight Bingo Caller, chokecherry wine that had been cured under a full moon, KFC gravy, and then some of the bannock dough of the original recipe. He felt a flicker, and flash of what should happen but in the end although one of his fingers had turned almost completely to flesh, it reverted back to wood.

ᐱᓄᑭᓂᕁ thought maybe he had made a mistake, maybe he had put too much of the secret ingredient in. Maybe he put too much of the flour in. Maybe it was the wrong kind of dough. Maybe he did too much kneading.

Maybe he did not do enough. A recipe was only a guide, and it needed the right hands to form the bannock.

ᐱᓄᐯᓂᒥ was at a loss and he did not know what to do next. He tried again. He prepared the bannock from the recipe and let it bake. While it was baking, he checked the recipe again just to be sure. Sure enough, it seemed right. He sang the song but it was getting harder to sing the song, as his vocal chords were becoming harder, becoming wood–like. He sang the song, but it was garbled a bit. He put the elements on again, and he felt the surge again, but he also felt the bannock energy retreat quickly again.

ᐱᓄᐯᓂᒥ knew that if he tried again his voice would quickly fade even more and by the time he got the bannock ready, he thought that he would have a voice that would sound like a swimmer under water, gargling his words. He summoned Bannock Slap and told him to get the Senator.

The Senator came in without saying anything. ᐱᓄᐯᓂᒥ brought him his favourite high class instant coffee in a long tall ceramic cup, and then Bannock Slap poured hot water into the cup. Then the Senator started clanking his spoon against the cup. The Senator put a heaping table spoon of sugar into his cup. The Senator was one of those guys who always had to have the fixings with his cup of joe.

Without really looking at ᐱᓄᐯᓂᒥ, the Senator knew that something was wrong. "You're turning back to a wooden Indian again. you're not making the recipe right."

"How do you know?"

"Because I heard what happened. I heard that Bannock Slap and Papoose Face got the recipe from the shipwreck in the north. The Senator paused for a minute and then sipped on his coffee. "You know there is nothing better than Folger's crystals, nothing better than instant coffee. You got to give the môniyâw credit when credit is due. They sure know how to make coffee delicious and also convenient. We don't have to drink that bush camp shit that we grew up drinking. That shit is ever harsh. Pretty much like molasses."

ᐱᴐᑭᓯᣵ had forgotten the slow pace of the way in which the Senator spoke and the way the Senator worked his way around words. Ever since the hustle of the expansion of Chief's Fried Chicken, he was used to the fast way that people often talked to him. It was the fast pace nature of the neechie hustle of recent times which had made everything so fast, so glorious and indeed which had made everything so epic.

"Well, you see there was the 8-track incident. My consciousness was put into an 8-track tape of CCR. I was trapped in between the tracks of the songs, and I thought I would forever be trapped between two CCR songs. But because of the help of Paskwâw-Iskwêw, I escaped. She helped me escape from the trap of the 8-track player and helped me get my consciousness back in my body. For her help, I agreed to keep an eye on you. You were said to be coming as the old Chicken bucket grease prophecies talked about."

"Kah," said ᐱᴐᑭᓯᣵ.

"They said that you were a very rare manifestation of the Bannock force, and that you would change things forever."

ᐱᴐᑭᓯᣵ could not talk any more because his vocal chords were turning to wood.

"Now you must come with me to go see old Paskwâw-Iskwêw." ᐱᴐᑭᓯᣵ nodded, and then they went to her house.

She knew they were coming and had tea ready for them.

"Tânisi nôsim. You have done a lot for the people, you have indeed changed their lives for the better. You have created a whole industry for our people. You have made chicken our new buffalo."

Everyone who could speak said, "ahâw."

"Now for that power comes a price. You had to

draw upon both the light and dark sides of the bannock."

Just then two hooded figures entered the room. One was Olaf, and the other was Pacinîs. "ôhi napêwak 'bannarchists' ka–isiyihkâsocik. They have been the guardians of the secret since the time of the bannock maker of kayâs ago Scotland."

"Now your circle is complete. I can give you the bannock dough, and we have the three other elements on hand. The choice is yours. You can take the form of a human again or fall back into your form as a wooden Indian. The choice is yours. But if you choose to be human, all of the power of Broken Elbow will leave for three generations."

There was a silence. He saw the Senator looking at a picture of Nadine. He looked at Pacinîs chewing his Copenhagen snuff and saw him pass some to Olaf. He knew that what they said was true. He could feel it in is his heart. He thought of the glory of Jingles and imagined more of the glory that could follow if he gave up his human form.

Years later when the Senator told the story he swore that a single tear fell from the eye of the wooden Indian.

Years later, when Broken Elbow Juniors would sing the ballad of ᐱᔪᐸᑐᕀ at pow wow, the old ones would speak of how he gave up his human form to become one with the bannock force and how the bannock force was allowed to continue to surge through the people and deeds of the Broken Elbow Cree First Nation. They spoke of how the funeral pyre of the wooden Indian was so bright that even people in Siberia were rumoured to have seen the flames lick the sky.

After Nadine got married to the Italian journalist, she flew Paskwâw–Iskwêw to live her last years of her life in her husband's villa in Tuscany. Nadine went on to write several bestsellers and many of her books were made into movies. Before she left the Broken Elbow reserve she passed the secret of the recipe to Jingles who was entrusted with the secret recipe. He was now the Bannarchist.

Cash ended up being the first casino manager in Saskatchewan in the 1990s. Pacinîs passed away a few years after. The Senator kept the Third Hand Pawn Shop going and he kept telling stories. He formed a group of people who would get together every Tuesday night and read from The Ancient Book of Cha and people would talk about its teachings. Some people called it a cult but the Senator just called it a book club. Napoleon was never heard from again, but the Senator did reserve regular orders for rabbit root from Paris, and he did receive a post card in the mid 1980s in what the Senator swore was Napoleon's handwriting. It said, "A little bannock never hurt nobody."

THE ÂCIMO CLUB

The storytelling that the Senator had shared with Mervin had really fired up the old kisêyinîs. The Senator started to tell stories again and it was what he did the best. Mervin had loved the stories from the very first time. The Senator had really felt honoured that people had wanted to hear his stories.

All of this got the Senator going, and all through the summer he kept telling stories. People started to call it the "âcimo club" and in many ways, it reminded the Senator of the TV Club that they had had all of those years ago. This young Cree man, Mervin, had asked the Senator if he could write his stories down and put them into a book. The young Cree wanted to preserve the old history of the people. At first, he tried to ask the Senator to tell him stories of Wîsakêcâhk, and the like, but the Senator kept gravitating back to the stories of the jousting, to the stories of the rocket ship that they tried to build, and over the course of the winter, the Senator told him the length and stretch of these stories that he knew. The young man was surprised and somewhat shocked at the stretch depth of the memory that Senator. To honour the Senator and his skill, the young man wrote the book.

Mervin came one more time to the old folks' home and asked the Senator if he had any last thing to say. The Senator nodded.

"You can take the neechie out of the hustle, but you can never take the hustle out of the neechie."